"You can tell me to mind my own business if you want to, but I'd love to know how you ended up divorced . . . twice. Aren't you a marriage counselor?"

Resigned, Grant nodded. "Yes, I am. But therapy and my personal life are apples and oranges. I'd like to say I've been unlucky in love, but the truth is, I've just made some really bad choices. My skills as a therapist don't hinge on my ability to choose the right woman for myself. People talk about women who are only attracted to bad boys—"

"Are you saying you're only attracted to bad *girls*?" Moni asked, winking at him.

Grant dropped the plate and heard it clatter on the counter. He didn't even look to see if it had broken. Instead he gripped the edge of the sink at either side of Moni's waist, trapping her against him.

Uh-oh, looking down was a mistake.

He now had a close-range view of those firm abdominal muscles that tortured him daily. She was a pretty little package, tightly wrapped.

What the hell, he thought. He'd never been any good at waiting until Christmas . . .

W9-DHX-473

By Robyn Amos

WEDDING BELL BLUES
BRING ME A DREAM

ROBYN AMOS

Wedding Bell Blues

HarperTorch
An Imprint of HarperCollinsPublishers

This is a work of fiction. Names, characters, places, and incidents are products of the author's imagination or are used fictitiously and are not to be construed as real. Any resemblance to actual events, locales, organizations, or persons, living or dead, is entirely coincidental.

HARPERTORCH
An Imprint of HarperCollins*Publishers*
10 East 53rd Street
New York, New York 10022-5299

Copyright © 2004 by Robyn Amos
ISBN: 0-380-81543-5

First HarperTorch paperback printing: May 2004

HarperCollins ®, HarperTorch™, and ❦™ are trademarks of Harper-Collins Publishers Inc.

Printed in the United States of America

Visit HarperTorch on the World Wide Web at www.harpercollins.com

10 9 8 7 6 5 4 3 2 1

This book is dedicated to John Pope.
Without his love and support,
I wouldn't have been able to finish this book.

❧ Prologue ❧

Grant Forrest stood naked in his remodeled bathroom, grinning with pride as his day-old hot tub filled with water. Anticipation had pulled him out of bed thirty minutes before his six o'clock alarm.

Just as he was about to dip his toe into the hot, bubbling water, he heard the *Union Tribune* land on his doorstep. Grant wasn't big on morning coffee, but the one thing he did need to get started was the daily news.

Without thinking twice, he grabbed a towel off the rack and wrapped it around his waist. A hot soak and the morning paper—what could be better?

Halfway to the bathroom door, he caught his reflection in the mirror and shuddered. He could just imagine what the neighbors would think if they caught him creeping around his front porch in nothing but a pink bath towel.

Thanks to his ex-wife, *all* his towels and sheets were pink. The day she moved out, she'd washed his crisp white linens with everything red she owned—approximately, half her closet.

It was true; he preferred things simple, if not plain. That fact had driven Katrina crazy during their short marriage. Leaving him with nothing but pink sheets to sleep on was her cheap attempt at revenge.

Eventually, he'd buy new white linens—or maybe even beige, but for now, he let the feminine hue remind him to be careful who he let into his heart and his home.

This wasn't a lesson he took lightly. As a marital therapist, he knew not to let one failed marriage sour him on love. But after *two* failed marriages, Grant was giving up on walking down the aisle. He'd seen enough battered relationships to know that marriage wasn't for everyone.

Marriage with Katrina hadn't been easy, but it was a picnic compared to his marriage with his first wife, Charlotte. How could two little words like "I do," change a woman so completely? He felt a dull ache in his chest and quickly pushed the bad memories aside.

Grant dashed downstairs, stepping over his twin white Persian cats, Dr. Ruth and Westheimer.

Gripping his towel at the waist, he cracked the door open, hoping the paper had landed within reach. Instead, he spotted it at the far corner of his doorstep.

"It figures," he muttered.

Moni Lawrence squinted at street signs in the hazy light of dawn. "Was that Bernardo Mesa?"

She slammed on the brakes, sloshing tepid coffee all over her handwritten directions.

"Poop," she swore, trying to mop up the spill with the first thing handy, her sweatshirt sleeve. Blue ink ran together on the page, and Moni couldn't make out if she was supposed to make a left- or right-hand turn.

If it weren't for each home's distinctive landscape, Moni wouldn't have been able to tell one neighborhood from the next. All the houses featured red Spanish-tile roofs and stuccoed facades.

Backing up to make a three-point turn, Moni hung the directions out of the window, hoping the air would blow them dry.

She'd been driving for most of the night, and for the last hour and a half, she'd been hopelessly lost. Six A.M. was way too early to start knocking on doors for directions to 1405 Paloma del Rio.

Moni was noticing that most of the streets in San Diego had Spanish names. Around here, they all sounded alike. She'd been searching for Bernardo Mesa and instead found Bernardo

Vista and Bernardo Valley. Things hadn't seemed nearly so confusing with the real estate agent by her side several weeks earlier.

The excitement of being the proud new owner of her first home had fizzled six hours ago when the eighteen-hour drive from her best friend's home in Portland had turned from an adventure to a scavenger hunt.

Moni made a left turn on Bernardo Mesa and crossed her fingers. Her eyes were so tired they burned, she had a painful crick in her neck, and to make matters worse, she was suffering from a severe case of cramps.

All she wanted was to find her new house so she could take a hot shower and a long nap. She didn't even care that her nap would have to take place on a sleeping bag because her bed wouldn't be delivered until the next day.

Turning up the radio, hoping to force some energy into her sleep-deprived brain, Moni almost missed her next turn. Jerking the wheel hard enough to screech the tires, she made a wide turn onto Paloma del Rio.

Grant scanned the surrounding houses relieved to see they were as dark as the early morning sky. Pushing the door open wider, he leaned all the way out. His fingertips had barely brushed the plastic sleeve, when he felt a rush of movement at his ankles.

He tried to close the door, but one cat had already slipped through his legs.

"Westheimer, get back here."

Still clutching his towel, Grant lurched forward, making a grab for the cat. He stumbled as Westheimer evaded his grasp and sprang into the yard in hot pursuit of a squirrel. The squirrel scampered across the street and the cat followed, right into the path of an oncoming car.

"Look out!" Grant raced after his pet, barely aware that he'd lost his towel.

Westheimer stood frozen as the brown station wagon sped toward him. Tires screeched and the car swerved sharply to the left, missing the cat by a whisker.

Just as Grant's mind registered Westheimer's safety, he realized that the car was now headed directly for *him*.

The station wagon jumped the curb and came barreling across the lawn.

Grant turned and ran. The anticipation of lethal impact fueled his heels. Like an Olympic sprinter, his body sliced through the wind.

His feet slid on the slick grass, and his head whipped around. The car was still coming for him. The woman behind the wheel was shouting, but he couldn't make out the words.

Grant picked up speed. There was nowhere to run. He'd never make it to his door before this woman flattened him.

Hurtling toward his fence, Grant leapt up and hooked his arms over the top. The fence shuddered and bowed as the car crashed through a few feet from where he hung.

Following a resounding splash, a cascade of water arched over the fence and rained down on him. At once, Grant knew the station wagon had landed in his swimming pool.

Grant dropped to his feet, and a sudden chill settled over him. He looked down and froze.

"Good Lord, I'm naked."

Chapter 1

"Ms. Lawrence." Judge Fox said, with as much amusement as southern charm. "Would you please explain your 'attractive nuisance' defense to the court?"

"Of course, Your Honor," Moni Lawrence said, taking a deep breath, still a bit stunned to find herself in a San Diego small-claims court.

She darted a look in Grant Forrest's direction. He bore a strong resemblance to the actor Taye Diggs—smooth skin the color of bittersweet chocolate, neatly trimmed hair and a clean-cut, handsome face. His khaki pants were pressed into a crisp seam, and his shirt and tie were perfectly coordinated and wrinkle-free. He was the picture of composure—and why shouldn't he be? *He* was suing *her*.

He'd stated his case against her in a strong clear voice, but now that it was her turn, she prayed her voice wouldn't crack.

"An attractive nuisance is an irresistible hazard—like an unenclosed pool would be to a child. The water is so seductive, the child is lured to it and, therefore, endangered."

"I object, Your Honor," Grant interrupted. "My pool *was* enclosed, in fact, Ms. Lawrence had to drive her car *through* my fence to get to it."

"Judge Fox, in this particular situation, it was Mr. Forrest *himself* that was the hazard. Not his pool."

Moni held her breath, afraid to glance in the plaintiff's direction. Any moment now, she was sure she would burst into flames from the sheer force of Grant's gaze.

Judge Fox chuckled, creases forming in his leathery brown cheeks. "And would you please tell the court how you came across this defense strategy, young lady?"

His eyes sparkled with grandfatherly amusement, and Moni felt like a five-year-old who'd just been asked to perform for visiting relatives.

"When I was in college, I took a business law course and remember going over attractive nuisances and how they can be liabilities for businesses or homeowners. So I did some research on the Internet to see how it might be applied in this case."

Moni could see that Judge Fox was amused by her defense. While she realized that didn't mean he was buying into it, she had to give it her best shot. Why couldn't she be Ally McBeal for a day?

She cleared her throat. "As the plaintiff stated

earlier, his cat ran into the street, and I swerved to avoid it. Now, I *might* have been able to regain control if Mr. Forrest hadn't been standing right there *stark* naked."

At that point, Moni made the mistake of looking over at Grant again. This time her memory took over. His clothes started melting from his body the way ice cream dripped from a cone. She could see every muscle in his lean, well-defined chest. His biceps were firm and he had a tight six-pack at his middle. Her eyes dropped lower.

She drew a sharp breath. For a moment, Moni forgot where she was. Clutching a hand to her chest, she gaped at Grant.

"Ms. Lawrence." Judge Fox banged his gavel to get her attention. "Ms. Lawrence, please continue."

Like a needle skipping across a record, her fantasy ended. She faced forward, pulling herself together.

"Yes, um . . . as I was saying . . ." She blinked. "Uh, what was I saying, Your Honor?"

Judge Fox sighed, his amusement fading. "Ms. Lawrence, you were about to explain to the court just how Mr. Forrest's nudity makes him an attractive nuisance."

"Of course, I'm sorry, Your Honor. I'm a bit nervous. I've never been in a courtroom before."

The judge smiled, his eyes softening again.

"Where are you from? Your accent is mighty familiar."

"Oh, I'm sure you've never heard of my hometown, Judge. I'm from Dunkin, Virginia."

Judge Fox laughed, smacking his desktop. "A little town about forty miles outside of Richmond, right?"

"Why, yes." Moni straightened with surprise. "You mean you've actually heard of it?"

"I was born and raised in Richmond, Virginia. We used to drive to Dunkin to go fishing twice a year. You know, I've been meaning to get back there."

Grant cleared his throat. Judge Fox gave the plaintiff a sharp look but took the hint and prompted Moni to continue.

Gaining confidence, she raised her voice. "Now, I realize that things are done a lot differently here than where I come from, but isn't it still against the law to parade around naked in public?"

"Objection, Your Honor, I wasn't *parading* around, it was an acc—"

"Now, now, Mr. Forrest, you've had your turn. Let Ms. Lawrence state her case. Then I'll hear from you again."

"Thank you, sir," Moni continued. "I was so caught off guard by the plaintiff's . . . uh, pe—uh, I mean his . . ."

Moni grabbed the water pitcher in front of her, poured herself a glass, and took a long sip.

Her cheeks felt hotter than a pancake griddle on Sunday morning.

"Let me start over. Mr. Forrest's *nudity* was so startling, I lost control of my vehicle a second time, and was drawn onto his property to my own misfortune. In fact, I think Mr. Forrest is lucky he wasn't arrested for indecent exposure."

From the corner of her eye, she saw Grant throw his hands up. "Your Honor, you can't possibly be taking this seriously."

"Young man, I've been doing this for many years without the benefit of your help. I think I can decide for myself what I should and should not take seriously. Now, tell me this, Mr. Forrest, did you and the defendant reach an initial agreement regarding the fence?"

"Yes. I told Ms. Lawrence that I would get a few estimates, and she agreed to pay for the repairs."

The judge nodded toward the defendant. "Is that true, Ms. Lawrence? Did you agree to pay for the repairs to Mr. Forrest's fence?"

"I did, Your Honor, but the estimates Mr. Forrest brought me were outrageous."

Grant raised his hand. "Your Honor, I have photos of the damage to my property."

"Please pass the photos and your estimates to the bailiff." Grant did as he was instructed, and the judge studied the folder of evidence.

"The cheapest estimate I see here is eleven hundred dollars," the judge stated. "Tell me,

Ms. Lawrence, why does that seem unreasonable to you?"

"Eleven hundred dollars? Judge, I could buy ten fences for that much money."

"And what facts are you basing that statement on?" he asked.

"Well, back home—"

"Ms. Lawrence." The judge smiled at her as though she were a two-year-old. "You do understand that the cost of living in a small town like Dunkin is considerably lower than it is here in San Diego."

"I can understand that, sir. But you'll notice on his estimates that the largest portion of the bill is for labor. If I bought the wood and replaced the fence myself, it wouldn't cost anywhere near eleven hundred dollars."

"And are you qualified to perform such a task?"

Moni wasn't a stranger to tools. She'd been raised in the country, where folks didn't believe in hiring someone else to do a job they could do for themselves. "Yes, sir. I'm very capable with my hands. I *know* I could do the job."

Grant held up a finger. "May I say one other thing, Your Honor?"

Judge Fox nodded. "Go ahead."

"After the incident, Ms. Lawrence mentioned that she'd just come into a large inheritance. Clearly, money isn't the problem here. In which case, I don't understand why she would rather dirty her hands making the repairs herself when a contractor could get the job done in half the time."

Judge Fox steepled his fingers under his chin. "Mmm, this is very interesting. Is that true, Ms. Lawrence, did you inherit a sum of money?"

Moni resisted the urge to roll her eyes. Why on earth had she told Grant so much of her personal business? She'd been flustered and, as usual, had become overly chatty.

"Yes, I did, Your Honor. My last living relative, my Aunt Regina, died eight months ago, and she did leave me a great deal of money. As Mr. Forrest stated, this isn't about money. I'm used to not having it, so it makes no never mind to me if I have to spend it. But folks back home in Dunkin were like family to me, and they made me promise to spend it carefully. They told me that when I moved to such a large city, people would be eager to con me out of my inheritance."

She threw a sideways glance toward the plaintiff. "Now, by no means am I calling Mr. Forrest a con man . . ."

"It certainly sounds that way to me."

"Mr. Forrest," Judge Fox scolded.

"I'm sorry, Your Honor." Grant straightened his tie.

Moni bit her lip. Had she gone too far? Maybe it was time to backpedal a little bit.

"Your Honor, I understand that it was my car that left a whopping hole in the plaintiff's fence.

I was raised with proper southern values. I want to make amends for Mr. Forrest's loss. I just want the opportunity to fix it myself. I'm certain once he sees what a good job I've done, we'll both be able to put this unpleasantness behind us."

Judge Fox nodded. "Okay, I've heard enough to make my decision. I'll adjourn to my chambers to review your testimonies and return with my verdict."

Grant had expected an open-and-shut case, but he should have known better once he'd gotten a look at Moni Lawrence.

Sure, she'd had that same fragile look when he'd fished her out of his pool, but he'd chalked that up to crashing through his fence followed by an unscheduled swim in a 1987 Buick LeSabre.

Yet, somehow, she maintained that same look this morning. How did she manage that wide-eyed look of innocence? A look he'd thought was reserved for those Precious Moments figurines his sister collected. Head lowered, nibbling on her full bottom lip, she darted nervous glances at him through her lashes.

Grant shook his head as his eyes traveled down her body. She was way too thin. The skirt of her plum-colored suit was too short, making her look like she was all legs. Or maybe it was the three-inch heels that created that illusion. Despite the fact that they were nice legs—a smooth expanse of honey-brown skin—she still looked like someone needed to take her home and feed her a big fat steak.

Obviously, she'd tried to tame her wild curls by knotting her hair at her neck. A few strands still managed to bounce free like couch springs, in addition to the two long corkscrews she kept batting out of her eyes.

"Please rise for the honorable Judge Fox," the bailiff announced to the courtroom.

Grant pulled his attention away from Moni, and held his breath as the judge took his place. At this point, it could go either way. Even with the truth on his side, it was hard to compete with Moni's hometown connection.

"Mr. Forrest, Ms. Lawrence, I've listened to both sides of your argument very carefully. This case is actually more straightforward than it initially seemed. Miss Lawrence accidentally drove her car through your fence, leaving behind a large hole."

Grant felt his body start to relax when he heard Judge Fox's matter-of-fact tone. Hopefully, the judge hadn't taken Moni's fanciful interpretation of the law seriously.

"Now, Ms. Lawrence doesn't deny that she's responsible for the repairs. The real dispute here is money. What is a fair price for fixing Mr. Forrest's fence? Is Mr. Forrest's estimate of eleven hundred dollars too high?"

Grant began to tense again.

"I made a phone call while I was in my chambers. It seems Mr. Forrest's estimate is not unreasonable, but it is at the high end of the spectrum."

Grant winced as his strong case was getting weaker by the moment.

"In most cases, that's irrelevant. As long as the plaintiff submits a reasonable estimate, the defendant is expected to pay."

Grant sighed his relief. Now you're talking, he thought.

"But, in this case, I find that there is some validity to the defendant's claim that the plaintiff shares some responsibility here." The judge looked him in the eye, and suddenly, Grant felt like a sixteen-year-old who'd missed curfew.

"Since attractive nuisance laws generally refer to property and not people, they are not particularly relevant in this case. However, it may have been early, and you may have only planned to go as far as your front porch, Mr. Forrest, but your state of undress did cause the defendant to lose control of her vehicle."

Grant felt his spine go numb. He wiggled a finger in his ear. He couldn't have heard that correctly.

"Therefore, Mr. Forrest will have to be flexible regarding the repairs. The court will draft an order stating that Ms. Lawrence must restore Mr. Forrest's fence, whether it be by hiring her own contractor or by repairing the fence herself. The fence must be mended within thirty days. If, at that time, the fence has not been repaired, or the repairs are not done to the plaintiff's satisfaction, Mr. Forrest can petition the court for monetary compensation."

Grant stood frozen in place. Had the whole world gone mad?

Chapter 2

Grant stared at the blinking cursor on his computer screen. He needed a synonym for stinky. Malodorous?

"The rotting corpse was *malodorous*," Grant read aloud. "Now *that* stinks." He hit the backspace key several times then scanned the thesaurus again. Finally, he typed the word "pungent."

Narrowing his eyes at the screen, Grant muttered, "No, no . . . keep it simple, stupid," and deleted the entire sentence. "Let me try, 'The rotting corpse stank like a—' "

Grant's thought process was interrupted by a clattering thud out front. He tried to ignore it, but a few minutes later, he heard it again—plink, plink, plink, thump.

He glanced at the clock. It was only 8:30 in the morning. Getting up from his desk, he walked over to the window. Looking out, he snickered. "You've got to be kidding me."

Grant saw a large pile of wooden planks stacked in Moni's front yard. One by one, she was carrying them across the street and dropping them on his lawn. At that rate, she'd be carting wood all morning.

He moved away from the window, glancing back at his computer. He'd been working since 6:30 and he hadn't gotten past the opening line of chapter one. But at least then it had been quiet. His concentration would be shot with Moni banging around out there. He couldn't get rid of the comical image of her trying to haul those enormous boards into his yard.

Deciding a break was in order, Grant went outside to his front porch. By now, Moni was headed back to his property with a large plank barely balanced on her shoulder. "Are you sure you can handle that?" he called to her.

"No problem," she called back, but her breathing was heavy and she looked over-heated. Finally, she plunked the board down with the others and stood with her hands on her hips as she gathered her breath.

Grant walked over to her. "Are you sure you want to do this? Do you *really* know what you're doing?"

"Piece . . . of cake," she said, inhaling deeply. "Don't you worry about a thing."

Grant looked from the stack of wood still on Moni's lawn to the three boards lying on his lawn, and suddenly he worried about *every*thing.

Would she be outside his house all day? All week? All summer?

What would his fence look like if and when she finally finished?

Was all this aggravation worth it?

Suddenly, he wished he'd told her to forget the whole thing. He could have had the fence fixed at his own expense and moved on with his life.

He'd known she was gung ho about this project in court yesterday, but he hadn't expected her to move so fast. Now that he'd seen her in action, he knew she was going to be trouble.

She was barely five feet tall, and her curls spouted like water fountains from pigtails on either side of her head. Her hair was a combination of colors; the rich browns of fresh earth and the orange-reds of fall leaves. Her honey-brown skin was flushed from exertion.

He knew she had to be at least twenty-five, but she didn't look a day over eighteen. She'd dressed in tiny denim overall-shorts with a tool belt strapped around her waist. But, it was her shoes that really caught his attention—neon blue work boots with pink shoelaces.

"Don't let me keep you from whatever you were doing, Grant. I've got everything under control." With that, she trotted back across the street.

Grant opened his mouth to tell her different, then instead, shook his head and went into the house to get back to work. He'd only been sitting at his desk for a couple of minutes before he heard talking out front.

Walking back to the window, he saw his next-door neighbor, Ed Jackman, helping Moni carry wood back and forth across the street. Grant sighed. "There's *definitely* gonna be trouble."

Ed was mid-fortyish, balding and his beer belly was in its third-trimester. He also had an eye for the ladies. He'd heard that every summer, he'd park himself at the community pool just to watch the young women in their bikinis. Ed's wife, Sandra, was aware of his roving eye, and as a result, she kept a close watch on him.

And, sure enough, Grant didn't have to wait two minutes before he saw Sandra marching across the street. He moved away from the window. He didn't have to watch to know what was going to happen next. Sandra would cause a minor scene and then drag Ed straight home.

Grinning to himself, Grant sat back down at his computer. Ten minutes later, he'd deleted more than he'd written. He'd had no idea writing fiction was going to be this difficult. His nonfiction books had practically written themselves. Writing about helping men to communicate better with women or helping women to recognize when they're in dead-end relationships came naturally. He did those things all day long.

Now that he was trying his hand at fiction . . .

well, he was trying too hard, that was all. Looking up every other word in the thesaurus wouldn't get him anywhere. He had to let the words flow and tweak them later.

With that in mind, Grant tapped away at his keyboard and finally started accumulating paragraphs. Just when he'd gotten into a groove, his telephone rang.

"What's wrong with you? How could you let that poor little girl do all that heavy lifting on her own?"

"Sandra? I . . . uh—"

"Ed and I helped her move the boards to your yard, but she refused to let us do any more. She said you wouldn't like it if we helped her. Why couldn't you *hire* someone to fix your fence instead of making that poor little thing get all sweaty in the hot sun? You must be violating all kinds of child labor laws."

"Moni is hardly a child—"

"What's the difference as tiny as she is. Those boards are twice her size. This is not how Rancho Bernardo residents welcome their new neighbors."

"Sandra, she insisted—"

"I don't like it. I don't like it at all. Now, you get out there and help that little girl before she hurts herself and sues *you*."

The next thing Grant knew, he was uttering a sheepish, "Yes, ma'am."

Sandra had already hung up the phone before Grant realized what had happened. His earlier amusement faded. How did she do it? How did Moni manage to keep turning things around on him like this? She hadn't been outside for more than an hour and already his neighbors were angry . . . with *him*, no less.

Shaking his head, Grant went outside. Now his neighbors thought he was some kind of fiend for letting her do work that was better suited to a professional anyway.

He burst out of his front door, and immediately came to a dead halt. "Omigod. Be careful." He rushed over to steady the sawhorse just before the whole thing toppled over on her.

Moni steadied herself. "Thanks. That was just a bit of a miscalculation. I'm fine, really."

"You see, that's exactly what I came out here to talk to you about—"

"It's the saw," she said, shaking her head at the offending tool. She gingerly laid it on the ground. "It's just way too big for me to handle."

Grant glared at the saw. Next to Moni's five-foot frame, it seemed monstrous. She could have seriously injured herself trying to wield that thing. Grant felt his anger rising. "What on earth made you think you had to cut all this wood yourself? You *do* know you can get it from the lumber yard precut."

She grinned, hooking her thumbs in the loops

of her tool belt. "Of course, but why waste money on something I can do just as well myself? My dear Aunt Reggie—God rest her soul—always said, 'If you want something done right, you have to do it yourself.'"

Grant resisted the urge to roll his eyes. *Everybody* always said that. He doubted Moni's dear Aunt Reggie—God rest her soul—had invented the phrase. "Look—"

"Besides," Moni continued. "I just know it's the saw. You caught me at a bad moment, but I really do know what I'm doing. The saw I used back home was much smaller than this. Aunt Reggie kept a whole shed full of custom-made tools. We Lawrence women have always been the smallest branches on the tree."

"Well, that's nice, but—"

"I don't know why I didn't think to bring the tools with me. I sold most of Aunt Reggie's furniture and such along with the house. I figured, what the heck? Why not start fresh? I'm moving to a whole new place. May as well get all new things." She rubbed her chin. "I just didn't know I'd be needing new tools so soon."

Moni bent down to pick up the gigantic saw again. "I thought this one looked uncommonly large in the hardware store, but it was the only regular saw in stock. The rest were power saws. Maybe I'd better see if I can borrow a smaller one until I can buy another."

"Why didn't you just get a power saw?"

She slanted her eyes downward with an attractive blush. "I'd like to finish this job without losing an arm."

"I've got a saw." Grant blinked. Why had he said that? "But . . ."

Before he could take it back, Moni's face lit up. "Really? Would you let me try it?"

"But . . . I'm not sure it's too much smaller than the one you've got there, so . . ."

"Can I see it?" She looked so excited, they could have been talking about diamonds instead of an old saw.

"I guess . . ." Before Grant knew it, he'd not only gotten out his saw, he'd cut through three boards and was about to tackle the fourth when Moni stopped him.

"Thank you kindly for your help, but I'd like to do the rest myself, if you don't mind."

"Oh, sure. Um . . . of course . . . I'm sorry." Grant backed away from the sawhorse, feeling a tiny bit foolish. How had he ended up helping her when he'd come outside to send her home?

"Don't worry, it's not your fault," she said, as though she could read his mind. "I'm used to it. My DDS strikes again."

Grant shook his head in confusion. "DDS? What's that? Are you sick?"

"No, it's just something I made up. DDS is short for Damsel-in-Distress Syndrome. I'm afflicted with it."

"What?" Grant couldn't help himself, he laughed out loud.

"I'm serious. For some reason, I seem to give off this vibe that makes people want to rescue me. I'm really not the helpless little thing I appear to be. But, you know how it is. I'm petite and, well, kinda perky. Plus, my Aunt Reggie always said I was cursed with my mother's eyes. When I was younger, I'd thought she'd meant the unusual gold-brown color. Now I know she just meant the fact that they're real big and round. When I see pictures of myself, I cringe because I've always got this stupid wide-eyed look on my face. Just like those dopey Precious Moments figurines Aunt Reggie collected."

Grant threw back his head and released a bout of laughter that came from deep in his belly. He'd had that same thought just yesterday. Now, as he studied her more closely, he wondered if he'd judged her too harshly.

Sure, she'd made an unusual first impression—driving into his swimming pool and all—but those had been unusual circumstances. What's more, it was pretty hard to stay mad at someone who looked as appealing as she looked with her curly pigtails and day-glow work boots.

She'd been so self-deprecating about her cuteness, he couldn't hold that against her, either.

Moni bent over to pick up the saw he'd dropped, and Grant noticed the way the cuffs of her shorts brushed against the firm muscles cording her thighs. He'd also been wrong about her being too skinny. She was small-boned, but didn't have that frail, bony look of undernourishment. Her body was lean and healthy.

Very healthy, he thought with masculine appreciation as his eyes skimmed over her round derrière. Eventually, Grant realized that while he'd been standing there gawking at her, Moni was busy sawing wood.

He walked around the sawhorse and noted that her face was set in a determined grimace as she worked. He'd be damned if his gut instinct, as he watched her, wasn't to snatch that big nasty saw out of her hands and take over. She was right, there was something about her that made people want to take care of her.

But he also had to admit that once she'd gotten her grip on that saw, she attacked the wood with tenacity.

Maybe he did owe her the chance to try to get the job done. She clearly had something to prove, if not to him, then to herself.

"Hey, listen, it's going to get pretty hot out here. Can I get you something to drink?"

"Gee, that would be great, but I don't want to stop just yet."

"No problem. I'll bring it to you." Grant returned a few moments later with two full glasses of lemonade.

Moni put down the saw and took the glass from him. "Delicious. Is this fresh squeezed?"

"I'm afraid not, it's a powder mix. I just added lemon slices."

"Well, that's quite a bit more trouble than I would have gone to. I used to spend a lot of time in the kitchen when Aunt Reggie was alive. Now I live off anything that comes in a box and can be fixed in the microwave."

Grant shrugged after taking a sip from his own glass. "I don't mind cooking. But, you're right, I'm a lot more motivated when I'm cooking for another person." His mind turned toward his ex-wives. For both of them, he'd done most of the cooking.

"That's right, didn't you mention in court that you're divorced?"

Grant swallowed, feeling that familiar sinking in his stomach. "Twice."

Now why had he told her that? It certainly wasn't because he was proud of the fact. No need to advertise that he was hopeless when it came to marriage. Especially when people paid him to be an expert on matters of the heart.

Before she could comment on his multiple divorces, he changed the subject. "You mention your Aunt Reggie a lot. The two of you must have been close."

"Yes, my parents were killed in a plane crash when I was fourteen." Her gaze was focused on the bottom of her lemonade glass and sadness crept into her soft southern voice. "My Aunt Regina raised me."

"That's right, you said she was your last living relative." Grant leaned against the sawhorse next to her. "That's rough. I'm sorry."

Moni sipped her lemonade. "Yes, it has been rough. Thank you."

He could see the pain etched in the normally smooth lines of her forehead. Perky suited her far better than melancholy.

"In Dunkin, Aunt Reggie was affectionately known as a crazy old bird," Moni said with a wistful smile.

"She wasn't a kook or anything," she rushed to add. "She just had her own way of doing things."

Grant nodded. "We all have at least one relative like that." Or more than one, he thought. Hell, everyone in his immediate family had quirks. His quirk was the marriage jinx.

"I never realized just how eccentric she was until after she died."

"Why is that?" Grant watched as she played with the condensation on her glass.

"It was the money she left me. None of us even knew she had it."

He shook his head. "What do you mean?"

"Well, we weren't poor or anything, but we definitely lived . . . modestly. All I expected to receive at the reading of the will was the house and the land it rested on—in itself, that's nothing to sneeze at."

"So where *did* the money come from?" Grant

asked. It never occurred to him that he might be prying. People shared their most intimate secrets with him on a regular basis.

"I had no idea Aunt Regina had been investing the money my parents left her. She never touched a dime of it. Can you believe it?" she asked, shaking her head.

"She owned a little flower shop," Moni continued, "and the income from that is what we lived on. Sometimes money was tight, and the interest alone would have set her up just fine."

"That's incredible. It was noble of her to save the money for you."

Moni's face clouded. "In the will, she said she wanted me to use it to leave my mark on the world."

Grant couldn't resist teasing her, hoping to bring back her smile. "Well, you're off to a good start. You've already left your mark on my front lawn." He pointed to the matted grass of her tire tracks.

She wrinkled her nose at him and shook her head, making her pigtails jiggle from side to side, but her expression *did* brighten.

"On a serious note," he said. "I'm curious. You inherited a house, property, and, I presume a flower shop in Dunkin. How in the world did you end up all the way out here in San Diego?"

Moni paused to drain her lemonade glass. "I needed a change. I wanted to see the world outside of southern Virginia. I picked San Diego because my college roommate used to live out here. I came for a visit and decided to stay."

His brows rose. "*Used to* live out here?"

"You don't miss a thing, do you?" Moni smiled sheepishly, and the sparkle returned to her eyes. "You're going to laugh at me. This kind of stuff only happens to me."

"What's the story?" he asked, folding his arms across his chest.

"My old college roommate, Akiko, married a Navy man, Jim, and he'd been stationed here in San Diego. Right around the time I went to closing on my house, Jim left the military and took a job in Oregon. I was driving in from their new home in Portland the morning of our, *ahem,* incident."

He shook his head in sympathy. "Well now, you've been having some rotten luck, haven't you?"

"You could say that," she said with a sigh.

"Did you consider moving back to Dunkin after your friends moved away?"

She winked at him. "I bet you wish I had, don't you?"

"I'm not saying that, I just figured it might be difficult for you out here alone. Sounds like you left your support system back in Dunkin."

Moni stared at her boots. "I can't go back."

Grant noted her heavy tone. She sounded so final. "Why can't you go back?"

She began to fidget, tracing one of her fingers

with her thumb. "I told everyone I was coming out here for a fresh start. I can't go running back home now."

His instincts told him there was more to the story. If she were a client, he'd probe deeper, but she wasn't. And for the summer, he wasn't a therapist; he was a novel writer.

"Well, that's enough about me." She handed Grant her empty glass. "I'm sure I'm keeping you from something important."

Grant thought about his nearly blank computer screen waiting for him upstairs. "Nothing that I wouldn't like to put off a little longer."

"I know that feeling. What is it? Cleaning the bathroom? Reorganizing the closet?"

"Nothing like that. I'm writing a book."

Her bright eyes went wide. "A book. That's great. You're a psychologist, right? What are you writing—some kind of self-help thing? Like *Men Who Love Women Who Don't Love Them Enough*?"

"No, I've written a couple of those, but this is my first stab at fiction. A psychological thriller."

"This is so exciting. Are you writing under your real name?"

Her enthusiasm brought a grin to his lips, warming him with pride. "No, since I wrote my nonfiction books under my own name, this one's going to be written under a pseudonym. Mike Diamond."

"Mike Diamond." Moni rolled the name around in her mouth. "Mike Diamond . . . isn't that a Beastie Boy?"

Grant frowned. "A what?"

"A Beastie Boy. You know, as in *The* Beastie Boys. It's a music group."

An image of three white guys rapping flashed in his mind. "Even so, I seriously doubt my reading audience would know the difference."

"You never know. You might want to consider changing the name . . . unless you want your work associated with the guys who told everyone to fight for their right to party."

"Um, I'll think about it," Grant grumbled. Mike Diamond is a Beastie Boy. He shook his head.

Moni shrugged and then bent over to pick up the saw she'd laid down. The sun was angled just right for him to see through the opening in her overalls.

Grant was unprepared for the ball of heat that socked him in the stomach and then spread downward to his groin. Moni's top was cropped, leaving him a stunning view of her torso.

She had the perfect six-pack. Her abs were sculpted in smooth ripples, just below the feminine curves hidden by her top. Grant raised his gaze, afraid she'd become aware of his sudden fascination with her body.

Fortunately, she was oblivious to his hot gaze as she brushed sawdust from her shorts. Grant didn't want her to catch him drooling over her like a teenager, so he turned away.

He hadn't been prepared to feel such a strong attraction to Moni. In fact, it was the last thing he needed right now.

The last time he'd allowed himself to get caught up in his physical desires, he'd ended up married . . . and divorced. Then married. And divorced again.

He was taking a break from relationships and the complications they brought to his life. Moni and her damned DDS were more trouble than he could take on right now. He had to put his libido in check—and the fastest way to do that was to avoid temptation.

He started moving toward his front door. "I don't want to distract you from your work any longer."

"Okay. I'll see you later?"

Grant waved his hand and went into the house. Right now, that was the only safe place for him.

Chapter 3

Moni tried to get back to work after Grant left, but as morning slid into afternoon the heat of the sun became unbearable. The muscles of her hands and arms were so sore, she found it difficult to lift them.

Thinking she'd only take a short break, Moni headed home to cool off and rest her aching limbs. Instead, she flopped onto her bed and fell to sleep for several hours.

The sound of the telephone ringing pulled her back into reality. She sat upright on the bed still feeling disoriented. "Hello?" she croaked into the telephone receiver.

"Is that my Moni-love?"

Moni snapped out of her sleepy haze at the rich southern tones of her ex-fiancé's voice.

Earlier that day, Grant had asked her why she couldn't go back to Dunkin when her friends had moved away. The real reason was the man on the other end of the line, Burt Reynolds—the tire salesman, not the actor.

"Hi, Burt. I thought I asked you not to call me Moni-love anymore."

"I know you've been through a lot lately—and that's confused you into thinking we need to be apart *for now*—but you'll always be my Moni-love. Nothing's going to change that."

Despite herself Moni smiled. She could picture Burt's disheveled blond curls and the uneven smile that always hung on his suntanned face. In many eyes they were an unlikely couple, but they had been engaged for almost a year, and before Aunt Reggie died, she'd been content with the idea of spending the rest of her life with him.

"That's sweet, Burt. In a lot of ways, you'll always be my best friend in the world"—she tried to keep her voice gentle, but firm—"but I just want to make sure you've grasped the concept that we're not going to be married. Ever."

"Mama asked me what she should do with the wedding dress that's still on her sewing machine. I told her to finish it so it would be ready when you get back."

"You know I'm not coming back, Burt." Losing the desire to be gentle, Moni's voice took on a hard edge. "Are you being hardheaded on purpose?"

Although his heart was usually in the right place, Burt could be more bullheaded than anyone she'd ever known. It wasn't uncommon for him to make decisions and move forward with them despite any protest she might make to the contrary.

Over time, she'd come to overlook his controlling behavior, but now she saw it as one of the many reasons they'd be better off as friends instead of husband and wife.

"Don't be cross, Moni. I'm not being hardheaded so much as optimistic. I miss you is all. So does the rest of Dunkin. If you don't come back to see *me*, you've got to come back to visit all the folks who ask me a dozen times a day how you're doing out there."

Moni sighed, suddenly feeling sad. She did miss her friends, but it was too soon to visit. First they had to see that she could survive on her own.

"Tell them that I'm doing just fine. And that I miss them, but I don't know when I'll be back to visit. I've got a lot of things to take care of out here for a while."

"What kind of things? Is everything all right?"

Moni thought of Grant's fence and bit her tongue. "Everything's great. I just need time to get settled," she answered, then quickly changed the subject. "How are things there? Did Rhonda Tucker have her baby yet?"

Burt laughed and proceeded to fill Moni in on the latest gossip. When she finally hung up the phone, the mix of emotions she felt surprised her.

Even though she knew it had been the right thing to do, breaking off their engagement had been difficult.

Moni smiled, remembering Burt's proposal.

Burt was a quiet, deliberate man who hated public displays of any kind. Therefore, Moni knew it had taken a Herculean effort on his part to arrange for MONI LAWRENCE WILL YOU MARRY ME to be placed on the marquee of the Dunkin Multiplex Theater. There was only one movie theater in the area, so on a Saturday night, half the town was present to witness the proposal.

Aunt Regina had strongly encouraged her to accept Burt's offer of marriage. This surprised Moni, because Reggie had always been known in town as free-spirited. Though she'd eventually settled into the simple life of a shopkeeper, no one had forgotten the wild exploits of her youth.

It wasn't until a few months before she'd died that Aunt Reggie had begun extolling the virtues of security and marriage. These sentiments from a woman who'd never had any interest in tying herself down to one man. Until the day she died, she'd been in demand by both the local dentist and the county sheriff.

Later, Moni discovered that Reggie had been made aware of a heart condition several months before her death. She never told a soul, and after

Burt's proposal Reggie would often comment that it would be nice to know that Moni had someone to take care of her.

Aunt Regina hadn't been the only one in town excited over Moni and Burt's engagement. It seemed everyone in Dunkin had volunteered to contribute. Janet Mosley at the bakery would have made their cake. Burt's mother had begun sewing her wedding gown. Carlos Mendoza of the Dunkin Plaza Hotel had donated a free night in the honeymoon suite, and of course, Aunt Reggie would have handled all of the flower arrangements.

Moni had gotten caught up in all the excitement and the plans to be made. She hadn't even realized that she had no desire to get married until after Aunt Reggie's heart condition took her from them.

Reggie had always said she'd rather blow out her candle than let it slowly melt away. Aunt Reggie had lived a full life, though she'd died too young at fifty-eight.

Although part of her had wanted to marry Burt, Moni knew now that she never would have been satisfied. She was only twenty-six, and before she settled into a quiet life, she wanted to have wild adventures like the ones Reggie had experienced.

When the lawyer had read the amount of her inheritance and Aunt Reggie's wish that she use it to make her mark, Moni knew this was her chance.

Despite wanting her to be taken care of, Moni knew her aunt would much rather she follow in Reggie's footsteps and experience life.

Unfortunately, explaining this to Burt had been the most difficult task. Burt was crushed by their breakup and blamed it on the shock of her aunt's death. Moni *had* been in shock, but she'd also known that once the shock wore off, she still wouldn't want to get married.

As usual, Burt had been convinced he knew what was best for her and had told all of their friends the wedding had been postponed instead of canceled. The town had rallied around her to show support. While she was touched by their loving concern, she couldn't blink without someone asking if she were all right, bringing over baked goods, or insisting on sleeping in the guestroom so she wouldn't be alone.

She'd gone to San Diego to visit Akiko just to get away from the watchful eyes that were certain she was going to crumble without her aunt to lean on. What Moni had discovered was that she loved the freedom and independence of being out on her own.

It was easier to mourn her aunt in private, and she felt Burt needed some time to accept that things were really over between them. So, she sold her aunt's flower shop and the house without looking back. She loved Dunkin, and she planned to visit eventually, but she couldn't resist the opportunity to feel out her independence.

People always wanted to do things for her, but all she really wanted was to do for herself. Burt was a wonderful man, but whenever their opinions or choices conflicted, he insisted on having the final word. She didn't want to live that way anymore. She'd loved him, but there was something more out there for her.

Moni got up from the bed and sent a fleeting glance toward the window and Grant's house. She really should get back out there and finish cutting those boards. She'd had no intention of wasting so much of the day sleeping.

"Ugh," she moaned, trying to rub the soreness out of her shoulders. All she really wanted to do at the moment was soak in a hot bath.

Retrieving her notes from the dresser, Moni studied the project outline that consisted of a list of supplies, diagrams and measurements, and a timeline for each day's work on Grant's fence. She liked to approach each new project in an organized, scientific manner.

"I'm not too far behind." She penciled her progress into the margin, and then headed to the bathroom to fill the bathtub. "I'll just have to get started a little earlier tomorrow morning."

The next afternoon, Moni was hard at work when the loud roar of a motor caught her attention. Seconds later, a yellow convertible screeched to a stop in Grant's driveway.

An attractive man stepped out of the sports car, wearing a black T-shirt fitted to his muscular chest and black slacks. Despite his shorter, stockier build, it wasn't hard to determine that he was related to Grant. They shared the same angled jaw and broad nose.

A second car door slammed, forcing Moni's gaze away from the handsome stranger. A petite young girl rounded the car.

"Hey there," the man called.

Moni waved, walking over to the newcomers.

"If I'd known handymen were so pretty these days, I'd have started home improvements long ago."

A hefty sigh came from the girl beside him. She rolled her eyes and folded her arms across her chest. *"Dad."*

"I'm just kidding, Tara," he said, putting an arm around the girl's narrow shoulders.

"I'm actually not a handyman." Moni pulled off her gloves and extended her hand. "I'm Grant's neighbor, Moni Lawrence."

He took her hand in a firm grip. "I'm Keith— Grant's brother, and this is my daughter, Tara."

"Nice to meet you both," Moni said, her eyes meeting the young girl's. Tara smiled back shyly.

"Neighbor?" Keith was rubbing his chin.

"Don't tell me you're the crazy—uh, the lady who drove her car into his pool."

Moni laughed, nodding. "That's me. The crazy lady."

Tara giggled and Keith was clearly embarrassed. "Sorry, I didn't mean—"

Moni waved off his apology. "It's okay. I don't blame Grant for describing me that way. Most people wait for an invitation before taking a plunge in the neighbor's pool. Me? I just drive right in."

Tara snickered. "You're funny."

Moni knew this was the highest of compliments coming from a representative of the preteen generation. Anxious to change the subject, she looked past Keith to the bright yellow sports car. "Oh, how pretty. What kind of car is that?"

Keith beamed with obvious pride. "Porsche Boxster. Although, pretty isn't quite the right word for a gem like this." He stepped back to run a loving hand over the hood.

"Oh yes . . . it's definitely a *hot* car," she said dutifully.

He rewarded her with a vigorous nod. "That's right. You should see the engine."

Before Moni could reply that she wouldn't know the difference between a car engine and a bicycle gear, Keith was already showing her the engine—which for some reason was behind the seats.

"Look at that. This baby is powered by a water-cooled, six-cylinder engine with four-valve technology."

Catching her blank stare, Tara came to Moni's rescue. "Dad, you're doing it again. You're the only one who cares about this stuff."

Keith turned to face them with a sheepish grin. "Sorry. As Tara knows, I can get carried away with my car talk. Clearly you're not a mechanic, and we've already determined you're not a handyman. What do you do for a living?"

Moni shrugged. "I guess you could call me an entrepreneur."

Once she finished mending Grant's fence, she was going to pour all of her energy into starting a business with her inheritance. Since she wasn't quite sure what kind of business to start, she was relying on the research skills she'd developed as a psychology major. She'd compiled a list of ten creative business concepts, and she planned to investigate the viability of each one thoroughly.

Keith raised his brows, looking impressed. "Really? What are you . . ." He paused as Grant came out of the house.

"Don't let me interrupt." Grant crossed the lawn, then reached down to hug his niece.

Keith clapped his brother on the back in greeting. "Your new neighbor was just about to tell us that she's an entrepreneur."

Grant smiled, winking at her. "What do you

mean? I thought you were a wealthy woman of leisure."

Moni knew Grant was just teasing her, but couldn't help taking offense to the implication that she would choose not to work. She was getting really tired of not being taken seriously because of her appearance. She'd graduated summa cum laude from the University of Virginia, but she knew if she told Grant that right now, he'd regard her with wide-eyed disbelief.

Everyone assumed that she wasn't smart just because she was girly and petite with a cheerful attitude and a southern accent.

"A woman of leisure? Not at all." Moni lifted her chin. "I'm in the process of starting a business."

His brow lifted. "Seriously? What kind?" Grant asked.

Now that she had his interest, Moni was too embarrassed to tell Grant that she hadn't figured that part out yet. Aunt Reggie wanted her to leave her mark on the world, and Moni planned to do exactly that. She had no intention of blowing her big chance on the wrong concept.

But instead of trying to explain all that to Grant, she decided to describe one of the concepts she was researching. "It's a Web service that I'm going to call Music Therapy."

A puzzled expression passed over Grant's face. "Are you in the mental health field?"

Moni shook her head. "No, this has nothing to do with the type of music therapy used to treat psychological disorders. But it did inspire the name of my site."

Grant shrugged. "A therapy Web site? I don't understand—"

"Shh, let her explain," Keith said. Through all of this, Tara was slumped against the car, looking bored again.

"The site will be a variation on the concept of Internet radio. You can choose a play list of music based on the mood you want to create. If you want to get into a cheerful mood, you can create a play list from a database of upbeat music. If you just broke up with your girlfriend, you can choose from the most popular breakup songs. You can pick workout music, haunting music or songs for a rainy day."

Grant still looked confused. "And you would listen to this music over the Internet?"

"You can listen to it directly from your computer speakers or download it to your MP3 player."

He shook his head. "What's MP3?"

Tara perked up. "Uncle Grant, don't you know anything? MP3s are the newest way to get music. It's an MPEG file created specifically for digital transmission."

Moni grinned. "Thanks, Tara, I couldn't have explained it better myself."

"Oh, of course. Well, um, good luck with

that . . . whole thing," Grant said, though he clearly didn't understand what they were talking about.

"Thanks. I'll let you know when I get the site up and running. You can all be my first customers."

Keith grinned wickedly. "Tara and I will be your customers. Tater needs to call tech support just to turn his computer *on*."

"Tater?" She studied Grant. "Is that your nickname?"

Grant glared at his brother.

Keith laughed. "Yeah, Tater. That's what the family calls him. When he was little we called him Tater Tot 'cause he was so small. Even now that he's bigger, we still call him Tater out of habit, right, little brother?" He patted Grant's shoulder.

Grant rolled his eyes, brushing Keith's hand away. "You're the only one who still calls me that."

Moni smiled. "*Little* brother? I don't know why I assumed Grant was older."

Keith grinned. "Yeah, you're not the only one. It's because Grant's such an old man. As for me, age hasn't been able to suppress my youthful exuberance."

"Youthful exuberance," Grant said, "also known as blatant immaturity."

Keith kept smiling, clearly unruffled, but Tara was squirming at his side, her patience wearing thin. "Well, Tater, I have to drop Tara off at cheer-leading camp this afternoon, so we need to get going. I just dropped by to give you this check for the anniversary party. Let me know if you need more. I hit it big in Vegas last weekend."

A wary look passed across Grant's face as he accepted the check. "Thanks. Have fun at cheer-leading camp, kiddo," he said, squeezing Tara's shoulder.

They exchanged goodbyes and Keith and Tara got back into the Porsche and drove away.

Moni played with the fingers of her work gloves. "What kind of anniversary party?"

Grant watched the car pull off with a distant look on his face. "I'm sorry. What did you say?"

"What kind of anniversary party are you having?" She pointed to the check in his hand.

"Oh, my parent's fiftieth wedding anniversary is coming up. My brother, sister and I are throwing them a huge surprise party at the Hotel Del Coronado."

Moni sighed. "Fifty years. That's amazing. Tell your parents congratulations."

He nodded. "Thanks, I will."

"You and your brother look a lot alike," she said as she studied Grant's face.

He frowned. "Are you kidding?"

"No. You *do* look alike. Especially around the mouth and nose." They were both handsome men, but Grant had more of a clean-cut style.

"That's interesting because most people view the two of us as day and night."

Moni nodded. "You don't have a lot in common, do you?"

Grant shrugged. "We actually get along pretty well, but our interests are very different. Keith is a mechanic," he said in a flat tone.

"Well, you don't have to say it like that," she said, noting the disappointment in his voice. "Auto mechanics is a respectable profession."

Grant blinked. "Oh, of course it is. Don't get me wrong. It's just that he's absolutely brilliant with numbers—practically a genius. He was accepted at Vassar but turned down admission. Keith wouldn't have applied in the first place if my parents hadn't insisted. Instead of going to college, he went to work at Mason's Auto World."

Moni mulled over Grant's words for a minute. "Sometimes people feel the need to make personal decisions that everybody else might not understand. Your brother is probably happy with his choice. I know a lot of my friends didn't understand why I passed up a full scholarship to graduate school, but it was something I had to do."

Grant looked over in surprise. "Do you mind if I ask why?"

"My Aunt Reggie needed me to come home and help out with the flower shop. It was an uncharacteristic request from her, but I didn't question it. After all that she'd done for me, I thought she deserved to have a little more time to herself. I know now that she knew she was dying and wanted me close to home."

His eyes softened. "That's different, Moni. You were helping a family member. Keith's first year out of high school he spent running back and forth to Las Vegas on the weekends."

"Ahh, I thought I noticed a strange look on your face when he mentioned Las Vegas. Is that the problem—gambling?"

Grant shook his head in resignation. "Keith could have done so many things with his inherent mathematical talent, but casinos and cars are the only things he puts any effort into. His wife, Janet, almost left him because of his lack of ambition."

She shook her head. "That's really a shame."

Grant nodded. "They've had some rocky times. They're separated right now, but I think they're still trying to work things out for Tara's sake. My brother's a good guy and an excellent father, but he's not a goal-setter. He doesn't plan for the future. It's hard to build a life with someone like that. I recommended they get counseling with a colleague of mine, but I don't know if they'll go through with it."

Moni smiled, trying to be reassuring. "Well, you never know. If they really love each other, they'll work it out."

"Or not," Grant said under his breath.

Moni wasn't surprised by his cynicism. After two failed marriages of his own, he probably expected the worse for everyone. She couldn't help wondering how that affected his work as a therapist. Before she could ask him, Grant started backing away.

"I guess I should let you get back to work," he said and turned toward to the house.

After he left Moni, Grant returned to his novel. Two hours passed slowly with minimal progress. That must be why it was suddenly much more important to do an exhaustive Web search for the origin of the term gumshoe rather than write another paragraph.

He'd just discovered a plausible theory— "gumshoe" referred to the gum-rubber soles detectives wore to get around quietly—when his phone rang. He should have taken the phone off the hook so he could focus on his writing, but since he wasn't getting much done, he picked it up anyway.

"Hello?"

"It's happening again. The anxiety. It's back."

"Samantha?" He slipped the pencil he was holding behind his ear.

"I had to go up to the attic this morning, and I was overcome with a feeling of panic. My palms got sweaty, and I had to rush back downstairs." Her voice was tight.

"Okay, take a deep breath and tell me what's going on." Grant heard her inhale and exhale. He resisted the urge to do the same.

"Whew. Okay," she said after another deep sigh. "I'm sorry to call out of the blue like this. I know you took time off so you could write. I didn't want to interrupt you, but you said I should call if the anxiety came back."

"That's all right. Don't worry about it, I wasn't getting much done anyway. Tell me what's going on?"

"Well, I know you said it's not obsessive compulsive disorder, because I, you know, don't do all the hand washing and everything, but—"

"Yes, and you don't have any other symptoms of OCD, either."

"Yes, I know, but, I wanted to tell you that I figured it out. I was reading *Psychology Today* last night and it hit me." Her voice rose in pitch as she became excited.

Grant was almost afraid to ask, "What hit you?"

"Ataxophobia. That's what I have." He could her hear her clap her hands together to punctuate the sentence.

Grant chewed his lip. He didn't have a mental list of every possible phobia, but he knew Samantha would be more than happy to explain.

"Why do you think you have ataxophobia?"

"You know how I like to have things neat and organized all the time? Well, I've decided I'm not your run-of-the-mill neat freak. I believe I'm actually *afraid* of things being disorderly or untidy."

"Of course, because ataxophobia is a fear of disorder. Samantha—"

"Wait, I know you're going to say it's all in my head. You psychologists love to say that, but hear me out."

Grant listened quietly as Samantha described the stress and discomfort she experienced when her two sons left their toys strewn around the house or when her husband left a pile of dirty dishes in the sink.

"There's good news and bad news for you, Samantha," he said when she finished making her case.

"Tell me the bad news first. I can handle it," she said with grim resolve.

"The bad news is that you *do* fixate on disorderliness and that *is* causing your anxiety."

"I knew it," she whispered. "Go on."

"But, the good news is that I don't think you have ataxophobia."

"Why not?" She sounded disappointed.

"Because, while you *do* like things neat and clean, and you *are* anxious when they're not, I don't think your level of anxiety is abnormal or debilitating. It's very common for someone to feel unsettled when their environment is unorganized. With three small children, it's hard to keep the house clean the way you did when you were single. The reason you're focusing on your anxiety is because being home full-time with the kids is a huge adjustment for you."

"I hear what you're saying." She was quiet for a moment. "But, what am I supposed to do about the anxiety? Even though you think it's not ataxophobia, the panic is real."

Grant thought for a moment. Whatever advice he gave her, she'd still be on the phone with him tomorrow.

"Carl makes enough money for the two of you to have a maid. Why don't you discuss the possibility with him?"

"A maid." She tasted the word like an exotic dish—reluctantly.

"Trust me, if you have someone come in and straighten up once or twice a month, it will take a large part of the burden off you."

"A maid." This time her voice filled with anticipation. "Okay, I'll see what Carl thinks. Thanks for listening, Grant. I know you must be getting sick of me."

"Not at all. How could I, you're my sister. I'm stuck with you."

"And don't you forget it. I'll talk to you later. I heard about a great band we may be able to get for the anniversary party."

Grant hung up his phone shaking his head. Even though he'd taken the summer off, he'd known he wouldn't be able to escape his sister's constant need for attention. Ever since she made the transition from accountant to stay-at-home mom, Samantha had become convinced something was wrong with her. She read too many self-help books for her own good.

In the past, he'd tried suggesting she work part-time to gradually adjust to the idea of staying home. But, she'd insisted on being home to raise the kids while they were young because she'd read in *Psychology Today* that these were important bonding years.

Grant stared at the blinking cursor on his screen. He hadn't thought writing a novel would be easy, but he also hadn't expected it to be this difficult. His first two books had been born directly from his experience as a psychologist.

He'd chosen to focus on counseling married couples because, despite his own issues with the institution, marriage was a concept he believed in. He knew he was helping people, even if that didn't always mean keeping couples together. Sometimes he had to help them face the reality that they'd be better off apart.

Counseling was rewarding work, but it could also be frustrating. It was difficult for him to face the games and lies that couples played with each other from day to day. He needed to take some time to sort out his own relationship issues. Spending the summer writing a thriller would be a welcome vacation from his normal routine—or so he'd thought.

At the moment, sitting in his office as the impartial observer would be preferable to facing this empty computer screen. His best friend and colleague, Mitch Taylor, thought he was crazy. But Grant suspected that was directly related to the fact that Mitch had to take over his case load.

When the summer was over, he'd be glad to get back to marital therapy. He'd be refreshed, and hopefully, he'd have a completed novel in his hands. His editor for *It Takes Two: Learning to Communicate with Your Partner* and *You're on Your Own: A Guide to Moving On* had promised to give his first attempt at fiction a serious look if he turned in a proposal for two more self-help books.

Grant didn't want to lose this opportunity by wasting the summer. He pulled his keyboard tray closer. He could still hear Moni bumping around out front and her words echoed in his ears. Mike Diamond is a Beastie Boy. Did that really mean he had to change the name?

His editor wasn't thrilled about this book in the first place. Maybe it would be better not to give him any reason to reject it on sight. He sighed heavily. That meant he would change the name.

He thought for a few moments and typed the name Michael Woodland on the title page. Michael was his middle name and Woodland was a play on his last name Forrest. "Should be safe enough," he said aloud.

At least retyping the name on all three pages

of his manuscript gave him something to do. Once that was done, he was back to square one.

He clicked open his Internet browser. "I wonder where the word 'cop' came from?"

Chapter 4

Moni pulled into her driveway with a raging headache. She slid out of the rental car, rubbing her temples.

"Hi, Moni," a male voice called. She turned and saw Grant unloading groceries from his car. Her heart rate picked up as she walked to the edge of her driveway and waved.

He set his grocery bag on the ground and walked over to her. "What's the matter? I expected to see you working on the fence bright and early this morning."

Heat rushed up her neck. Two days had passed since she'd done any work on Grant's fence. She knew he was secretly hoping she'd already given up.

Although she'd rather die than give him the satisfaction of quitting, she *had* run into a rather embarrassing snafu that had delayed her progress.

After cutting all of her boards, she'd begun stacking them to one side to keep Grant's lawn uncluttered. She'd stacked several boards before a problem became apparent. Each board seemed to get ever so slightly shorter than the one before it. There was nearly a five-inch height difference between the boards she'd cut on the first day and the boards she'd cut on the second day.

Since she hadn't cut all the boards evenly, she'd had to order more planks from the lumberyard. In hopes of saving face—and energy—this time she ordered the wood precut.

Having been taught to be frugal all her life, she couldn't bring herself to pay twice as much for a rush delivery. Since she needed to replace her car anyway, she figured she might as well buy a sport utility vehicle and haul the wood herself.

Moni didn't want Grant to know how complicated she'd managed to make things, so she kept these details to herself.

She forced a bright smile, resisting the urge to rub her temples. "Have no fear. I haven't given up on the job. I had to special order a stain that would match the rest of your fence. Once it arrives, I'll be back to work."

Grant winked at her. "Is that a threat or a promise?"

She narrowed her eyes at him.

"Seriously, I'm not rushing you. I was just wondering why I hadn't seen you in a couple of days. You know, working on the fence."

Moni winked back at him, unable to resist the

urge to put him on the spot. "How sweet. You missed me hanging around, didn't you?"

She didn't have much experience with flirting, but it seemed to come naturally with Grant. Cute and preppie as ever in his standard uniform of Dockers and polo shirt, he took her breath away. Today he wore a white shirt that flattered his deep mahogany skin.

To her surprise he played along. "You know, I did. I was just starting to get used to the sweet lull of sawing wood."

"Really? I'll make you a tape so you can sleep at night. In fact, maybe I should start a series, soothing sawing, plinking planks and . . ."

"Don't forget my favorite, the relaxing whoosh of cars being dropped into swimming pools."

Moni held up a hand as if to solemnly swear. "I'm sorry that was a one-time performance. You'll have to rely on your memory for that one."

Grant laughed and Moni realized they'd come a long way since that fateful day in court. Already, they could laugh about the situation. That made her feel so good, she almost forgot about the nagging pain in her head.

"I hope you've been making good use of the peace and quiet. How's the book coming along?"

Grant's rolled his eyes. "Well, there's really only one answer to that question. Slowly. It's coming along slowly."

Moni nodded, sensing it was best not to continue with that topic. "Well, good luck. I hope to get an autographed copy when it hits the stores." She reached up, pressing two fingers to the throbbing pain at her right temple.

"It's a deal." His gaze followed the motion of massaging fingers. "Do you have a headache?"

She nodded. "I think it's more psychological than physical. I've spent the last two days car shopping."

"That's right, I guess you had to scrap that old junker they pulled from my pool." He glanced at the white Toyota in her driveway. "Is that a rental?"

"Yes, and I'm starting to think it might be worth the extra money to *keep* renting, if it means I don't have to face any more car dealers. I thought if I did my homework and showed up well informed, they'd have to take me seriously, but they're crooks. Every last one of them."

Grant laughed. "Is this your first time buying a new car?"

"Yes, I bought my first and last car—the one that ended up in your pool—for next to nothing from Akiko and Jim. That car and I didn't have a very long relationship."

"So, what's the problem? Is it that you know what you want, and they're just not giving you a fair price?"

"Exactly. It's as if they don't believe I could possibly know what I'm talking about. At first, I thought it was just the men, but the women are just as bad. I thought all you Californians were supposed to be laid back. This morning I had two different dealerships on the line going back and forth in a bidding war. I finally got so frustrated I hung up on them both."

"Look, I did pretty well last time I got a new car, would you like me to go with you?"

He felt sorry for her. She could read it in his eyes. "No, but thanks for the offer. I couldn't ask you to do that."

Grant shrugged. "It's okay. I really don't mind."

She gave him a shy smile. "Oh no, I'm not letting you use me as an excuse to avoid your writing. Don't worry about me. I'll have a brand-new SUV by this time tomorrow."

Moni fought to keep her voice light as her head began to pound harder. "Maybe I'll break down and order one over the Internet. I think they can drive it right to your door."

"Yes, but you're guaranteed to pay much more that way."

Moni sighed wistfully. "You may be right. I do need to save money for my business."

Grant nodded. "Yes, the music therapy thing. How's that coming along."

Moni fidgeted, sliding an imaginary ring on and off her ring finger. "I'm still researching it. But, I hope to get it off the ground soon."

"Ahh, I see," Grant said, but Moni knew that he didn't.

She didn't want to confess that she was just about ready to cross music therapy off the list.

The easiest thing to do would have been to come to San Diego and become a florist. After all, she'd been in the business all her life and knew the industry from the inside out. But, that had been Aunt Regina's dream. She wanted to make her *own* dreams.

Until now, she'd always thought she'd go back to graduate school and complete her Ph.D. degree in psychology. But even that dream didn't seem to fit anymore.

Moni started backing toward her house as Grant picked up a grocery bag. "Well, I'd better let you get your groceries inside. I hope you don't have any ice cream or anything in there."

"If you change your mind about car shopping, just give me a call."

"I'll do that." Moni crossed the street and let herself into the house. As she passed the phone, she saw there were seventeen messages on the answering machine.

"Ugh, more car dealerships." Clutching her head, she raced upstairs to search for some aspirin.

A gold-tinted pink haze was just spreading across the sky as Moni left the house for her morning jog the next day. She paused just long enough to note that the sunrise was the exact color of her new passion fruit nail polish, before pulling on her headphones and loping down the street.

She fell into her breathing rhythm, and as her body sliced through the air, Moni let her mind wander. It felt good to finally get back into her old exercise routine. It had been easy to slack off while she'd been working out the details of moving and preparing for court. But those excuses no longer existed.

On each run, she'd find a new route to explore, allowing her to feel more in touch with the unique landscape of San Diego. Moni loved to run first thing in the morning. The city was still asleep, and she could pretend she was the only person in the universe. At least that had been the case back home in Dunkin. San Diego had more than its share of the physically fit. She took note of several joggers, bikers and even inline skaters on her runs.

The exertion helped her expend all the tensions she'd built in the last few months. It was also a good opportunity to think things through. She'd done her best business brainstorming during that time, and she'd even sorted out the new feelings she'd been experiencing lately.

She'd felt joy with Burt. She'd felt warmth, comfort and pleasure with Burt, but she'd never felt passion. When she talked to her girlfriends, she'd never been able to relate to that irresistible force they'd described. Quickened breath, a surge of energy, followed by a tingling spine, fluttering tummy, and the blind emotion that drove all rational thought from the brain.

An image of Grant Forrest's nude body flashed in her mind and Moni's body became flushed. Passion? She felt a flutter in her tummy.

Grant was an attractive man. What luck that she'd moved in across from an eligible bachelor as delicious as he was. Her feminine intuition told her that he found her attractive as well. That and the lusty look she'd spotted in his eyes on occasion.

Yes, Grant was an attractive neighbor, and she wouldn't mind at all if he decided to ask her out. But something told her that despite their mutual attraction, he wasn't going to be the one to make the first move.

It didn't matter anyway. She'd just gotten out of a relationship. It was much too soon to pursue a new one.

It was a simple case of physical attraction. Just because she considered Grant handsome, didn't mean they had to have a relationship. Plenty of people shared attractions and never acted on them, right?

She caught another glimpse of Grant's nude body in her mind's eye and promptly tripped over her feet. Luckily she regained her balance before she went all the way down.

Moni forced thoughts of Grant from her mind and let herself focus on running. She ran until she reached that peak that extended beyond fatigue, beyond muscle soreness and beyond breathlessness. When she hit that pace, it was like reaching the placid center of a tornado. She felt like she could run forever and feel no pain. It was the closest thing to euphoria she'd ever felt.

When she rounded the corner of Paloma del Rio, Moni turned up the volume on her walkman and picked up speed for her homestretch sprint.

As her feet pounded to the thundering techno beat of her music, she couldn't help mourning the loss of her music therapy Web site. It was a shame that sorting through the copyright issues made the project cost prohibitive.

She still thought it was a wonderful idea. Nothing could affect her mood more than music, and Moni just knew her Web site would have been a fresh approach to the concept of Internet radio.

She began to slow down until she'd completed the transition to a brisk walk. Still riding the high of a good run, she refused to let her first setback upset her. Smiling, she lifted a hand to touch her chest. Next on her list was an even more promising initiative.

Grant prowled around his office after being pulled out of bed by his restless lead character, Trent Black. So much for his plans to sleep in. Instead, he turned his plot this way and that in his head, trying to get Trent out of the corner he'd backed him into. As it stood, his story was over in chapter three, and it didn't look like Trent was going to make it.

He passed the window noticing that he wasn't the only early riser on this block. The lights were on across the street at Moni's house. A flash of movement caught his attention, and he backed up to look closer. Moni was returning from her jog, circling the cul-de-sac at a brisk walk.

Grant watched her for a moment—only because it was something to do, he told himself. As his mind began to wander back to Trent, he saw Moni dip her hand into the neck of her T-shirt and pull out the end of a straw.

He leaned his nose against the glass, certain his eyes were deceiving him. Then, his delusions continued as she placed the straw in her mouth.

Grant blinked twice. Where was the water bottle, he wondered when he didn't notice a fanny pack or holder of any kind. He was watching so intently, he didn't notice Moni pausing in front of her house to wave up at him.

When her motions became exaggerated, he suddenly realized what she was doing and hastily waved back. Then she bent over and began doing knee bends and stretches.

Grant stood there for a moment, then his curiosity got the best of him. He just had to know what she'd been up to with that straw.

Throwing on an old T-shirt and tugging a pair

of jeans over his boxers, Grant rushed downstairs, hoping to get outside before Moni went
into her house.

"Hey," he called from his front porch, and
then jogged across his lawn.

Moni stood up and waited for him to cross the
street. "Good morning. Looks like it's going to
be a beautiful day."

"Yeah. Yeah, it's going to be nice, um, can I
ask you a question?"

"Sure, what's up?"

"I thought I saw you"—he was at a loss for
words—"drinking something?" He felt ridiculous. Had he really run out of his house to ask
her that absurd question?

But, to his surprise, Moni's eyes lit up. "Yes.
That's my new invention. I'm testing the proto-
type right now." She pulled the straw out of her
neckline again.

Grant shook his head. "What is it?"

"A beverage bra."

"A beverage bra . . . uh . . . ?" He stared un-
blinking, not sure how to process this new information.

"Yes, it's the next step in athletic support bras.
Want to see it?" She grabbed the hem of her
T-shirt and began to strip it over her head.

"Wait, I don't think . . . I mean . . . maybe you
shouldn't—"

"It's okay. You have to see it to really appreciate the design."

She whipped off the shirt and Grant's eyes went wide. It looked like a regular sports bra except the bottom half seemed to be covered with a rubbery material. If Moni hadn't already made it clear that the bra was filled with liquid, he would have thought her chest had doubled in size.

Grant almost felt ashamed of himself for staring at her chest so intently. "Isn't that, I don't know, heavy . . . up top?"

"Not at all. I can barely feel it. See your drink of choice is carried here. And the length of the straw is adjustable. You close off the straw with this rubber cap," she said, displaying the straw that protruded from her left shoulder strap.

"And you *invented* this?"

"Yup. I'm thinking about selling it on the Internet. The plan is to start with one product, then eventually expand to other things. I'm working on ideas for a similar athletic accessory for men—a beverage backpack or something."

"I see."

"Yes, water bottles are so cumbersome. With the beverage bra a woman can work out and stay hydrated at the same time."

"Amazing." His voice was flat.

"I think it could be a big success. When you have a chance, check out my Web site at www.beveragebra.com. Right now it's just a preview of coming attractions, but it should give you the basic idea. I have an online survey posted to see what kind of interest the public has in this idea."

"Wait a minute. What happened to your Music Therapy idea?"

"The research didn't support its viability. Too many copyright issues. I didn't want to go out the way of Napster."

"Yes, of course." Napster? It sounded vaguely familiar. It had been in the news awhile back, but the details escaped him.

He started backing toward his house. "Well, good luck with the, uh, beverage bra there. I didn't mean to interrupt your workout. I'll talk to you later."

"Oh, okay. Hey, and if you know of anybody who might be interested, let them know about the beverage bra."

Grant threw a wave over his shoulder. When was he going to learn to mind his own business where Moni was concerned?

That afternoon, after swimming several laps in the pool, Grant entered the house, knowing his dreaded writing was waiting. When he'd taken the summer off, he'd been excited about the prospect of spending his days pounding out page after page of the thriller that he'd been kicking around for years.

In reality, he'd spent most of the day writing garbage that he knew would eventually have to be thrown out. He'd hoped getting a little exercise in the pool would leave him with a clear head, so he could pick it up later.

As he passed through the kitchen, he grabbed a peanut butter energy bar, then jogged upstairs to check his machine. Anything to prolong the time before he had to go back to work.

He hit Play on his answering machine and Samantha's voice filled the room.

"Hi, I'm sorry to bother you again, but I need you to call me back right away. I think I'm developing an eating disorder. I haven't thrown up anything, but Carl agrees that I've been eating like a bird lately. My appetite is definitely deteriorating. Call me back. It's Samantha."

Grant erased the message and tucked a newspaper under his arm as he headed for his office. There was no way Samantha had an eating disorder. It was safe to read the sports section before calling her back.

As he flipped through the paper, he came across an ad for a Jeep Grand Cherokee and thought of Moni. She'd said she didn't need his help. It was best to leave it at that.

He caught himself tearing out the ad. What was he doing? Looking for an excuse to call her? He answered himself, finally being honest. The fact was, he had a little bit of a crush on her.

He loved her southern drawl, slow and sweet like honey. And she had a cute way of phrasing things, especially when she quoted her "dear Aunt Reggie—God rest her soul." He'd never met anyone like her.

It wasn't a relationship he wanted to pursue. Crushes led to dating, dating led to sex, and sex led to marriage. He wasn't going there again.

He picked up the ad. That didn't mean he couldn't offer her a helping hand if she needed it.

With the newspaper ad under his arm, he crossed the street to ring Moni's doorbell. After he rang it three times and was about to head back home, the door opened a crack and Moni peeked through the opening.

Then the door swung wide open. "Oh, thank goodness it's you."

Grant frowned. "Who were you expecting?"

She stepped to one side and gestured for him to come in. "Those vultures from the dealerships have started e-mailing me with counter offers. I wouldn't have been surprised if they had the nerve to show up at my front door."

Grant laughed. "That's why I dropped by. I thought you might want to look at this ad. It sounds like a pretty good deal."

"Oh, thanks." Moni took the page and pointed toward the couch for him to have a seat.

He scanned her place while she looked over the ad. "You've made a lot of progress in just a few weeks. I was still unpacking a year after I moved into my place."

"Thanks. I still have a few boxes left, but it

wasn't too difficult to unpack because I bought almost everything new."

He watched her wiggle her pink polished toes in the plush carpet. Pink sandals were in a corner by the door. He couldn't miss the fact that Moni loved shoes. As he watched her now, it was just as clear that she loved to be barefoot, too.

His gaze traveled up her slim legs, over her pink cotton shorts and came to a screeching halt at her belly button. She was wearing a pale pink tank-top that stopped just inches above her waistband.

She sighed, and he watched her flat stomach move with the exaggerated breath. "I'm fed up. This whole process is consuming way too much of my life. If your offer to help is still open . . ."

"Absolutely. Just tell me when and where."

As the words left his mouth, Grant felt a rising sense of warning. Why did he think he might regret getting involved at all?

That evening Moni parked her brand-new silver Jeep Liberty in front of her house. As she got out of the car she threw a glance toward Grant's house, but he'd already dashed inside.

Once they'd gotten off of the highway, he'd pulled his car in front of hers and sped off. Clearly, he'd wanted to avoid any further contact with her.

Shaking her head, she trudged toward the house. She couldn't blame him. The test drive hadn't quite gone as planned, but Bart, the car salesman, had managed to keep his cool. Thank goodness Grant's head injury hadn't been serious.

Still, the joy of having a brand-new automobile was dimmed by the fact that Grant may not speak to her again.

Moni entered the house and the telephone was ringing. She rushed to pick it up, hoping it was Grant.

"Hello?"

"Moni?"

"Akiko, how are you?" She hadn't spoken to her best friend in nearly a week.

"Ugh, can I just tell you how much I hate Portland."

"Give it time. You'll get used to it." Tucking the phone into her neck, she moved over to the sofa and flopped down.

"I doubt it." Akiko went on to complain about the neighbors, the traffic and the local restaurants. "Anyway, enough about me. I called because I have a fabulous idea for your business."

"You do? Well, I already have some ideas, but let me hear it." She reached down, picking at the chipping polish on her big toe.

"Shoes," she shouted.

Moni pulled the phone away from her ear. When Akiko got excited, she got loud.

"What do you mean? Like *selling* them?"

"Of course," Akiko said, so thrilled, she could have been talking about a 50-percent-off sale at Nordstrom's. "No one on earth loves shoes more than you do."

"That's true, but—"

"You could hire a designer and start your own line."

"Akiko—"

"I've even got the perfect name. You can call them *Monies*. You know, kinda like Candies?"

"I don't know . . ."

"Why not? It's a fabulous idea, right?"

She sat up, trying to choose her words carefully. "Well, it's fabulous except for one thing."

Akiko finally noticed that Moni wasn't as excited as she was. "What's that?"

"My passion for shoes is the one untainted thing in my life right now. Having a bad day? I can hit the mall for some fire engine red pumps. Feel like dancing? Orange retro platforms. Feeling mellow? Ferragamo ankle boots or Fendi loafers. Don't you see?"

Her friend's voice was softer now. "Not really."

"If I make the transition from shoe connoisseur to . . . shoe*maker*, I run the risk of corrupting my only true passion. I could never look at a strappy sling-back the same way once I'd seen it without its sole."

Akiko was silent for a moment. "That is so

true. Forgive me, I don't know what I was thinking. So, back to the drawing board. Knowing you, there must be charts and graphs tacked up all over the place. What's next on the list?"

In college, Akiko loved to tease Moni about her meticulous study habits. Her notes were color-coded, and she'd plot her study schedule on a timeline. Naturally, she wasn't going to do any less for her business plans.

There was a long list of concepts that Moni had crossed off right away. She'd dismissed going into the restaurant business because, while she was a great cook, she loathed doing it or anything related to food service.

When Moni had been in high school, she'd worked part-time at Lou's Diner. After three months in that place she'd been ready to give up eating food altogether.

She did like the idea of providing a product or service. The concept of an original invention appealed to her the most. Unfortunately, it was hard to think of original ideas that didn't require a degree in chemistry or physics.

Moni smiled, knowing her friend really wanted her to succeed. "I'm focusing on the beverage bra right now. Did you get the sample I sent you?"

"Yeah, I haven't tried it yet. I try to avoid working out whenever possible. What else is new?"

Moni winced. "I bought a new car today."

"How exciting. What did you get?"

"Actually, it was a little too exciting. I got a Jeep Liberty, but I really had to work for it."

Akiko picked up on her tone right away. "Uh oh, what happened?"

"Remember my neighbor, Grant?"

"The one who looks like the guy in *How Stella Got Her Groove Back*? Whoa, are you trying to get your groove back?"

"Hush now. We're just friends. Or at least we *were* starting to be friendly. That is, until today."

Akiko giggled wickedly. "Don't tell me you drove another car into his pool."

"Will I ever live that down? Of course not."

"Honey, that's not something a person forgets. So, what happened?"

"Grant volunteered to come along and help me haggle with the car dealer. Now, keep in mind that I didn't ask him. He *offered*. I didn't even accept his offer right away because I wanted to do it by myself."

"No luck, huh? You know what I do? I use a credit union buying service. They give you a flat rate so you don't have to haggle."

Moni rolled her eyes. "Sure, now you tell me. The point is, Grant offered to come with me. We went to a dealership this afternoon."

"Did you get a good price?"

"Ultimately, yes. That wasn't the problem. The problem was the test drive."

Akiko groaned.

"It started out just fine," Moni continued. "We

were on a nice straight road. Smooth ride. It was kinda fun. I'd never sat in a vehicle that high up before."

"Get to the disaster. Did you wreck? End up in a ditch? What?"

"Well—" Moni could picture the impatient expression creasing her friend's smooth Japanese features. "—All I know is they're supposed to be all-terrain vehicles, right?"

"You went off the road, didn't you?"

Moni shook her head, starting to feel flustered all over again. "I didn't mean to jump the curb. The truck just, kind of, did it on it's own. One minute road. Next minute grass. The only reason it was so scary was because we ended up in the mountains and the road became very curvy. Sometimes it looked like we were going to drive right off the edge."

"The car dealer took you up a mountain for a test drive?"

Moni's skin burned hot with embarrassment. She was glad her friend couldn't see her.

"No, I took a wrong turn. Once we started climbing, we couldn't turn around until we reached the top. While I was trying to turn the thing around, I jumped the little wooden marker that blocked the road from the grass."

"Dear Lord!"

"But we didn't get too far downhill before I managed to get us back on the road. It was just so narrow and steep—and you know I'm afraid of heights."

"This stuff only happens to you, Moni."

"Grant wanted me to stop the car and let him drive, but he was in the back seat. I just wanted to get us off that mountain."

Akiko sighed heavily. "Well, the important thing is that you got the car back in one piece, right?"

"Yes. I didn't crash into anything, but Grant's still upset with me."

"Why? I think you did well for someone who's only had her driver's license for three months."

"That's just it. He didn't know I'm a new driver until then. I think he's mad because, if he'd known about my limited driving experience before we'd gone to court, he could have convinced the judge to make me pay for the damaged fence outright. And then, of course, there's the accident."

"Accident? I thought you said you didn't hit anything."

"*I* didn't. Grant did. He was so shaken up by the ride that he couldn't get out of the car soon enough. He jumped out so fast, he banged his head on the doorframe. He has a huge gash just above his left eyebrow."

"For heaven's sake. No wonder the guy's barely talking to you."

"I know. The good news is that after all we'd been through—with Grant standing there bleeding and all—the car dealer didn't have the heart to haggle with us. Within ten minutes we had a deal for 2 percent above cost, fully loaded. I drove it right off the lot."

"I'm glad everything worked out for you, but how are you going to make it up to Grant? What if he tries to sue you again?"

"I know. We'd finally gotten to a point where we could laugh about the whole car-in-the-pool thing. Now I'm going to have to live this down, too."

"Okay, this is still fixable." Akiko was matter-of-fact. "Let me ask you something."

"Yes?"

"What would Aunt Reggie have to say about this?"

Moni snagged one of her curls and wound it around her finger. "Hmm, good question." After thinking about it for a moment, she began to smile.

"You're a genius, Akiko. I know exactly what she'd do."

Chapter 5

Grant's doorbell rang at 10:30 the next morning. He wasn't the least bit surprised to see Moni standing there. He squinted, noting her bright orange University of Virginia sweatshirt.

"Hi, how's your head?" she asked in a tentative tone.

Grant touched his forehead just below his Band-Aid. "Getting better. How's your new SUV?"

"Still in one piece, I'm happy to report."

He nodded, his gaze dropping to the bundle she held.

"Oh, I brought this just in case you were still upset about what happened. My dear Aunt Reggie—God rest her soul—always said, nothing says I'm sorry like a fresh-baked loaf of banana love bread."

"Banana *love* bread?"

"Yes, I baked it this morning. It's a Lawrence family secret. Trust me, you'll fall in love with it once you try it." She held it out to him.

"Trust you, huh?" Grant gave her a skeptical once-over before finally backing away from the door. "After what you put me though at the car dealership, my only question should be, do you know the Heimlich maneuver?"

She followed him into the kitchen. "If you're worried, I'll try a piece first. Where do you keep your plates?"

Grant reached into the drawer for a bread knife. "They're in the cabinet above the sink."

She laid two plates on the table and Grant sliced the bread. "This smells incredible. Like banana bread, but different." He inhaled deeply as if to figure out the secret. "What's in it?"

She gave him a sly smile that made his toes curl. "Uh-uh. You'll just have to taste it, cause *I* ain't tellin' ya."

He tore off a piece and started to raise it to his lips. "I'm not joking, you first."

Moni shrugged and took a huge bite out of her slice. "Mmm, delicious, if I do say so myself."

Grant popped a corner of bread into his mouth, and as if on cue, Moni started choking and gasping for breath.

"Very funny," he said, barely getting the words out as he tore off another piece and crammed it in his mouth. "This is incredible."

"Told ya," she said, sitting down at the table.

"Would you like some coffee?" he asked her, pouring himself a cup.

She thought about it for a moment then shook her head. "Normally, I'd say yes, but I don't know if you've noticed how hot it is in here."

Grant nodded. "Yeah. I'm sorry about that. My air conditioner is on the blink. They can't come out to fix it until Friday."

Moni fanned herself with her hands, finally giving up. "I actually thought it was a little chilly outside this morning, but, it's sweltering in here. Do you mind?" She grabbed the hem of her sweatshirt and started to pull it up.

"Of course not. Make yourself comfortable."

He moved over to the counter to slice another piece of bread and almost lost a finger when he caught sight of her from the corner of his eye.

She was wearing another of her impossibly scant tank tops that showed about five inches of bare skin above her low-riding jeans. Despite the fact that he saw the same style on countless women every day, it seemed so much more provocative on Moni's tiny frame.

"That's got to be illegal somewhere," he muttered under his breath.

"Did you say something?"

"Uh, I was thinking about taking a swim a little later. You're welcome to come over and cool off if you like." As soon as Grant heard himself speaking, he knew he'd made a mistake. Moni in bikini? That was sure to kill him.

He was barely hanging on as it was. His only

hope was that she'd turn him down. She'd been talking about getting back to work on the fence today, so maybe—

"Sure, I'd love to."

"Great." He sat down across from her and tried to concentrate on anything other than his raging libido. "So, you went to UVA?"

"Yup, the Virginia Cavaliers."

"What did you study?"

"Psychology. If I'd pursued it, you and I could have been colleagues."

"You mentioned that you didn't pursue it because your aunt needed you close to home." One of his brows rose in curiosity. "Now that you have the time and the money, why haven't you gone back to it?"

Moni started playing with one of her fingers again. "I don't know. I guess the moment has passed. There may be something else in the cards for me now."

Grant continued to nibble at the bread, studying Moni as she spoke. "And do you know what that is?" He didn't mention the beverage bra. He had a feeling she was referring to something bigger than that.

"Not yet, but I think the journey toward that discovery will be very exciting." She looked up and smiled at him. "Now, stop picking my brain. Don't think I haven't noticed that you always get me to talk about myself, but we never talk about you."

Grant straightened in his seat, feeling a flush creep into his face. "Sorry. Force of habit. Getting other people to talk is my job."

"It's okay, because now you have to give me the chance to turn the tables on you," she said with a sly grin.

"What do you want to know?" Here it comes, he thought, holding his breath.

"You can tell me to mind my own business if you want to, but I'd love to know how you ended up divorced . . . twice. Aren't you a marriage counselor?"

Resigned, Grant nodded. This is the way it always went down. Once people knew he'd been divorced twice, they questioned his role as a marital therapist.

"Yes, I am, but therapy and my personal life are apples and oranges. I'd like to say I've been unlucky in love, but the truth is, I've just made some really bad choices. My skills as a therapist don't hinge on my ability to choose the right woman for myself. My job does rely on my ability to be a good observer, and my ability to facilitate communication between two people—"

Moni made a time-out signal with her hands. "I'm sorry, it seems I've hit a nerve. Believe me, I'm in no position to pass judgment on your skills as a therapist. I just meant, it's ironic. You don't *have* to talk to me about your marriages. I understand if it's too personal."

Grant released the breath he'd been holding.

"No, don't apologize. Once again, I'm the one who's sorry. I can be a little defensive about this topic."

Moni nodded. "I understand."

"It's not that I don't want to talk about it. It's just that my story isn't much different from anyone else's. Often the women I'm attracted to aren't the ones that are good for me. People talk about women who are only attracted to bad boys—"

"Are you saying that you're only attracted to bad *girls*?" Moni asked, winking at him.

"Not so much 'bad' girls as women who are . . . let's just say they have issues. After a while, high-maintenance relationships like that usually burn themselves out."

As far as he was concerned, his first marriage should have worked out. He and his first wife were perfectly matched in every way—or so it had seemed.

When he'd met Charlotte she'd been a fiercely independent and ambitious woman. It was one of the many reasons he'd fallen in love with her. Charlotte had a shine about her, like a freshly minted coin. She would glint in the light, and every man around took notice. All sex and sophistication, most often she'd worn her straight black hair in a ponytail that hung to her waist. She would wear her designer suit jackets over nothing but a bra.

As a feature writer for a prestigious newspaper, Charlotte had vowed to have her own column in less than a year. It had been Charlotte who encouraged Grant to write his first book. He'd loved that she had the same appreciation for order and simplicity that he had. Restaurants, movies and books were also easy picks for the two of them. In fact, they had so much in common, they should have had a long, happy life together. There had been only one, rather significant, disparity.

Charlotte didn't want to have children—a fact he discovered only after she'd aborted his child without telling him. He might never have learned the truth if her sister hadn't let it slip in the middle of a drunken tirade during Thanksgiving dinner. Charlotte and Grant had started divorce proceedings before the New Year.

He refused to let Charlotte's lies and betrayal turn him bitter on all women. He'd continued to date, hoping true love was still out there waiting for him.

Two years later, he'd met Katrina. If Charlotte was the moon, Katrina was the sun. Grant had been sure she was the one. Katrina couldn't tell a lie to save her life, and her desire for a career came second to her desire for a family. She was sweet and soft with an earthiness he'd never experienced before. She wore her hair short and natural, and she loved to dress in simple flowing designs.

Grant had loved her guilelessness—her lack

of pretension. But what had seemed at first to be raw innocence, eventually turned out to be full-blown helplessness.

After their marriage, Katrina remained in a constant state of emotional neediness. She couldn't defrost a chicken or buy new curtains without calling for his opinion.

Grant had been standing on the edge of his wits by the time he discovered Katrina cheating on him with the instructor of the assertiveness training class he'd encouraged her to attend.

He'd divorced Katrina over a year ago.

"I can understand how you feel about women who are high maintenance," Moni said, breaking into his thoughts. "But, now that you're aware of that tendency, how do you fix it? Do you try and trick yourself by dating someone who is the opposite of your normal type?"

He rubbed his chin, thinking about her question. Grant was surprised that talking about his failed relationships with Moni wasn't as difficult or painful as he'd expected. It was as if she'd opened a closet door and his pent-up emotions came tumbling out.

"I don't think trying to fool myself is the answer. If I tried to do that, I probably *could* remain emotionally invulnerable. But, more than likely, I'd end up hurting the other person."

Moni nodded. "I see. I guess I can understand that. So, you're taking a break from dating?"

Grant looked away, suddenly the conversation began to feel awkward. He couldn't answer that question truthfully without either exposing his attraction to her or limiting his options for the future. He would not be getting married again. Period. That made him undesirable to a large chunk of the single female population.

Grant moved back over to the counter to refill his coffee cup. "My priorities this summer are finishing my book and planning my parents' fiftieth anniversary party."

He shrugged, trying to make it sound casual. "No room for dating in the agenda right now."

Moni smiled, but was quiet for a brief moment. "How is the party planning coming along?"

"Aside from dealing with my siblings—who have two separate sets of taste—it's going just fine."

"That's great." She stood up and carried her empty plate to the sink.

When she turned on the water and started to rinse her plate, Grant came up behind her. "You don't have to do that. I can get it later."

"Oh, it's no trouble at all." She whipped around and suddenly Grant found himself nose to nose with her.

She was pinned between him and the sink and there was nowhere for her to go. Moni held the wet plate out and Grant reached over and plucked it from her grasp. "I'll take that. You're a guest. Guests don't do the dishes."

She was so close, he could feel her breath on

his neck. A wild stirring built inside him quickly. He wasn't prepared for the sudden tightening in his groin.

He dropped the plate and heard it clatter on the counter. He didn't even look to see if it had broken. Instead he gripped the edge of the sink at either side of Moni's waist, trapping her against him.

Uh-oh, looking down was a mistake.

He now had a close-range view of those tight abdominal muscles that tortured him daily. She was a pretty little package, tightly wrapped. What the hell, he thought. He'd never been good at waiting until Christmas.

Feeling his control quickly slipping, he dragged his heavy gaze up to hers. If he'd seen any kind of hesitation he would have pulled away.

Instead, her usually wide, gold-brown eyes were hooded. She peered at him through the fringe of her lashes, her lids half closed. He needed no further invitation.

Grant leaned forward and brought his mouth down on hers. She released a delicate moan immediately, and her arms curved around his back.

Her full lips were supple against his, stirring lusty impulses inside Grant that had been all but dead for a long time. He'd pull back, then seek her mouth again, as if irresistibly drawn to their contact.

Grant didn't know when or if he would have

released her, if he hadn't felt her back straighten and the light but firm pressure of her palms against his chest.

He stepped back right away, already breathing raggedly. He wasn't sure why, but he was overwhelmed by the feeling that he should apologize. He forced himself to remain silent. Though he wasn't sure of many things at that moment, the one thing he did know was that he wasn't sorry he'd kissed her.

Not sure what else to do, he shoved his hands deep into the pockets of his shorts and watched for her reaction.

Her fingers were pressed to her lips, and her eyes were bright. Finally, she motioned toward the window. "Well, I'd better get out there. I've got work to do, and I know you do, too. I'll look forward to that swim later, okay?"

Grant nodded. "Sounds like a plan. Hey, thanks for the banana *love* bread." His body was still hot from the kiss they'd just shared. He rubbed his chin. "Are you sure you don't want to tell me what's in it?"

Moni reached up and twirled one of her buoyant curls around her finger. Her lips tilted into a sexy little smile he'd never seen before. "Why ruin a good secret. My dear Aunt Reggie always said, leave 'em wanting more."

With that, she grabbed her sweatshirt off the chair and skipped out the door, tossing a light goodbye over her shoulder.

*   *   *

Moni stood in front of the hole in Grant's fence, wearing what she *knew* was a silly grin. She just couldn't help herself. As had become the routine since moving to San Diego, she'd experienced yet another first.

Passion.

She finally knew exactly what it was. It had overwhelmed her just before she realized Grant was about to kiss her. She'd actually been a little bit scared. She'd felt . . . out of control. Wild. And, more importantly, she'd felt those same feelings emanating from Grant.

Since the feelings had been unfamiliar and uncontrollable—they'd freaked her out. She'd had to back off.

She'd felt so hot. Too hot. She fanned herself. That was the closest she'd come to being incinerated.

Moni was so caught up in her fantasy loop, replaying Grant's kiss over and over, that she stared at her stacked planks for several minutes before she remembered she was supposed to be doing something with them.

Finally, she pulled herself together and began laying out the wood. She hadn't wanted Grant to see her exchanging the original boards with the precut boards from the lumber yard, so she'd done it yesterday, in the middle of the night.

Unfortunately, she almost blew her cover

when the sprinklers came on while she was stacking wood. She'd forgotten that it rained so little in southern California that many homes had underground sprinklers to water the lawn overnight.

She'd managed to finish her job without calling attention to herself, but she'd gone home looking like a drowned rat.

Moni was glad the cutting and measuring of the boards was behind her, because now the real challenge would begin. Luckily, she'd crashed through a section of fence that was between the grounding posts. She wouldn't have to worry about drilling holes in the ground or laying cement.

Though the houses in the neighborhood were similar, each home had its own distinctive style. She was glad Grant liked things simple, because she would have had significantly more trouble if he'd had a lattice fence like Ed and Sandra had.

Moni began working up a sweat as she moved the boards around, preparing to stain them. She was grateful for the hard work. It gave her a bit of a distraction from the sexually charged images that flashed in her mind every time she thought of Grant.

She and Burt had been close, but nothing they'd shared came anywhere near what she'd experienced today. Plus, she had the added anticipation of their swim date later that afternoon.

Who could predict what would happen then? She hoped Grant would kiss her again. If he did, she wouldn't pull away this time.

Grant stalked into his office and kicked the door shut with the heel of his sneaker. That was it— no more interruptions. His body was threaded with energy—the kind he usually stirred up from the bottom of a coffee cup. The writing that he'd been slogging through all morning like a kid with a term paper suddenly called to him. Nothing like a little sexual frustration to put him in the mood for murder.

Even if it was only fictionalized murder, it still felt good to release his tension in some form. It wasn't the form of choice, but it would have to do.

His fingers clicked rapidly on the keyboard, his thoughts flying almost too fast for his hands to keep up.

Finally, he paused to work a kink out of his wrist, and as if on cue, the phone started ringing. He considered not answering it, but found himself speaking into the receiver without even checking the caller ID. "Hello?"

"Oh, thank goodness. I was hoping you'd be home."

"Samantha . . . you okay?" He asked anyway, even though he knew she wasn't. She never called to tell him things were fine.

"I'm not sure . . ." She paused on the other

end of the line and Grant could imagine her raking her salon-manicured nails—her one indulgence for a woman with three small children—through her short curls.

Fighting to keep the sigh out of his voice, Grant asked her to tell him what was wrong. His encouraging murmurs were second nature as he tucked the cordless phone in the groove of his neck and started for the kitchen. He might as well have a sandwich while she described her latest malfunction.

"I heard on the news last night that women who spend all their time around children can sometimes lose contact with their adult selves. I have noticed lately that I enjoy the programs the boys watch so much more than daytime TV and even the news. Do you think I'm—"

"Samantha, who wouldn't choose cartoons over talk shows and soaps. Daytime television gets old pretty fast. I'm sure that isn't unusual." He opened the refrigerator.

"You always say that, but this morning I caught myself having a ten-minute conversation about Sponge Bob Square Pants with the grocery store clerk."

"Were you buying something with Sponge Bob on it?"

"They were having a sale on beach pails."

"And that's what got you and the check-out person talking?"

"Well, yes, but—"

Grant laid mayonnaise, roast beef and wheat bread on the kitchen counter. "Look, Samantha, do you really want to know what I think?"

"Of course, that's why I called." Her tone was cautious.

"Fine, if you think you're not getting enough adult contact, why don't you call one of your friends and go to lunch. I could baby-sit—"

He winced as soon as the words were out of his mouth. He saw three screaming boys under the age of eight playing hide-and-seek around his stereo speakers. His mind flashed images of peanut butter and jelly fingerprints on his computer keyboard, dirty footprints on his beige carpet and puddles of grape juice on his kitchen floor.

"Or Mom and Dad can—"

"Oh, speaking of M-Mom and D-Dad."

He stopped spreading mayonnaise on his bread. Something was up.

There was a long pause on the other end, and Grant felt the muscles in his stomach tighten with tension. "What's going on?"

"It's about their anniversary p-party."

Whenever his sister felt put on the spot she reverted to her childhood habit of stammering.

"What's wrong? You reserved the Hotel Del Coronado for September, right?" He stacked a liberal amount of luncheon meat on his bread, covering it with a slice of bread.

"Yes, everything is fine. Th-that's not the problem."

"What's the problem?" he asked, licking mayonnaise from his thumb.

Samantha sighed. "I ran into Katrina at the mall yesterday. We st-started talking and I mentioned our parent's fiftieth wedding anniversary."

"And?" He cut the sandwich in half and carried it to the table.

"And, um, K-Katrina's planning to come."

He forgot about his sandwich as he stood blinking at the phone. "You invited my ex-wife to the party?"

"It was an accident. She—she just assumed she was invited. I didn't know how to tell her no."

Grant felt himself losing patience—a formerly unfamiliar feeling that had been coming more frequently lately. He resisted the urge to hang up on his sister. Inhaling deeply, he forced himself to sound calm. "Don't worry about it. I'll take care of this. I'll call you later."

"Are you sure, because I c-can—"

"Yes. I'll call you. Goodbye."

He stood shaking his head at the receiver in his hand. "Unbelievable," he muttered, stabbing a pattern of numbers he'd been hoping to forget.

A second later a tiny voice came over the line. "Hello?"

"Katrina? It's Grant."

"What a pleasant surprise. It's really nice to—"

"Look, I don't want to beat around the bush about this. Why on earth would you want to come to my parents' anniversary party?"

"Oh that," she said, giggling in her typical childlike fashion. "I was so thrilled when Samantha invited me. I'm really looking forward—"

His jaw was so tight, he could barely speak. "Don't you think your presence will make things a little awkward?"

"Why should they be awkward?"

He clenched and released his fist, picturing her blank stare. It was an act. It had to be. No one could be that naïve. "Because we're divorced. Remember?"

"Of course I know that, but I don't see why that should make us enemies. There's nothing like a party to bring friends together."

"Katrina, we're *not* friends."

"But, we could be," she said sweetly.

Grant tried to calm himself. "I don't think that's a good idea."

"I'm sorry you feel that way, but that doesn't have to be a problem. It's not like I expect you to dance with me or anything." Her voice took on a note of cheerful resolve. "We can maintain a civil distance."

"Fine. This is my idea of civil distance. Me—at my parents' fiftieth anniversary party. You— anywhere else."

"That's not very funny, Grant."

He rolled his eyes. "Gee, that must be because I'm not joking."

"When did you become so mean? I really don't remember you ever being this mean."

Grant blew out his breath, taking a moment to gather his thoughts. It was time to try another approach.

"Look, I'm not trying to be mean. What I'm trying to say is ... having you at my parents' party would make me uncomfortable. The fact that things didn't work out between us is still ... *painful* for me," he lied.

He began pacing the room. "If it were an issue of mutual friends, I'd back out myself. But these are my parents. I have to be there. It would be a lot easier for me if you didn't attend the party."

Katrina was silent and Grant found himself holding his breath. Maybe he'd actually gotten through to her this time.

"I'm sorry, Grant. I didn't know this had been so hard on you. It's not my intention to make you uncomfortable."

He released his breath in relief. "Thank you. I appreciate your understanding."

"But I think we're losing sight of what's really important here."

He paused. "What are you talking about?"

"Your parents. Don't you think we can put our differences aside for one night ... for their sake?"

Grant held his head, trying to contain the building pressure. "What?"

"I'm sure it would make them feel good to see us getting along."

"No, I really don't—"

"You'll see. Having the two of us there together, showing that we've put our problems behind us . . . it will put their minds at ease."

"Katrina, I really think my parents would understand if you're not there. In fact—"

"Well, if you're so sure . . ."

"I'm very sure."

"Then let's ask them."

"What?" Grant stared at the receiver incredulously.

"Let's ask them if they'd mind having me at their party."

"Katrina, we *can't* ask them. It's a *surprise*. Understand? Asking them would spoil the surprise." He knew she was baiting him, but he couldn't seem to regain control of the conversation.

"Then you'll just have to take my word that they won't mind my being there."

A nerve started pulsing in his temple. His entire body was hot with frustration. "You're being deliberately thick-headed."

"There's no need to be insulting. We can resolve this very simply. Ask them. If you don't want to do that, then I'll see you at the party."

When had she gotten to be this vindictive? "That's blackmail. You're practically threatening to tell them about the surprise party if I don't let you attend."

"Now, Grant, there's no need to be so negative. Samantha invited me to the party. Clearly that shows that your family doesn't feel the same way about me that you do. You're just going to have to get over me, because I'm going to be at the party. Now, I'll see you there."

Then she disconnected the line.

He held the phone until the off-the-hook tone broke through his red haze. He had to get out of there. A long drive might help.

Grant paced then finally headed toward the door, grabbing his keys off the counter. His sandwich was left, untouched, on the kitchen table.

His thoughts were so focused, he was barely aware of Moni until she called out to him.

He looked up and saw her waving. "Where are you headed?" she asked.

Shaking his head, he didn't stop to talk. "Errands to run," he called over his shoulder.

"Oh, okay. So we'll go for that swim when you get back?"

This time Grant did stop, turning to face her. "Uh, I don't think I'll be back in time. Feel free to take a swim, though. You can have the whole pool to yourself."

He felt a twinge of guilt as he caught the bewildered expression on Moni's face. Pushing it away, he backed his Toyota down the driveway. One woman complicating his life was enough for now.

❧ Chapter 6 ❧

Early the next morning, Grant stood on the golf course surveying the tenth hole. He measured his swing once, then let his arms fly back in an arc, coming forward to whack the ball with tremendous force. The ball caught air and traveled an impressive distance over the fairway.

Mitch Taylor sighed as he gathered his clubs. "I've gotta tell you, buddy, your game has improved considerably since the last time we played."

Grant *had* been doing well that morning. Although he'd calmed down considerably since talking to Katrina yesterday, an ever-present tension still lingered within him. He'd been able to focus that into his golf game.

He barely spared his friend a glance as they advanced toward his ball. "I've discovered that tension is a great resource for my writing. I guess it's good for my golf game as well."

"Tension? What do you have to be tense about? I figured you'd signed yourself up for a cushy summer—rolling out of bed around noon, fiddling with your computer a little, then finishing up your day on the golf course or lounging pool-side."

Grant gave him a light punch in the arm. "Jealousy is a bitch, Taylor. It sounds like you resent taking over my caseload for the summer. I think that's why you can't admit that book-writing is actual work."

Mitch shrugged it off. "Yeah, yeah . . . says you. Watch out, next year *I'm* taking the summer off to write a book."

"Oh yeah? What are you qualified to write about?"

"Many things—golf, hot-wings, women—"

"Women? You'd better check with Shelly on that one. Any man who could date the same woman for eight years without marrying her, isn't what I'd consider an expert on the topic."

"That's *exactly* what makes me an expert. I've been with Shelly for eight years and still managed *not* to marry her. It takes skill to avoid the marriage trap. You could learn a few things from me."

Grant hit his ball hard, and it flew several yards past Mitch's ball. He nodded smugly at him. "You see that? You just keep talking trash."

His friend grunted. "Seriously, I'm working up to marrying her. One of these days, I'll call you and tell you the deed is done. Las Vegas-style—none of that fooh-fooh tulle and lace for me."

"Yeah, right. You're lucky she puts up with you."

Mitch looked uncomfortable, and after a few minutes of silence, changed the subject. "Anyway, you never told me what's making you so tense."

"What else could it be? Women, of course."

"Who is it now? I thought you'd all but sworn off women."

"You'll never believe what my ex-wife is up to."

Mitch's brow rose in question.

"Samantha let it slip that we're having an anniversary party for the folks and Katrina mistook that for an invitation."

Mitch paused mid-swing. "Are you kidding? She's coming to the party?"

"Can you believe it? I tried to talk her out of it, but she's still playing the same old games."

"Well, you know everyone handles divorce differently. Maybe this is her way of trying to hang on to you."

Grant cringed in horror at the thought of having Katrina in his life again. "That's just too bad. If she wanted to hang on to me, she could have been faithful. She had the nerve to imply that my parents would *want* her to be there."

He stopped lining up his swing to laugh out

loud. "My parents couldn't stand Katrina when I was married to her. Sure, they were always polite, but they made it clear to me that they didn't think she was *the one*. You should have seen the looks my mother would give me whenever Katrina would offer to read her tarot cards or check her aura."

"Maybe it won't be as bad as you think. There will be so many people there, you might not even notice her," Mitch said.

Grant snorted. "You know my ex-wife. It's impossible not to notice her."

Thinking about Katrina was starting to throw off Grant's golf swing. He forced himself to concentrate on the game, so he could maintain his lead.

"Can we please talk about something else?"

"Sure." Mitch grinned. "How are your fence repairs coming along? Are you getting along with your neighbor?"

He sighed. "Actually, I've tried to steer clear of her, but that's nearly impossible to do. I catch myself thinking about her all the time—which is strange because the last thing I want is to get mixed up in another relationship."

"Is she interested in you, too?"

Grant remembered their kiss. "I think the answer to that would have to be yes."

"You sound so sure." Mitch studied Grant's face.

He looked away. "I kissed her yesterday. I wasn't planning on it. But, she was looking up at me, and . . . she knew, and . . . I knew . . . then it was happening. We were both a little shaken up. She even got a bit shy afterward. But there's one thing I can say for sure—she's interested."

"Then you've got to leave her alone." Mitch started shaking his head vehemently.

"What?" Grant's aim was off and he ended up swinging at air.

"You're not looking for a relationship. Grant, you just said so yourself. You're just going to hurt this girl."

"Thanks a lot." Grant frowned, feeling defensive. "I don't want to hurt her, but what's wrong with indulging a mutual attraction? We're both adults. Dating just for fun is—"

"Out of the question," he said firmly.

"Why?" Grant hadn't planned on dating Moni, but being told he couldn't made him want to do it all the more.

Mitch slung his arm across Grant's shoulders. "You're still carrying around baggage from two—that's right, count them—*two* divorces. You know from experience that dating leads to sex and sex leads to marriage—which you're not prepared to offer her. You're a sinking ship, my friend. Do you really want to bring her down with you?"

Grant glared at Mitch. "Thanks, buddy.

You're really cheering me up with your glowing optimism."

"Look, I'm not trying to be a killjoy. You'll eventually be fit to date again. You've just got to give yourself some more time."

Grant felt sick to his stomach. He didn't want to admit that Mitch could be right. "Are you this tactless with my clients? Because, if you are, I'm taking them back."

"I'm your friend, not your therapist. With clients we sugarcoat the truth. I'm giving it to you straight. I think you're man enough to take it."

Grant knew Mitch wasn't entirely off base. Now *wasn't* the ideal time to start up something new. But maybe if he were honest with Moni, she could decide for herself if she wanted to risk dating him.

The two men played silently through the next few holes. Grant's game, which had been stellar at first, deteriorated to merely average.

Finally, Mitch broke the silence. "Attractive nuisance," he said, seeming to contemplate the phrase.

Grant looked up. "Yeah. I told you that was Moni's defense in court."

"I have to admit that was a pretty clever tactic."

"Hey, whose side are you on?" Grant frowned at Mitch.

"No, seriously, I just thought of something kind of interesting."

Grant lined up his next shot. "What now?" he asked, not certain he really wanted to know.

"Well, Moni considered *you* an attractive nuisance when she drove through your fence, but there's also a parallel for you."

"What are you talking about?" He sent the ball in a smooth arc to land on the green.

"I mean *she's* an attractive nuisance. You said yourself, she's cute, and she has this thing she calls DDS—I love that by the way. I'm going to use it. Anyway, you're constantly compelled to do things for her—to take care of her."

"Yeah?" Grant didn't like where Mitch was going with this. He'd already heard an earful.

"Well, after Katrina and Charlotte, the last thing you need in your life is another high-maintenance woman. Another woman you'll be forced to burn all your energy on, right?"

"Right. But, we've already established that I can't get involved with Moni."

"But, you kissed her."

Grant sighed heavily. "What's your point? You're saying I'm drawn to Moni, even though I know she's not good for me?"

"Exactly. Before you know it, you're helping her saw wood. Then you're going car shopping with her. Now you're kissing her. Even though you know getting involved with her will only get you in trouble. You can't resist trying to take care of her. She's *your* attractive nuisance."

Grant felt as though he'd been punched in the stomach. When Mitch laid it out that way, he couldn't deny the truth—even though he really wanted to.

Rather than confirm the revelation, all Grant said was, "It's your shot."

He was starting up the same old pattern again. The one that he'd had with Charlotte and then Katrina. If he continued down this path, Moni could be ex-wife number three.

He couldn't go on this way. They said the definition of insanity was repeating the same behavior and expecting different results each time. Grant already knew how this story ended, which meant he *couldn't* indulge his attraction for his cute neighbor.

All he had to do was keep his distance until she finished working on the fence, and then he'd be home free.

That afternoon, Moni was hard at work on Grant's fence when he pulled into the driveway. She tore off her gloves and walked to the edge of the pavement.

"Hey, I saw that you got an early start this morning. I didn't know you played golf."

Grant opened the passenger door of his sedan and tugged out his golf bag. "Yup."

Her smile was eager. "How'd you do?"

"Played a good game. I finished nine over par."

"Wow, I'm impressed. I'm not a *big* golf fan, but I have seen Tiger Woods on television a few times."

Grant swung his bag over his shoulder and started for the door.

"Uh, I'm making good progress with the fence. I think I'll be done well ahead of schedule."

"Great. The sooner the better." He turned slightly and nodded in her direction. "See ya."

Then he was gone.

Moni walked back to the fence and resumed working, stepping up her pace. The only problem was that the monotony of layering coats of stain on the wood wasn't enough to distract her from her mounting apprehension. She'd recognized that look in his eyes just now. She'd been dismissed.

It had happened more times than she could count in her twenty-six years. People, especially men, would pat her on the head and smile as though she were a puppy to be played with, then set aside when it was time for serious business.

Grant was no longer amused by her, and he was going back into the house to get back to his book. Obviously, the kiss they'd shared yesterday was already forgotten. It didn't take a rocket scientist to see that she wasn't his type.

Sometimes Moni got tired of being seen as

cute and perky all of the time, but the way she saw it, she didn't have much choice. Every time she tried to go against the grain, she wasn't taken seriously.

People would look at her with that my-aren't-you-cute-when-you're-angry grin, and then go on as though she'd never spoken up. But, that was okay, because she'd learned how to get around her terminal cuteness. She knew how to use it to her advantage. Since everyone insisted on underestimating her, she let them.

Not unlike the tortoise and the hare, Moni would get ahead while no one was looking. She'd come to San Diego to make it on her own. That's why she'd insisted on the chance to fix Grant's fence herself, and she wasn't going to take any more shortcuts. When all was said and done, Grant would have to stop doubting her.

Sure, she couldn't deny that she had a bit of a crush on him. For a while, she'd thought he liked her, too. But, she could imagine the kind of woman he really went for. Polished and sophisticated. Someone with a sleek hairstyle, not wild curls like hers. A career woman who dressed in DKNY.

"That sounds pretty boring to me," she muttered.

She didn't have time to waste on romance anyway. If she'd wanted to be tied down in a relationship, she could have stayed home and married a perfectly good man.

Her new business was top priority. She'd bought a computer, opened a business account, and she'd converted her basement into an office. Next, she would take on bigger projects like fleshing out her business plan and getting licensed.

Unfortunately, Moni couldn't move on these projects until she'd made a clear decision about the product or service she could provide. The beverage bra was her current favorite, but she needed a little more information on e-commerce.

That's why Moni was hoping the Internet business seminar she was attending downtown that evening would help. Not only was she counting on getting some constructive advice, she was also looking forward to meeting new people.

Although being under constant scrutiny could get tiresome in a small town, Moni missed the comfort of being surrounded by friends in Dunkin. That's why she was anxious to become active in the San Diego community. She couldn't wait to make new friends.

"Well, that was a colossal waste of my time," Moni muttered as she maneuvered her SUV around the busy streets of downtown San Diego.

The seminar had been a disappointment on many levels. For starters, the speaker had been nervous and difficult to hear. But worse yet was the discouraging message the seminar had pre-

sented. Without the financial backing of an established corporation, her enterprise was unlikely to succeed.

Her psychology background had not pre-
pared her for the cut-throat world of business.
Despite collecting a few business cards for her
Rolodex, she was back at square one.

Moni pulled up to the next light. She was so
caught up in her thoughts, she almost missed
the frantic young woman on the corner, trying
to get her attention. Normally, Moni might have
tried to ignore the stranger, but this woman was
difficult to brush off.

The first things Moni noticed were the thigh-
high shiny red leather boots the woman wore
with her short black dress. She had dark skin
and long black braids that curled down to the
middle of her back.

One word flashed like neon in Moni's mind.
Hooker.

Moni looked up and down the street. They
were in the heart of the city, yet it still didn't
seem like the right place to find a hooker solicit-
ing out in the open.

When Moni turned her gaze back, she almost
jumped out of her seat. The girl was leaning
against the passenger door of her vehicle. She
knocked on the window.

Moni held her breath as she lowered the window. "Can I help you?"

Just then the light turned green and a car behind her honked its horn.

Before Moni realized what was happening, the woman slipped her skinny arm through the open window, pulled up the door lock and climbed into the seat. "Yes, drive!"

More cars started honking and one even pulled out and raced around her. Moni sat frozen with her jaw hanging open. "What . . . you can't—"

The woman looked anxiously over her shoulder. "Now, go!"

With her mind numbed, it was easiest to just do what she was told. Moni stomped on the gas. After a few blocks, she darted a glance at her uninvited passenger. "Um, where can I drop you off?"

The girl stared back at Moni with eyes wide with fear. "Keep driving. If you stop now, he might catch us."

Chapter 7

Grant looked out the window and saw his sister's minivan pulling into his driveway. Tonight would be his first crack at baby-sitting without having Samantha or his parents as a safety net. It wasn't his ideal Friday-night activity, but after his gloomy discussion with Mitch this morning, he certainly wasn't going on any dates. At this rate, his three young nephews were much safer than women.

Still, his heart rate pitched as the boys tore out of the back seat of the minivan and raced toward the door.

He couldn't let on that he was nervous. Children could smell fear.

He opened the door and the house was immediately caught up in a flurry of activity. He hugged and kissed all three of the boys, as they ran past him into the living room. Right away, they dumped a huge bucket of Legos onto the floor and began dividing them among the three of them.

Grant kissed his sister on the cheek, noticing the two large bags at her feet. "I thought they were only staying for a few hours. You have enough luggage for a week."

"These are their games and toys, plus a few of their favorite snacks. They can be very fussy. But they should be fine for a while. They spent the whole day at Legoland, as you can see, and they brought back plenty of goodies. I didn't want you to feel obligated to entertain them."

She pulled a list from her pocket. "I wrote down some emergency numbers for you just in case one of them chokes on a Lego piece or something. There's poison control, Carl's cell, my cell, his work pager and—"

"Got it." Grant snatched the list and began ushering her toward the door. "I'm sure we'll have a great time. All you need to worry about is enjoying your night out with the girls."

"I also told Mom and Dad to be on call in case Marshall throws a tantrum. She can sing 'Are You Sleeping' over the phone. That always calms him down."

"We'll be fine," he said, holding the front door open.

Samantha never did anything half way. Her career as an accountant had been a healthy outlet for her obsessive tendencies, allowing her to be fairly balanced in the rest of her life. Now she split her time between worrying about the kids and worrying about the state of her mental health.

Samantha started to turn, then paused. "Were you able to talk to Katrina?"

Grant rolled his eyes. "I talked to her. It didn't do any good."

"I'm s-sorry she found out about the p-party. I should have kept my mouth sh-shut."

He rubbed her shoulder. "Don't worry about it. But, if you're really feeling guilty, feel free to bring me some tamales from Casa de Bandini."

"It's a deal. Thanks for doing this, Grant. I should be back by ten, ten-thirty at the latest. I'll call to check in around—"

"Don't call unless the restaurant is on fire, you hear me? Just take your time and have fun."

Grant went into the living room and immediately gasped in horror. "Alex, don't put that in your mouth!"

Moni and her unhappy hooker drove for several more blocks in silence until Moni couldn't take the curiosity any longer.

"Forgive me if this sounds rude, but are you running from your pimp?"

Feeling a blush on her cheeks, Moni realized that the concept was just a tiny bit exciting. Nothing like this ever happened in Dunkin.

She felt the woman staring her, and Moni darted a look in her direction. She saw that her passenger was even younger than she'd realized, probably in her early twenties.

"Pimp? Omigod, you think I'm a hooker?"

Moni blanched. "I'm sorry I didn't mean to offend you. I just thought . . . because, you know—"

"I am *not* a hooker," she said, raising her sculpted brows indignantly. She had a softly rounded face with smooth brown skin. Her features were attractive under her heavy layer of makeup.

"I'm a dancer at the Silver Spur."

Moni shot her another look. "Is that a strip club?"

"Topless dancing."

Moni nodded. "Oh, of course." She started to slow down. So far she'd been driving in a circle and was dangerously close to getting lost.

"So, where should I take you?"

"Where were *you* headed?"

Moni wasn't about to take this strange woman back to her house, so she pulled into the parking lot of a fifties-style diner. "Are you hungry?"

Grant's doorbell rang at a quarter to eleven, and he ran downstairs to answer it.

Samantha rushed in. "I'm so sorry I'm late. I haven't seen these friends in ages, and we got to talking—"

Grant held a finger to his lips. "It's okay. The boys are upstairs sleeping."

"How did it go? Did Johnny take his vitamins? They're chewable, but he always frets about taking them."

"Yes. Everything is fine. It *was* a little hairy at first, but they finally settled down. Actually, we had a good time."

Samantha took a moment to digest this, then a smile slowly spread across her face. "Careful, or you might become my regular sitter."

"Any time."

Samantha looked stunned. "Don't forget you said that when the time comes. I had a lot of fun tonight, too. It did feel good to spend a little time with some people my own age."

He slipped an arm around her shoulder. "I knew it would be good for you."

"By the way, I have some catering menus to go over. All I need is to give them a deposit."

"Fine. Call me tomorrow, and we can conference-call with Keith. He already gave me some money. I told him we could wait for the final bill and split it three ways, but he was anxious to pay up front." His voice sounded flat even to his own ears.

She followed him upstairs, pausing outside the bedroom door. "Don't sound so thrilled. Try not to let this little snag with Katrina change the way you feel about the party."

"Little snag." He snorted. "I'll try not to, but I'm only human."

She squeezed his arm. "Well, we'll just pretend she's not even there."

Grant led Samantha into the bedroom where her three sons were curled up on his king-size bed. He helped her carry their sleepy forms out to the car, surprised at how sorry he was to see them go.

He'd enjoyed being a kid for a while, playing with the boys that night. They'd built Lego monsters, played video games and made a big mess eating pizza. Even though he preferred his place to be neat and orderly, he hadn't thought about its current state of disarray.

Grant looked around his empty house that had been bursting with activity just a couple of hours earlier. If one of his marriages had worked out, he would have expected to have his own children by now.

He was the kind of guy who was meant to be a family man. His ideal life revolved around marriage—sharing a home with his wife and a couple of kids.

Twice now, he'd thought he was on his way to having those things. It was a hard dream to put on the shelf. Marriage wasn't right for everyone. He wasn't sure if it could ever work out for him.

He'd made a living helping couples communicate with each other, but all his skills had been irrelevant to his personal life. What good was communication if he couldn't find the right woman?

Feeling a headache pounding in his temple, Grant turned off the lights and went to bed.

"Summer Rain? Is that a stage name or something?" Moni asked her companion as she stared across the table at her.

"Cute, isn't it? It's almost like my mother knew what my future profession would be. Actually, it's not R-A-I-N. Rain is spelled R-A-Y-N-E."

Moni nodded. "I was never crazy about *my* name. Everyone always thinks it's short for something like Monique or Monica. But it's not. It's just plain Moni."

"You have a nice name. You're a nice person, too. I know I must have freaked you out by jumping into your car like some crazy person."

"You can say that again." Moni took a sip of her coffee. "Are you going to tell me what's going on?"

Summer played with the straw in her diet soda. "It's the same old story. Girl meets boy. Boy treats girl like dirt. Girl finally leaves. Boy goes crazy."

"Then we're talking about your ... boyfriend?"

"Yeah, Nigel." Summer sighed heavily.

Moni snickered. "Nigel? That's such a quiet, 'I-work-in-a-library' kind of name."

"I know." Summer snorted. "He seemed to

have that kind of mild personality at first." She pinned Moni with a hard look. "Let me tell you, honey, I don't know what your romantic situation is, but one thing is for sure . . . men are never what they seem."

Moni mulled over that statement. That sounded true enough. She'd thought, at first, that Grant was so different, too. Despite their rocky start, she'd really thought he was genuinely interested in her. Then, without any warning, he blew her off.

And, of course, there was Burt, the most predictable man alive. Consistency was his middle name. In fact, that had largely been the problem. If Moni had married Burt, she was certain she could have been happy, but life would have been incredibly dull. Maybe that was where Summer's theory kicked in. On paper, Burt seemed like every woman's dream—handsome, stable job, gentle personality and as faithful as a golden retriever. In reality, he just didn't flick her switch.

"I see your point. I'm not in a relationship right now, but my limited experience with men supports your theory."

Summer tapped her acrylic nails on the table. "Believe me, I know what I'm talking about. I thought Nigel was a dream come true when we first met. You should see him. What a baby face. These puppy-dog brown eyes to go with the boy-next-door 'aw shucks' grin. I was waitressing in a diner, not unlike this one, when he rolls in wearing Ralph Lauren. He slides into a booth, and when I come for his order, he drops his keys on the table so I'll notice the Mercedes logo on his key ring."

"Subtle," Moni said sarcastically.

"I know. It didn't take long for him to start all the talk about how he would take me away from all this. I didn't believe him. Mama didn't raise no fool, and I know a player when I see one. I mean I *really* made him work for it."

"Work for what?" Moni asked.

"A date. Don't let the fact that I'm a dancer fool you. I'm not *easy*. I made that clear to him up front. Besides, I wasn't even dancing then."

"Of course," Moni said, nodding.

"Anyway, he came to the restaurant every day. That was no small thing since the food at Mickey's stunk. Finally, after about four or five weeks, I went out with him. It was all over for me after the first date. He was so damn charming. He said he owned a 'club' and could afford to take care of me. I'd been on my own, taking care of myself and my baby sister since I was seventeen. It was nice to let someone else take over for a while."

She could see the bitter cynicism in her eyes. Summer was already older than her years. Although, Moni knew she was a couple of years older, next to Summer she felt like a child who'd never experienced the world.

"By the time I found out his 'club' was a strip joint, I was already too far gone—thinking I was in love. I have to hand it to him. He made it sound good, even respectable by the time he was through. All that talk about women taking control of their sexuality. Dominating men for a change. Financial independence."

"Whew, he sweet-talked you into seeing snow in July, didn't he?"

Summer's lips curled, showing mild amusement at Moni's choice of phrase. Then she continued.

"I know, it's crazy, but I fell for it. He talked me into dancing for him. Said I'd have it better at the Silver Spur than I would at the other, low-class joints. I have to admit, it's a rush getting the attention. And the money . . . Girl, I'd have to work at Mickey's for the rest of my life to make what I get from one weekend dancing."

Moni wondered why strippers always referred to it as "dancing." If they were as proud as they claimed to be, they should call it like it is.

She didn't want to be judgmental. In the twenty minutes she'd known this woman, she was surprised by how much she identified with her. Any woman could fall victim to loving the wrong man. She'd been lucky so far, and she'd grown up with a strong support system, despite losing her parents. Summer had been on her own.

"So you've been dancing at Nigel's club all this time?"

"Yeah. I mean, as far as clubs go, the Silver Spur is pretty classy, so I never guessed . . . I mean, I have to draw the line somewhere, you know?"

Moni shook her head, and her curls bounced against her ears. "What do you mean?"

"Nigel, that rotten little—"

"What did he do? What finally made you leave him?"

"He wanted me to . . ." Summer took a deep breath and started again. "He had some investors who owned a chain of clubs in San Antonio coming in for the weekend. He wanted me to give one of them a *private* dance."

"Lap dances or something?"

Summer raised one brow. "Much more like *or something.*"

"Omigod—"

"I know. I told him if he really loved me, he wouldn't want to share me with another man. He said this was business, and if I really loved *him* I would help him. That was the last straw. I mean, what the hell was he thinking? I am *not* a hooker. I'd been building up to dumping him for a while now, but that just sealed the deal."

"Good for you. You gave him the heave ho and you bolted. Why did you have to make such a hasty getaway?"

"Nigel's the possessive type."

"I can see that, but once you dumped him, what could he really do?"

Summer studied Moni carefully. "You're a small-town girl, aren't you?"

Moni blushed. "Is it written on my forehead?"

"No, but the accent and the Pauline Pure-Heart act are a dead giveaway."

Moni averted her gaze. She didn't think she was a prude. Maybe she could be naïve about some things—there weren't any strip clubs in Dunkin, so she'd never rubbed elbows with exotic dancers—but she did have some clue about what went on in the world. She had cable television.

"Don't get that look on your face. I wasn't trying to be insulting. I just meant you have an innocent way about you. Actually, it's nice. Don't let these people out here change you."

Moni grinned. She'd heard that from at least a half dozen people when she'd left Dunkin.

"Anyway, I had to bolt because Nigel threatened to come after me. He'd never gotten violent with me; I wouldn't have put up with that. No matter how stupid all this sounds, I draw the line there. I knew what I was getting into. I made these choices because they seemed right at the time. I wanted a different life. One where I didn't have to work so damned hard all the time."

Moni reached across the table and touched Summer's hand. "I'm not judging you. I hope you know that."

"Thank you. But I also know how it looks to someone like you. Some dumb, down-on-her-luck ninny lets a guy lead her astray. It may have taken awhile for his lies to wear thin, but when I make up my mind, I stick to it. There won't be any on-again-off-again crap for me. I let him know that when I left him. It's for good."

"I guess he didn't take that news very well?"

"Like I said, he's never gotten violent with me, but he made it clear that we're not through until *he* says we're through. I didn't stick around to see if he meant it. I ran out of the club and down the street two blocks. I saw Danny and T-bone, those are his bouncers, run after me. So I couldn't take the chance of going back to my car. Nigel has a key to my apartment, so I sure as hell ain't going back there tonight."

"Where do you plan to stay? A motel?"

"That's the problem. All I have is what's in my purse." She fished out a handful of singles. Until I can go back for my car and the rest of my stuff, I'm screwed."

A thought popped into Moni's head. She knew it was risky, but her instincts were strong. "Well, my dear Aunt Reggie—God rest her soul—always said, 'It's all right to get a little wet, if you can save a fox from drowning.'"

Summer's brow furrowed. "Honey, are you feeling all right?"

"I'm sorry. What I'm trying to say is, would you like to stay at my place tonight?"

Chapter 8

Moni hadn't been to a slumber party since she was fourteen, but having Summer stay with her was the next closest thing. They watched videos, snacked on junk food, and stayed up all night talking.

By morning, it was as though they'd known each other all their lives. Despite their different backgrounds, they still had a lot in common. They were both addicted to MTV and reality television shows. They both felt running was the only tolerable form of exercise, and they'd both lost their parents at a young age.

It wasn't until she'd finally had another person around that Moni began to realize how empty her house had been feeling.

After their late night, the girls didn't stumble down to the kitchen until just after noon on Saturday. Summer opened the double doors of Moni's pantry. "Oh, thank goodness you have Chocolate Crispies. That's my favorite cereal."

Moni smiled, turning on the coffeepot. "Mine

too. I've become a little bit of a junk food junkie since I've been in California."

Summer reached directly into the box and pulled out a handful of cereal. "Don't you just hate all that wheat germ, tofu crap they love to peddle around here? Give me a chili dog and a Mountain Dew, and I'm in heaven."

Moni pulled two bowls out of the cupboard and set a carton of milk on the table. "Aunt Reggie and I used to make everything from scratch. We didn't even own a microwave. Nowadays, if you can't cook it in a microwave or take it out of a prewrapped package, I don't buy it."

"Amen, sister," Summer said, taking a chair at the kitchen table.

Moni picked up her watering jug and walked over to the windowsill to give Marley his break-fast. "Good morning, Marley," she said as she filled the planter.

Summer whipped around. "Who are you talk-ing to?"

"This is my fern, Marley."

"You name your plants?"

Moni shrugged. "I don't usually, but my aunt and I had a flower shop in Dunkin. This fern, Marley, is the only plant I brought to San Diego. It's kind of become like my pet." She ran a finger over one of the leaves.

"I named it Marley because its fronds remind me of Bob Marley's dreadlocks."

Summer shook her head. "Honey, I've never met anyone like you before."

"That's not the first time I've heard that." Moni poured them each some coffee and sat down across from Summer. "I always choose to take it as a compliment."

"Don't worry. It is one."

"What are your plans for today?" Moni asked.

She shrugged, staring down into her bowl of crispies. "Keep a low profile. Avoid Nigel. I'll probably have to leave the city."

"You're going to run away?"

Summer twisted the end of one of her braids between her fingers. "I can't go back to my apartment. I'm sure he's got one of his thugs watching my building."

Moni thought for a moment. She would never get to sleep that night if she had to worry about Summer. "Well, this Nigel guy doesn't know me. He'd never find you here. If you want, you can crash at my place for a few more days."

Her eyes went wide for a moment, losing their weathered look. "Are you serious? You'd let me stay here?"

Moni shrugged, trying to seem casual. "It's a big place. I'm here all by myself. You'd actually be doing me a favor—I'd like the company."

Summer's face lit up. "Wow, that would be great." Then she looked down at herself. Moni had lent her a T-shirt and shorts to wear for the night. On Summer's taller, more voluptuous frame, the shirt looked like a baby-doll tee and the shorts were snug enough to be underwear.

"I can't keep wearing your clothes, and if I go back for mine, I'll probably run into Nigel."

"That's true," Moni said, chewing on her lip. "Do you have enough money to buy a few things?"

"I have twenty-two dollars. Nigel owes me another paycheck, but I'm sure I can forget about ever seeing that."

Moni sipped from her coffee cup. "Maybe I can stop by your apartment and pack some things for you. None of Nigel's friends would recognize me. I'd probably look like any other visitor going into the building."

"That might work. Hold on." Summer dashed upstairs and came back carrying a purple suede purse. She dug around inside and pulled out a set of keys. "You can use these to get into my apartment. I'll write down the directions for you."

Moni took the keys, taking note of the red plastic lips hanging from the key ring. "Okay, no problem. I have to do some work across the street this afternoon, but I'll stop by your apartment this evening."

Summer smiled, pulling her into a tight hug. "Thanks, Moni. A lot of people wouldn't be so quick to help a stranger like this. Jumping into your car last night was the smartest move I've ever made."

* * *

Grant arched his back and dove into his swimming pool in one smooth maneuver. He savored the cool shock of the water, and he began his laps. It was a lot easier to face his computer terminal after a little physical exertion.

His head rose from the water and a flash of movement caught his eye. He paused, trying to clear his water-blurred vision. Was Moni watching him from the gap in the fence?

By the time he'd wiped enough water from his eyes to see her clearly, her attention was consumed by the wood grain of the fence. Grant couldn't help feeling a twinge of masculine pride. She *had* been watching him.

He had the urge to get out of the pool and walk over to her. Instead, he sank back into the water and continued swimming laps. It was best to let her finish her work without interruption. The sooner she completed the job, the better. He had enough on his plate right now between trying to finish his book and planning his parents' anniversary party. Not to mention trying to convince Katrina that she didn't belong there.

Grant forced his mind away from everything but the feel of his body slicing through the water. When he finally grew tired, he floated over to the ladder to pull himself out.

As he reached for his towel, the sound of feminine laughter pricked his ears. His head snapped around.

Through the hole in the fence, he saw Moni. She was talking to someone, but he couldn't see who it was. He ran the towel over his body in a hasty motion, already moving toward fence.

Then he heard it again and winced. It was the unmistakable, childish giggle that could only belong to his ex-wife Katrina.

He didn't take the time to find shoes, Grant wrapped the towel around his neck, and still dripping, stepped through the gap in the fence.

"Katrina," he called. "What are you doing here?"

Moni turned immediately, wiggling her fingers in a shy wave, but Katrina took the time to complete her sentence before slowly shifting her gaze to his. She wore a floppy straw hat and a long brown floral-print dress.

"Grant? What do you mean?" A sly smile curved her round cheeks. "You invited me over. Don't you remember?" Her voice was filled with faux concern, as though she actually thought he might be afflicted with amnesia.

His grip tightened on the towel around his neck. He'd called her this morning and asked her to stop by. He was hoping to reason with her in person.

"Of course, I remember. I *remember* you saying you couldn't make it this afternoon."

"Oops." She raised a hand to her mouth and giggled once more. "I'm free after all."

Grant counseled himself to breathe deeply.

Stay calm. Don't let her get to you.

He opened his mouth intending to sound relaxed. Instead, he said, "You didn't see fit to call and let me know this?"

Moni coughed and did an uncomfortable shuffle from side to side. Grant nodded to her. "I'm sorry, Moni. You two haven't been formally introduced. This is my ex-wife, Katrina."

Moni blinked. "Oh—she's your—oh. Um, well, it's nice to meet you." She darted a look from Katrina to Grant, then back to Katrina. "I'm just gonna . . . I have some work to do, so . . . I'll just be, uh, over here." Then she skittered back over to the fence, once again deeply enthralled with the grain of the wood.

Taking another deep breath, Grant forced himself to relax. He'd promised himself he wouldn't lose his temper this time. Finessing Katrina took a great deal of patience, and he'd been short on that virtue lately.

"Katrina, why don't you come inside so we can talk?"

"It's a lovely day. I'd much rather sit out here." She sauntered past him, then smiled politely at Moni as she stepped through the hole in the fence. She made herself comfortable at the patio table and removed her hat.

Shaking his head, knowing she was being contrary just to tick him off, Grant followed her, taking a seat across the table. "I'm glad you were able to stop by after all, Katrina. I was hoping we'd be able to reach an understanding."

Katrina didn't answer as she busied herself fluffing her short afro. When she was certain every hair was in place, she acknowledged Grant's statement. "I thought we settled this on the phone, Grant. Even though we're divorced, I'm still a Forrest. I have a right to attend your parents' anniversary party."

Grant was prepared for Katrina's stubborn attitude, and he was ready to counter her arguments. During their short marriage he'd learned her habits. He planned to stay calm and even-tempered, and once she'd decided she'd tortured him enough, she'd give in.

After ten minutes of back and forth, Grant was starting to lose his cool again. "Come on, Katrina. We're both adults. Why do we have to play these games?"

He'd once had an infinite amount of patience for this type of situation. Those days were gone. He resented the fact that she insisted on coming more to spite him than out of a genuine desire to attend the party. Inch by inch, he felt his temper growing.

"Be reasonable. I'm asking you, straight out— please don't come to the party."

"Why are you stressing yourself out over this, Grant? You should let me cleanse your chakra."

"Grant." Someone called behind him.

He turned. "What is it, Moni?"

"I need your help for a minute. Can you come over here, please?" she called.

He blew out his breath. What the hell? He wasn't getting anywhere with Katrina anyway. "I'll be right back," he said, and jogged over to Moni.

"What's wrong?"

Moni took his arm and led him over to a stack of wood on far end of the yard. "Let me start off by saying I wasn't *trying* to eavesdrop on your conversation with your wife."

"Ex-wife."

"Right, but I couldn't help overhearing your predicament."

Grant shook his head, impatiently. "Moni, if you're about to impart some advice from your dear Aunt Reggie, I have to tell you, I'm not in the mood right now."

Moni tugged on her ponytail. "Well, there was something about if you have a raccoon in your garbage can, and hoping the neighbors had fish for dinner—"

"Moni."

"Never mind. I really don't remember that one, anyway. Listen, you obviously don't want your ex-wife at the anniversary party, right?"

Grant sighed. "I think that's obvious."

"Well, I was just thinking . . . maybe she'll have something better to do that night."

"She doesn't have something better to do,

that's why she's hell bent on coming. She just likes the attention."

Moni nodded. "All I'm saying is, maybe you could make *sure* she has something better to do. You know her interests better than I would, but there has to be an invitation more irresistible than yours. Or—"

Suddenly, the light bulb lit in Grant's mind. "Wait a minute, I see what you're getting at. If she gets distracted by a better offer, she'll lose interest in the party. Maybe I *can* arrange something."

His gaze settled on Moni. She was just as cute as she could be, wearing a baseball cap with her curly ponytail wagging out from the back. "Thank you. That's not a bad idea."

"No problem. I hope it works out. I can see your ex-wife is . . . well, as Aunt Reggie would say, she's ornery."

"You can say that again."

Moni smiled. "I would, but I think she's looking over here. Pretend we were talking about this wood." She held it up for him to admire.

Grant laughed out loud, wondering if he should tell her she wasn't fooling anyone with that act. He turned around, raising his voice. "Yeah, that's exactly the right stain. Make them all that color."

He went back to Katrina and formally surrendered. "I'm tired of arguing about this, Katrina. If you insist on attending the party, suit yourself."

She looked surprised for a moment, but recovered quickly. "I'm glad you're going to be reasonable about this, Grant. Your parents will appreciate your maturity."

Once Katrina had finally left, Grant went to his office to make some phone calls. Distracting his ex-wife with another invitation just might work.

If things went as planned, he owed Moni a favor.

It was late evening when Moni finally made it over to Summer's apartment. She'd felt a little nervous on the way in because the building was across the street from the strip club Nigel owned. Thankfully, no one appeared to be watching her, and she slipped inside without any trouble.

Summer's apartment had a courtyard view, which allowed Moni to turn on the lights without worrying about being seen from the street. Packing, on the other hand, *was* an issue. Moni needed an eighteen-wheeler to transport all of Summer's clothes.

The woman's tiny one-bedroom apartment was like one big wardrobe, complete with four mobile racks of clothing and two armoires. Moni found two large pink suitcases in the closet and began filling them with random items. She made sure she collected essentials first, underwear and toiletries, and then she filled the luggage with all the colorful skirts, pants and tops she could fit in them.

She may have been inconspicuous going in, but there was no chance of Moni getting out that way. She huffed and puffed, half carrying, half dragging the bright pink luggage down three flights of stairs.

Fortunately, she'd parked her SUV on the curb in front of the building. If she could load the bags quickly, she would get away clean.

Trying to move as fast as possible, Moni struggled to shove the heavy bags into the back of her truck. One last look around proved there were no suspicious men watching her, and Moni hopped into the driver's seat.

She was about to put her key in the ignition, when a flash of purple caught her eye. She did a double-take unable to believe her eyes. Wearing a shiny lavender raincoat, Summer was entering the Silver Spur.

"She must be crazy," Moni muttered under her breath.

Hopping out of the car, she ran across the street, trying to catch up to Summer.

She got as far as the smoky doorway, before she was stopped by a meaty bouncer. "That's gonna be a ten dollar cover."

"Wait, I'm not here for the show. I just need to talk to that girl for a second. She's over there. The one in the purple raincoat."

The bouncer, who had more spare tires than the Michelin Man, didn't blink. "Ten dollars."

"Poop," Moni swore, digging into her purse and pulling out a wrinkled twenty.

She threw it at the guy and raced after Summer, hoping to reach her before she disappeared backstage.

"Hey lady, your change—"

"Keep it," she called over her shoulder. Summer was standing at the curtain that led backstage. She was talking to one of the dancers. "Summer, wait!"

She turned around briefly, but didn't acknowledge Moni's wave. "Summer!"

Moni sped up finally reaching her new friend. "What are you doing here? I just picked up all of your things. Why didn't you just tell me you were coming back here?"

Summer just blinked at her. "Who are you?"

"What do you mean? You slept in my guestroom last night and suddenly you don't know who I am?"

The girl bit her lip, leaning in close, she whispered, "Oh, I'm Candy, not Summer. Shh, I'm covering for my sister tonight."

Moni shook her head, trying to absorb the knowledge that the woman standing before her was *not* Summer. "Twins? *You're* her baby sister?"

Candy narrowed her eyes. "Only by two and a half minutes."

"She didn't tell me . . . you work here, too?"

Candy lowered her voice. "No, I'm covering for Summer. Nigel called and said—"

"Nigel? He called you."

"Yes, he said he'd fire Summer if I didn't show up, and she really needs this job, so—"

Moni grabbed Candy's sleeve and started tugging her toward the exit. "You've got to get out of here."

Candy pulled away. "No, it's okay. I filled in once before when Summer had food poisoning. Her regulars didn't even notice the difference."

Moni took the girl's arm once again. "You don't understand, Candy. Summer quit this job. She's at my house right now, and Nigel—"

"And what about Nigel?" asked a male voice.

Moni turned around to find a young man with a baby face and an expensive suit smiling at her. He winked. "Good job, Candy. You brought me a new girl."

"Oh, my stars." Moni blanched. "We were just leaving." Still gripping Candy's arm, she dragged the taller woman toward the door. She heard Nigel screaming obscenities and demanding that they tell him where Summer was.

Somehow Candy ended up in front, and she managed to stumble out of the open door before the bouncer caught her. Moni wasn't so lucky. The bouncer caught a corner of her T-shirt.

Moni maintained her forward motion, and with a little wiggle, she slipped free of his grasp. Without looking back, she headed straight across the street for the car, jumped in and started the ignition.

She made a U-turn and started after Candy, who was still pounding down the street in her spiked heels. Moni had to chase the girl for another half of a block before Candy slowed down enough to recognize her.

"Get in," Moni called. "I'll take you to your sister."

On the drive back to her house, Moni explained the events of the previous night to Candy. "So, she sent me to pick up some of her clothes, and that's when I saw you going into the Silver Spur. You know the rest," Moni finished.

Candy sat in the passenger seat, shaking her head. "I can't believe she didn't call and let me know what's going on."

Moni chewed her lip. "I'm sure she would have, once she was sure it was safe."

"Well, I'm glad she finally dropped that loser." She gripped her forehead and sighed. "Whew, and I'm *so* glad I didn't have to go on stage tonight."

"I thought you said you'd covered for her before."

Candy nodded. "I did, and it was fine . . . at first. I was sick to my stomach immediately afterward. All those nasty, sweaty men, drooling and groping. Blech! I honestly don't know how she goes through that every night."

Moni glanced over at her, feeling a bit confused. "If you don't like what your sister does for a living, why would you cover for her so she wouldn't lose the job?"

"Because the only reason she's working so hard is to help me get through school. We have a deal. Right now, she's paying my college tuition. Then, once I graduate, I'll work and help *her* go to college."

"That's amazing." Moni pulled into her driveway and Candy nodded her head with appreciation.

"This is a nice neighborhood."

"Thanks. I haven't lived here long, but so far I like it."

Moni opened the front door and called Summer's name.

"I'll be down in a minute," she called back.

A few minutes later, Summer started down the stairs. "Girl, your bathtub is to die for. If I wasn't starting to prune, I might have stayed in there all night."

"There's someone here to see you."

Candy came out of the kitchen carrying a diet soda. Summer squealed, "Kiki!" The two girls embraced. "Omigod, what are doing here?"

The sisters were identical, and now that Moni saw them side by side, it was clear just how close they were. They were so excited, words flew out rapidly between them in disjointed bursts.

If Moni hadn't already been familiar with the

details, there wouldn't have been any hope of her keeping up. Still, their excited chatter was exhausting, and Moni quickly gave up.

Her stomach was rumbling anyway. "While you two catch up, I'm ordering a pizza."

By the time the pizza arrived, the three of them had decided that Candy should stay at Moni's too—just to be on the safe side.

They were halfway through a spicy chicken and pesto pizza when Summer stated that she had just one more tiny favor to ask.

Moni dropped her crust on her plate. She never ate the crust. "What is it?"

"Would you mind if a couple of my girlfriends drop by tonight?"

Moni dabbed her mouth with a napkin. "Girlfriends?"

"Just a couple of the girls from the Silver Spur. I called them this afternoon to explain what was going on. I didn't want them to believe whatever lies Nigel was telling them. Some of those girls are like sisters to me."

Candy made an indignant sound as she popped chicken from her last pizza slice into her mouth.

"You already invited them over?"

"It's not going to be rowdy or anything. Just a couple of girls. They want to stop by after their shift. You don't mind, do you?"

Moni sighed. "Um, I guess not."

Summer gave her a quick hug. "Thank you so much, Moni. I think you'll really like these girls. We'll have fun."

Grant was up late, trying to make progress on his novel that night. He'd spent the better part of the day lining up concert tickets for a reggae band Katrina loved. They were playing in town the weekend of his parents' anniversary party and all the shows were already sold out. The tickets cost him a fortune, but it would be worth it.

With a solution to that problem finally in sight, Grant's mind was clear to get some writing done. He leaned back in his chair, reaching for a clever retort to one of Naomi's angry barbs.

His muse had finally made an appearance, bringing a new character with it. A mysterious young woman had suddenly taken form around chapter five. She was turning out to be a challenge for Trent Black.

Grant hadn't planned on giving Trent a love interest. But now that Naomi joined the cast, his story was more fun to write.

The new character was unpredictable, often surprising him with her clever wit and quirky habits.

The sound of cars pulling into the cul-de-sac caught his attention. The clock on the bottom of his computer screen read 1:45 A.M.

Curiosity got the best of him, and he moved

over to the window. "What the hell is going on over there?" he muttered, watching three scantily dressed young women enter Moni's front door.

Grant stared out of the window for a few more minutes, wondering what three half-naked women would be doing in Moni's house at nearly two in morning.

"I know she was interested in starting her own business, but . . ." He shook off the notion that she'd abandoned her beverage bra in favor of a brothel. She was off-beat, but she wasn't *that* crazy? Right?

He turned away from his window and sat back down at his computer. "I'm just going to mind my own business. When I get too involved in Moni's life, I only get *myself* in trouble."

Determined to stay focused, Grant tapped at his keyboard, but he was doing a dismal job of keeping his mind off the potential activities across the street. He kept substituting Moni's name in place of Naomi.

He was on the verge of giving up and going to bed when someone started pounding on his door. That can only be Moni, he thought as he made his way down the stairs. He cracked open the door without bothering to check the peephole.

Three men stood on his doorstep. One younger, wearing an expensive suit, the other two looked like fugitives from the state penitentiary.

"Where is she?" The Suit asked, trying to move through the doorway.

Instinctively, Grant's arm came up to block the entrance. "Who are you looking for?"

"Don't play dumb with me. I know she's in there."

Grant shook his head. "I don't know what you're talking about, but I think you'd better—"

"Fine. You don't want to send her out. We'll come in after her."

"Wait a minute—"

The biggest thug behind The Suit hit the door with his meaty fist, and it flew all the way open. The men brushed past him, leaving Grant standing in the doorway looking after them.

The Suit circled the room while the two thugs rushed around opening doors. "Summer! Summer, come out. I know you're in here."

"That shows how much you know," a female voice shouted from outside.

Grant turned and saw a tall woman, wearing skin-tight red pants, platform shoes and a white baby-doll shirt with a huge red heart in the center, standing behind him. Her long black braids swung back and forth as she spoke.

"Nigel, I can't believe you! Why are you harassing this poor man? We saw you from across the street."

Nigel turned to the smaller of the two men and smacked him on the side of his bald head.

"You wrote down the wrong address, you dyslexic fool."

The short man shrugged. "All these houses look the same to me."

The three women Grant saw entering Moni's house appeared behind the first woman, who had to be Summer.

Grant didn't know what was going on. He just knew it was getting out of hand. "Look, I don't know what this is about, but I'd appreciate it if you would all just—"

"Stay out of this, pretty boy." Nigel shoved Grant in the chest, and he stumbled backward.

"Hey, leave him alone," a tiny voice piped up.

From the corner of his eye, he saw Moni push through the crowd. "Summer's not going anywhere with you, Nigel. Leave before we call the police," she said in a firm voice.

Nigel threw his head back and laughed. "You again. I should have known." He walked over to Summer and grabbed her arm. "Let's go."

Grant stepped between them. "I don't think she wants to go with you." He looked in Summer's frightened eyes. "Do you?"

Summer shook her head emphatically.

"There, you see," Grant said. "You're going to have to leave without her."

Nigel laughed again. "Oh, and *you* think you're going to stop me?"

He sighed. "If I have to."

Nigel let go of Summer's arm to square off against Grant. "Whatcha gonna do, pretty boy?"

Grant faced him without flinching. Nigel laughed, and pretended to turn away, only to cock back his fist.

His body reacted on instinct. Grant blocked with his forearm, swinging it down so his fist could connect with Nigel's stomach. Nigel doubled over, going down to his knees.

Before Grant could enjoy the afterglow, someone grabbed him from behind. He heard women squealing and saw a blur of movement around him as he struggled to breathe against the muscled arm at his throat.

He heard a loud thud and the sound of shattering glass. Then he was released.

He turned around and found Moni holding a broken lamp in her hand. "Are you okay?" she asked.

Police sirens whined in the distance.

Grant rubbed his temple, muttering under his breath. "That's a matter of opinion."

Chapter 9

"Mmm-mmm-mm, what is that heavenly smell?" Summer asked, coming into the kitchen Sunday morning.

Moni leaned over to pull the loaf out of the oven. "My Aunt Reggie's banana love bread." She set the pan on the cooling rack and pulled off her oven mitts.

"Sounds divine. Break me off a piece of *that*."

"Sorry, I'll make you and Candy another loaf later. This one's for Grant."

"Oh yeah, the hunk across the street. What is it? Some kind of peace offering?"

"Exactly. It's impossible to stay mad after a bite of Aunt Reggie's secret recipe."

Summer nodded, eyeing the bread with open lust. "Girl, Grant's gonna have to learn to share. Let me have a piece of that bread."

Moni slid the pan out of Summer's reach. "Uh-uh. There are some frozen apple fritters in the freezer if you're that hungry. After what we put Grant through last night, there's no way I'm going to let you eat his bread."

"Wow, what's that smell?" Candy walked into the kitchen trying to rub the sleep from her eyes.

Summer opened the freezer. "Don't bother, Kiki. She's not about to share the bread. Apparently, the hot guy across the street rates better than her new best friends." She turned to wink at Moni.

Candy giggled. "Oh, you baked it for him. Did you bake some cash into it? Because I saw two broken lamps when we left last night."

Moni chewed her lip. "Good point. I'll bring my checkbook, too."

"Ohh, these look good. They're homemade aren't they?" Summer asked, peeking into the foil-wrapped pan she pulled from the freezer.

"Yes, they are. When I get in the mood for home cooking, I make a large amount and freeze it."

Summer slid the pan into the oven. "You can keep your old bread, I think I just found something better."

Moni placed the bread into a paper bag. "You two help yourselves to whatever's in the refrigerator. I'm going to take this across the street. If I don't return in a reasonable amount of time, call the police. It means he's strangled me to death."

Summer looked over her shoulder. "You're

not going over there like that, are you? I thought you wanted him to forgive you."

Moni looked down at her oversized chambray shirt and white capri pants, which she wore with white huarache sandals. "What's wrong with my clothes?"

"You've got to show a little more skin."

Moni blanched. "What?"

"Here, I can fix this." Summer unbuttoned the bottom of Moni's shirt, then she knotted it just under her breasts. "Men are much easier to distract when they can see skin. Nice abs by the way."

"Um, thanks." Moni picked up her peace offering.

Summer nudged her toward the door. "Any time, sweetie. Have fun."

Armed with that sage advice, Moni marched across the street with her banana love bread in one hand and her checkbook in the other. Standing on Grant's doorstep, she began to get nervous.

Maybe she should put down the bread, ring the doorbell and disappear before he answered. She chewed her lip and mulled it over. No, maybe she should just come back later—after he'd had a lot more time to cool off.

She turned around and stepped off his porch. No, she should just get this over with. Even if he did want to yell at her, she deserved it. Aunt Reggie taught her to stand up and take her punishment.

She turned around again, and this time she got as far as opening the screen door before she turned back.

Moni was halfway across the lawn when she heard the front door open. "I hope you don't think a little of your Aunt Reggie's banana *love* bread is going to fix things this time," he called to her.

Holding her breath, she walked back up to the door. "Oh, then you don't want it."

Grant reached out and plucked the bag from her hands. "I didn't say that." He moved aside so she could follow him into the house.

She stepped inside and closed the door behind her. A fluffy white cat marched up to her and brushed against her legs. Stooping, she ran her hand along the cat's back.

"Hi, sweetheart." She looked up at Grant. "Is this the poor cat I almost maimed?"

"No," he called from the kitchen. "That's Dr. Ruth. Westheimer is the one you nearly made into a pancake. Here he comes. He can't stand it when Ruth gets all the attention."

Westheimer slid in between Moni and Ruth and began to purr expectantly. She did her best to pet both cats. "I'm glad he's not the type to hold a grudge. Hint, hint."

"Nope, Westheimer's a sucker for anyone who'll show him a little affection."

Moni stood, causing both cats to mewl in disappointment. She joined Grant in the kitchen. "Look, I can't tell you enough how sorry I am about last night. I had no idea things were going to turn out that way."

Grant didn't answer her. Moni tried not to take it personally since his mouth was full of banana love bread. After he swallowed and took a long swig of milk, he turned back to her.

"I just want to know one thing?"

"What?" she asked, holding her breath.

"How do you manage to function with your life in this constant state of upheaval? If it's not one thing, it's another."

Moni thought about his question. She reached back and grabbed a strand of hair from her ponytail and began twirling it around her finger. "You're not going to believe this, but this is the most exciting my life has ever been. Back in Dunkin things were simple. I had a good life, but nothing out of the ordinary ever happened."

Grant nodded. "I see. Now that you're in San Diego, you're making up for lost time."

"It's not that I'm creating these situations intentionally. Stuff just keeps happening."

"And for some reason, I always seem to be in the middle of it."

"Maybe *you're* a jinx," she teased.

He gave her a stony look.

"I'm sorry, that was a joke. In reference to your

earlier statement, I don't expect the bread to make up for everything. This time, I brought my checkbook." She pulled it from her waistband.

"You don't have to sue me this time. I'll write a check for whatever you want."

He laughed. "Whatever I want, huh? A couple of lamps. That's not going to put you out too much, but the pain and suffering, the emotional damage, now that's going to cost you."

Moni didn't bat an eye. "Have you got a pen?"

Grant leaned his hip against the kitchen counter and surveyed Moni carefully. He always had big thoughts about how he was going to maintain a hard front, until he was face-to-face with this woman.

Mitch had been right on the money when he'd called Moni an attractive nuisance. Whenever Grant got involved with her, his life tripled in complexity. But all he had to do was look into those wide brown eyes and, suddenly, he just didn't care.

He didn't care that wherever she went, trouble followed. He didn't care that trouble for Moni usually meant *more* trouble for him. And he definitely didn't care that she was just the type of woman he was supposed to avoid.

"Come here, let me show you something," he finally said, and led her into his living room. "You see these?"

He pointed to the two end tables that each supported a lamp.

"Aren't those the lamps that were broken last night?" she asked.

"Yup, it's called Miracle Glue and it's a buck ninety-nine at the drugstore. You want to write me a check for that?"

"Just because you fixed them doesn't mean you're not entitled to have them as good as new. How much would it cost to replace them?"

"Forget about it."

Moni grabbed a pen from the end table. "Fine, I'll estimate." She scribbled a number on a check then tore it off and handed it to him.

Grant looked down at the check. "This is ridiculous. I'm not going to take it." He tried to hand it back, and she pushed his hand away.

He sighed. "Take this back."

She turned around so he couldn't force it on her. He grabbed the collar of her shirt and stuck the check inside.

"Stop it." Moni wiggled and contorted until she'd retrieved the check. "Look, I don't want to go through what we did with the fence. Just take it."

She tried to grab him, but he jerked away. Moni ended up chasing him in a circle around the room.

"I don't want it."

She stopped. "Why not?"

"Have you ever considered that it may be

worth more to me just to have you out of my hair?" He'd meant to be flippant, but his words came out harsher than he'd intended.

"Oh, I see."

He reached for her arm. "Look, Moni—"

She turned away. "Of course, that makes perfect sense. I thought you'd been behaving differently toward me." She was deep in her own thoughts. "Yes, that does make sense. I've really been getting on your last nerve, haven't I."

"No, I didn't mean it that way."

She balled the check up into her fist and picked up her checkbook. "I hope you enjoy the bread. And, don't worry, the fence should be fixed shortly."

She moved toward the door, and Grant grabbed her by the arm. "I don't want you to leave thinking I don't like you."

"Oh . . . no . . ." Moni was trying to laugh but her voice sounded forced. "I don't think that. I mean, everyone just loves me. I know that."

He could hear the sarcasm in her voice, and it was killing him. He grabbed her by the shoulders and shook her lightly. "Listen to me—"

Her head was lowered, and she wouldn't meet his gaze. "Don't bother. Really, it's not necessary. I know you've got a lot to do, so—"

"I like you. The problem is, I think I may like you a little bit more than I can handle right now. Do you know what I mean?"

She was looking up at him now. Staring with wide doe-eyes.

He couldn't tell if he was getting through to her. "I don't think it's any secret how attracted I am to you. It's just . . . this isn't a good time for me to start up something new. Do you understand?"

Moni shook herself out of his grip and fidgeting with her hands. "Of course."

The muscles in Grant's stomach tensed. "There's still a lot of things I have to figure out."

She nodded.

"If it were a different time or a different place." Wow, he'd never noticed how smooth her skin was. Golden honey. That's what it looked like.

"I get it."

"Then maybe we could see what happened. That is, if you were interested . . ." He was staring at her lips now. They looked so soft.

"Sure, if it had been another time . . ."

"Because I know we could have been . . ." Suddenly, Grant didn't know what he was babbling on about. All he saw was a pair of lips he really needed to kiss. Right now.

His fingers slipped behind her neck, and he tilted her head up toward his. She knew what was coming because she moved into his embrace naturally, her lips parting softly when he pressed his mouth over them.

Their lips moved together, and he was drawn to her softness. Her arms curled around his waist, and he could feel her small hands pressed to his back. Grant didn't know what he'd been expecting. To kiss her briefly then pull away? To take a small taste without sitting down for a meal?

Whatever Grant had been prepared for, it wasn't the sudden rush of passion that overtook him.

Moni felt fragile and delicate in his arms, but her effect on him was strong. He stroked the soft skin at the nape of her neck with one hand and rubbed her back with the other. His left hand moved in a circular motion over the fabric of her shirt until a finger slipped off and made contact with skin.

The other four fingers were drawn to her bare lower back like magnets. Suddenly, such limited contact wasn't nearly enough. He wanted to touch more skin. All over.

Without breaking contact with her mouth, Grant pulled Moni backward until he felt the sofa against his legs. He sat down and dragged her onto his lap.

She straddled his hips and leaned forward, reaching up to frame his face with her hands. She pressed her mouth over his and took control of the kiss.

Grant heard a guttural moan, and vaguely

recognized it as his own. He didn't care. His body felt like steel and Moni's cushioning softness was addictive.

His fingers found the fabric knotted under her breasts and pulled it loose. She reached up to help him unfasten the buttons and seconds later her shirt was fluttering to the floor.

Grant reached behind her to unhook her bra, and when he finally did, it followed the shirt to the floor. His eyes burned at the beautiful sight of Moni's bare torso.

Dipping his head, Grant brought his lips to the curve of her breast, brushing them gently. He inhaled her sweet scent, and struggled to control his raging ardor. Lifting his head, he began to massage one nipple with his fingertip as his mouth caressed the tip of the other. He alternated back and forth and Moni's soft, wild sounds drove him to the edge of his restraint.

"I want to see you, too," she whispered, reaching for the hem of his sweatshirt.

He helped her raise the shirt over his head revealing his bare chest. Her eyes were bright and eager, raking over every inch of his skin. His excitement intensified.

Her fingers traced the muscles of his torso with a feather-light touch. He was in agony. Gritting his teeth, he endured the intensity for as long as he could, then he grabbed her around the waist and flipped her under him. He stretched her out on the sofa, and their bodies pressed together from ankle to shoulder.

"Is this okay?" he whispered in her ear.

Her eyes were hooded, giving her a sensual look. She nodded before her eyelids fluttered shut.

Grant leaned down and kissed Moni once again. When he lifted his head and looked down at her, the look of innocence in her face compelled him to say something else.

"Moni, what I said earlier about not being ready for a relationship . . . that's still true . . . do you understand?"

She opened her eyes. "I understand. No commitment." Then she reached behind his neck and pulled his mouth back down to hers.

Satisfied that he wasn't taking advantage of her, Grant let himself relax and enjoy the moment. Her lips were soft and with each gentle swirl of her tongue against his, he became more impatient for her.

He wanted to sink into her softness and feel her legs locked around his back. He needed to hear her uncontrolled sighs of pleasure.

Raising his body, Grant began to unfasten her pants. With Moni's help, he removed them. His hands moved to her panties. They were covered with tiny blue flowers and were edged with a thin band of lace.

He tucked two fingers of each hand into her

underwear and was about to tug downward, when he felt her hand on his chest, stopping him.

"Grant, before we continue, there's something I need to tell you."

"What is it?"

"Um, technically . . ." she paused. "I'm a virgin," she whispered.

For some reason, it took a moment to break through his passion-fogged brain. His mind stalled on the first part of her phrase.

"Technically?" He stared, pronouncing the word as though he didn't know what it meant.

"What we're doing here?" she said. "*Technically*, I've never done it before. I'm still a virgin."

Reality soaked through him like ice water. He sat up, leaning against the arm of the sofa, away from Moni.

Moni sat up also, pulling her legs up to her chest and wrapping her arms around her knees. "I take it that's a problem?"

"Whoa," was all Grant could manage. He ran a hand over his face, trying to think this through. "That's—that's . . . whoa."

"I didn't want you to stop. I—I just thought you should know."

"No. No, I'm glad you told me." He reached down, snagged Moni's shirt from the pile of clothes on the floor and tossed it over to her.

Moni slipped on the shirt. "So . . . you don't want me anymore," she asked with a tiny voice.

Grant's heart ached at the hurt he heard in her

question. He stood and began pacing the living room. "Moni, it's not that at all. It's just . . . you're first time should not be like *this*."

"But this is what I want."

He stopped pacing and knelt in front of her. "I'd never be able to live with myself—"

Moni rolled her eyes. "Why? I'm twenty-six years old, not eighteen. I know what I'm doing. I'm more than ready."

"There must be a reason for your waiting this long."

She pinned him with a hard look. "You want to know the reason? I'll tell you why I'm still a virgin. It's not because I'm a prude or anything like that."

"I'm listening."

"I was in a relationship back home. I dated my high-school sweetheart almost exclusively until a few months before I moved out here."

"Almost?"

"We broke up for a while when I was in college to try dating other people, but he was my only serious relationship."

"And the two of you never—"

"Actually, we'd tried a few times." She looked way, suddenly shy. "It never worked."

He frowned. "What do you mean 'it never worked'?"

She chewed on her lip, staring at her hands. "He said, you know, it was too small, or something. He couldn't get in."

Grant opened and closed his mouth. There wasn't much he could say to that.

"Finally, we decided we should wait until marriage. Honestly, I was just relieved. It seemed like a lot of work for something that might not even be worth the trouble. But, just now, with you, it felt . . . different. Suddenly, I think I've figured out what all the fuss was about."

"Moni—"

"Passion. I'd read about it in books and talked about it with friends, but I'd never actually come anywhere close to it until you started touching me."

His body went hot at her words. He wanted to forget what she'd just told him, pick her up and finish what they'd started. But that wasn't smart. Women developed emotional attachments to men they made love with. The fact that he would be her first would guarantee him a significant place in her heart. He couldn't take that responsibility.

He took both her hands in his. "Moni, your first time should be romantic. It should be with someone you love and who loves you in return."

She pulled her hands out of his grip. Her eyes flashed. "What gives you the right to tell me what I need? Can't I decide that for myself?"

"Of course, but this particular choice involves me, and I can't in good conscience—"

Moni stood, stepping over Grant and grabbing

her pants. "Give me a break. You're acting like I'm a twelve-year-old who doesn't know what's good for her. Contrary to popular belief, I'm not naïve. You never even considered the possibility that I'm the one who's not looking for a relationship. If that's what I was after, I would have gotten married when I had the opportunity."

Grant watched as Moni hastily dressed. "Look, I know you're upset now, but when you look back on this later, you'll realize this would have been a mistake."

Moni adjusted her clothing. Stuffing her bra into her pocket, she marched toward the door.

"Do you understand?" Grant followed after her. "The first time should be for love. This would have been—um, something else."

Moni tossed a sharp look over her shoulder before letting herself out. The door closed behind her with a thud.

Chapter 10

"Nothing like a little shopping to beat the boy-next-door blues," Summer mused, bending over to breathe in the sent of handmade soap.

They'd covered less than a block of the charming old-fashioned shops at the center of Old Town San Diego State Historic Park, but it was becoming blatantly clear to Moni that something vital was missing.

"Where are the shoe stores? I realize this isn't supposed to be Bloomingdales, but a few hand-stitched slippers and some dusty wooden clogs from the General Store isn't gonna cut it."

"I hear you, girl." Summer flipped her braids over her shoulder as they walked out of the store. "But I figured a nice country girl like you could appreciate the old-school vibe happening here."

Moni looked around again. She did enjoy experiencing life as it was for the first Spanish settlers in the 1800s. She and Summer had toured an old schoolhouse, unique little shops and a beautiful mansion built around a garden courtyard. It was a dramatic contrast to Colonial Williamsburg, which she'd visited often in Virginia.

"Actually, I like it a lot." Moni felt a pang of guilt for her low spirits. "I'm sure I'd enjoy it even more if I came back when I'm in a better mood."

Summer leaned close and peered at her.

Moni leaned away. "What are you doing?"

"I've been taking you at your word that you're feeling down. But I'd never know the difference. You're perky even when you're upset."

Moni rolled her eyes. "It's the curse of the Lawrence women. My aunt was in her fifties when she died, and the woman still had the look of a wide-eyed virgin."

"That's the way to do it," Summer said, oblivious to the two men that nearly broke their necks trying to catch her eye as she passed. "So, you want to go home?"

"Yeah," Moni said with a sigh. "Thanks for coming with me, though. It's nice to have something to do with my time besides work on Grant's fence and research my business."

Summer stopped dead in her tracks, clapping her hands together. "I've got an idea."

Moni jumped. "For what?"

Summer squeezed her shoulder. "I know what you need. Not only will it be fun, but it will solve your virginity problem."

She pulled away. "Whatever it is, I'm not doing it."

"Oh, my bad, I didn't mean that literally. What you need is a slutty makeover."

She raised her eyes toward the sky. "Dear Lord."

"I bet we could get that hot neighbor of yours to take you seriously after that."

Moni regarded her friend in disbelief. "I don't think that would make any difference to him."

Summer snapped her fingers. "He has eyes, doesn't he?"

"His eyes aren't the problem. I think he notices me plenty. He just doesn't want to get involved right now. He's officially off limits."

"Sorry, chica," Summer said with a shrug. "Let me know if you change your mind about my makeover offer."

Distracted, Moni nodded, her attention suddenly taken by a little shop across the park. "Look over there."

Summer turned around in a circle. "At what?"

Moni pointed. "Do you mind if we stop in that flower shop for a second?"

"Why? Gonna buy your man some roses? It's worth a shot, but I don't think guys dig that stuff the way we do."

"No, it just reminds me of the shop my aunt and I used to have in Dunkin." The block-lettered sign read FLOWERS—plain and simple, but the calico awning and the flower boxes filled with tulips under the windows were a familiar and comforting sight.

They walked into the shop and Moni closed her eyes, inhaling the scents of jasmine and roses. In each corner were wooden barrels filled popular flowers, including daffodils, lilies, and sunflowers. Moni felt the prickle of moisture in eyes. The flood of memories was so strong, she could almost see her aunt standing behind the counter, wrapping long-stem roses in green tissue paper.

"Are you just gonna stand around? Or are you actually gonna buy something," snapped a tight voice.

Moni blinked away the nostalgia to see that instead of her aunt, a narrow-faced, shriveled old woman with white spiky close-cropped hair stood behind the counter.

Swallowing hard, Moni approached the woman. "Do you have any *Strelitzia reginae*."

The woman's eyes went wide and her head darted around, reminding Moni of a startled ostrich. "What in carnation is that?"

"The common name is bird-of-paradise or crane lily." She'd researched the local flora when she decided to move to southern California. Compared to her native green Virginia, the landscape here was any horticulturist's dream.

"Well, why didn't you just say so? There may be some of them over there." The woman waved a bony finger toward the back of the store.

Moni shook her head. Aunt Reggie always said, "You treat rudeness like any other handicap—you have to overlook it." So, while Summer stood outside flirting with one of the many men who'd been ogling her during their tour of Old Town, Moni moved toward the back of the store.

After several minutes, she walked back to the woman. "I didn't see any bird-of-paradise plants back there. I thought they were common in this area."

The woman's expression didn't change, and if her lips hadn't started moving, Moni would have thought she was made of stone. "Well, we don't have any."

Moni's brow furrowed. She hadn't come into the store looking to buy flowers, but now she was quite committed to the idea.

She shifted her weight. "Um, is there anyone else here who can help me?"

"Nope." The woman picked up a folded newspaper from the counter and started reading it.

Moni tugged on one of her curls. "Well, who's the owner?"

"Me." The woman didn't spare her another glance.

It figured. Moni shifted her weight and tried again. "So, you're sure you don't have any crane lilies?"

"Yup."

"What about blue irises?"

The woman shrugged.

Suddenly, it became a challenge to see if she could get this old bat to give her any kind of service, or at least, show some human emotion.

"No disrespect, ma'am, but are you always this disinterested in helping your customers?"

The old woman shrugged again.

Moni's sighs got heavier. "You know, you'd probably get more repeat business if you'd just—"

"What you know about it," the woman grumbled, still reading her paper.

"Well, actually, I used to work in a flower shop in Virginia and we—"

She slapped the paper down on the counter and Moni jumped back two steps. "Oh, so you're saying you think you can do better'n me?"

"The point I'm trying to make is—"

The woman untied the apron around her waist and tossed it at Moni's head. "Good. I could use a break, Mary Sunshine. Knock yourself out."

Moni stood dumbstruck as the woman tucked her paper under her arm, pulled out a pack of cigarettes, and strolled out of the front door without looking back. Moni hadn't realized that she'd been frozen in place until someone tapped her on the shoulder.

She turned to see a tan blond man holding hands with a shorter red-headed woman. "Hi. We were wondering if you had any *Strelitzia reginae*."

At two o'clock on Friday, Grant was still sitting in front of his computer, pounding away at his keyboard. As usual, he'd started early, but this time, when the opportunity came to eat, shower and shave—he couldn't tear himself away.

It had been over a week since Moni had left his place in a heated rush. She'd been embarrassed by their encounter. He knew because he'd barely caught a glimpse of her since that day. She was still working diligently on the fence, but she'd started scattering her hours from early morning to just before dusk. She would come quietly and disappear before he'd even realized she'd been there.

Grant hated the idea of her avoiding him, but he knew it was what was best for both of them. That truth didn't change the fact that he couldn't stop thinking about her. At night he'd wake up sweating from steamy dreams about Moni. He'd see flashes of skin, feel her soft hair, and inhale her fresh baby powder scent.

Thoughts of her were driving him up the wall, but they were also helping him in an unexpected way. When the tension in his gut became unbearable, he found that he was able to channel it into his writing.

He had to be careful that Naomi didn't take over the story.

He enjoyed writing the dialogue between Naomi and Trent. He was never sure what witty or smart remark might fly from the little minx's mouth. She was sharp and sexy and wouldn't take any lip. Grant knew he was probably transferring his own desires onto the page, but writing about Naomi gave him something to look forward to when he sat down in front of the screen.

Grant moved away from the computer and stripped off his shirt, heading for the shower. Before he'd taken two steps, the phone began ringing.

He held his breath as he took note of his brother's number on the caller ID.

"Hey, Keith. What's up?"

There was a pause on the line. "Uh, it freaks me out when you do that. Can't you just say hello?"

"Sure." Grant hung up the phone.

The phone rang again, and this time when Grant answered it, he said, "Hello?"

"Smartass," Keith grumbled.

Grant laughed wickedly. "I'm sorry . . . Smartass? I don't know anyone by that name. You must have the wrong number."

He hung the phone up.

The phone rang again. Grant picked up the receiver but didn't speak.

"Very funny," Keith said, laughing. Grant was rarely playful. "I'm glad you're in a good mood, because I need to ask you for a favor."

Grant was tempted to hang up the phone again. "I knew I shouldn't have answered the phone."

"No, listen. This favor isn't for me, it's for Tara."

"I hope you haven't stooped to using my niece to get favors out of me. If you tell me she needs a satellite dish so she'll be able to do her homework . . ."

"No, that was a joke. Anyway, she just got back from cheerleading camp, and I promised that she could invite some of the girls over for a slumber party."

"I don't know where this is going, but it's not looking good."

"Well, as it turns out, there's a plumbing problem in my apartment building, and next week they'll be turning off the water while they make repairs."

"Don't tell me. You want me to have Tara and a bunch of her girlfriends over for a slumber party?"

"Tara worships you. She'd be thrilled if you let her have this party."

Grant massaged the bridge of his nose. "And where will you be during this time?"

"Janet and I thought we'd go to a hotel. We're trying to work things out."

"How convenient. While you and Janet sort through your troubles in a cushy hotel, I get your kid and her cheerleading friends."

"Come on. Like I said, this is for Tara, not for me."

Grant rolled his eyes. "I know I'm going to regret this."

When he hung up the phone and finally made his way into the shower, he realized that he'd just agreed to have a bunch of twelve-year-old girls spend the night in his house.

He turned his face into the spray. Oh, well, he thought, he'd managed with his sister's boys. Somehow how he'd figure out how to handle the girls, too.

By the end of the summer, he'd be qualified to run his own baby-sitting service.

That evening, Moni followed Summer into the living room, where Candy was punching and kicking along with her Tae Bo video.

Summer pressed pause on the VCR, and Candy released a startled, "Hey!"

"Kiki, you've got to hear this," Summer said, giggling. "Moni got a job today."

Moni dropped her shopping bags and slumped on the sofa. "I don't think it's a very amusing story."

Candy grabbed her towel, mopping her face and neck before sitting down beside her. "A job? You mean, like, a project for your business?"

Summer came out of the kitchen peeling a banana. "No, an actual nine-to-five job. Some old lady walked out of her flower shop and left Moni in charge."

Candy shook her head in confusion. "What? Why would she do that?"

"She didn't go far. She was on the front porch smoking a cigarette the whole time." Moni reluctantly explained the events leading up to the woman, whom she now knew as Vera Schonefeld, walking out on her. "When she got back she offered me a job. At first, I wasn't going to accept."

"What made you change your mind?" Candy asked.

"Vera, the old lady, has a very irreverent attitude about the shop. It just killed me to see how she was running it into the ground."

Candy shook her head. "You walk in off the street and she just hands you a job? I wish things like that would happen to me. Once I get my graphic arts degree, I'd like to get into Web design. But, there's a lot of competition."

Moni curled up into a ball, cradling a throw pillow to her chest. "Don't congratulate me. This isn't a good thing. The last thing I need right now is a job. I'm supposed to be planning my own business. Which, I might add, has just been one major failure after another."

"Don't look so depressed," Candy said, patting her arm. "Just because your first couple of ideas didn't pan out, doesn't mean the next one won't make you the next Bill Gates."

"That's so true," Summer said, nodding. "You're so smart—I've never seen so many damn charts in my life. The way you lock yourself in the basement every night with the computer is gonna pay off."

Moni rolled her eyes. "I'm not so sure about that. In fact, this job falling into my lap is probably a sign. The cosmic forces of the universe are telling me to give up and work a normal job, just like everyone else."

Summer sprawled out on the floor beside the couch and took a large bite of her banana, leaving red lipstick around it.

"Girl, you've got the blues," she said, after swallowing. "I know exactly how to cure that."

Moni threw a hand over her eyes. "No, Summer, I already told you. I'm not interested in *any* kind of makeover."

Summer made an exasperated sound. "I'm not talking makeovers, this time. I'm talking techno music, flashing lights and dancing with gorgeous men. Nothing boosts a woman's ego like dancing the night away."

Moni didn't lift her head. "I don't think I feel like dancing."

"Nonsense," Candy said resolutely, jumping up from the couch. "We're going dancing. You may not feel like it now, but you'll thank us for this later."

"That's right," Summer said, also getting to
her feet. "We need to pick a sexy outfit for you.
Once you turn a few heads, you'll forget all
about your troubles."

Moni reluctantly got up from the couch. By
the time she'd slogged up the stairs, Summer
and Candy were already going through her
closet.

"What are you two doing?" she asked, even
though she'd already guessed.

"We're trying to find something for you to
wear," Candy said, holding up a pale pink sun-
dress for Summer's inspection. Summer shook
her head and held up a pair of red tights she'd
pulled from the dresser.

Moni snatched the tights from her hand. "I've
been dressing myself for years, thank you very
much."

Despite Moni's best efforts to convince her
new friends that she could pick her own clothes,
the twins insisted on helping her choose an outfit. Eventually they determined that Moni's
wardrobe just wasn't sexy enough and began to
accessorize her strappy black dress with body
glitter courtesy of Summer. Candy fastened a
shiny silver choker around her throat and
clipped a silver spiral just above her elbow.

The girls took turns fussing with her hair, and
Moni began to realize what it would have been
like to grow up with sisters.

"It's too beautiful to tame," Summer shouted, removing a hair clip. "Let it be free."

When Moni looked into the mirror, she felt like a different person. Curls vibrated like bolts of electricity from her head. And, to her surprise, she liked it. She'd bought the slinky black dress on a whim when she'd moved to San Diego. With the glitter and jewelry, Moni felt like a twinkling star.

"Wow," she murmured.

"Welcome to California, baby," Summer said, blowing a kiss to her reflection.

Moni opened the second closet in the master bedroom, where she kept her most prized possessions.

Candy stood in the doorway and simply sighed in awe. "I have never seen anything like this."

Summer released a shrill whistle. "Check out Imelda junior."

To complete the bonding process with her new roommates, Moni did something she never did. She let them borrow her shoes.

Chapter 11

Saturday morning, Moni stood before the bathroom mirror, examining her torso. She'd gotten her belly button pierced last night. It had seemed like a good idea at the time, but now it just hurt like hell.

With a deep sigh, she frowned at the small ring of silver punctuating her navel. The pounding of her temples reminded her that she may have gotten carried away with the margaritas last night. She vaguely remembered walking past a tattoo shop on the way to the parking garage at two A.M.

To their credit, Summer and Candy had tried to talk her out of going inside. But Moni had been tipsy and giddy after having so much fun at the dance club. For a few hours, she'd let go of the stress of trying start a business. She forgot about Grant's rejection and let the music carry her away. It was the same tension release she got from running, except that the addition of bright lights and good-looking California men had overloaded her senses just a bit.

One throaty female voice had commanded from the loud speakers to "Just let go!"—and Moni had. The result was waking up with a hangover and a shiny silver hoop in her belly.

Moni tugged on a pair of faded jeans, but when she pulled her cotton T-shirt over her head, the material irritated her navel ring. She had to settle on a white halter top instead.

Donning a pair of sunglasses to shield her sensitive eyes, Moni trudged across the street to finish working on Grant's fence. She only had one or two final touches to complete.

She'd been trying to avoid running into Grant directly since their last humiliating encounter. Thank goodness she expected to complete work today.

Unfortunately, since she'd slept in that morning, she didn't make it across the street until late afternoon, when the sun was high. She was already moving slowly because of a slight headache. The hot sun immediately sapped her energy. She'd had big plans for the progress she wanted to make, but most of her effort was spent resting on the grass and squirting herself with the water bottle.

This is how Grant eventually found her. Sitting on the grass, knees to her chest, with her forehead resting on her arms.

"Are you all right?"

The sound of Grant's voice startled Moni, and her head snapped up. She shielded her eyes against the sun, trying to focus on his face.

"Uh, yeah, I'm fine. Just taking a break." Immediately, she could feel her cheeks growing hot, knowing she'd been caught slacking off.

"Yeah?" He stooped to bring their eyes level. "Looks like you've been breaking more than working today."

She started to get up and he touched her knee to stop her. "It doesn't bother me. It's just that you don't seem to be feeling well."

She sighed. "Don't worry about me. It's just the aftereffects of a late night out on the town. I'm fine."

"If you say so." He shrugged. "I haven't seen you around much lately."

"Because my schedule has been a little more hectic, I've been working on the fence sporadically. You should be thrilled to know I'm almost finished—with time to spare."

He chose to focus on her initial statement. "Is it really your schedule, or have you been avoiding me?"

Moni looked down to trace the letters on her water bottle. He looked wonderful in his khaki shorts and blue tank-top. She could see the lean muscles of his legs and smooth mounds of his biceps. She'd always been a sucker for nice bi-

ceps. She took a long swallow of water, unsure
how to respond.

She decided to take the easy way out. "I've
been busy."

"Okay." He nodded, clearly not believing her.
"How is business? The beverage bra Internet
thing—how's that coming along?"

"I had to scrap any plans that had to do with
the Internet," she said with a sigh.

Thinking about her business plan gave Moni a
queasy feeling in her stomach. She knew she
was wasting time and a golden opportunity. She
needed to refocus, but she was allowing other
things to divert her attention.

She averted her eyes from Grant's attentive
gaze. "I have a few balls in the air, but the truth
is I'm between projects right now."

He patted her shoulder. "You sound discour-
aged."

Moni couldn't help responding to his genuine concern. "I guess I am. I knew starting a
business wouldn't be easy, but my first two
ideas have already flopped. I feel like a squirrel
in a briar patch—I don't know which way to
turn."

He nodded. "What I hear you saying is that
you haven't made as much progress as you'd
hoped to by now."

"That's right."

"And that's making you feel down?"

"Exactly." Moni smiled, feeling as though she should be lying on a couch and paying Grant by the hour.

"Don't you think starting a business is a huge endeavor and that a few false starts should be expected?"

"Yes, that's true . . ." Moni sighed. "But, have you ever had an opportunity to do something really special and halfway through, you started to feel like you were blowing it? Or worse than that, like you were crazy to think you could do it in the first place?"

Grant laughed softly. "Have I *ever*."

She studied his face. "You mean your book?"

"Yup. Many times I've asked myself why I didn't stick to what I know best. Stretching yourself is uncomfortable, but that's because it's supposed to be. Every time I start feeling like I'm not banging out enough pages or that I'm not talented enough to carry the whole story, I try to remember that if it were easy, everyone would do it. So, I keep plugging away."

"I try to keep plugging away." Moni continued to hug her knees to her chest, resting her chin on her kneecap. "But lately, it's easier to distract myself with other projects than to focus on a business that isn't going anywhere."

"So, rather than do something that will further your business, you let yourself get caught up in . . . what?"

She grinned at him. "Working on your fence.

Rearranging furniture. Shoe shopping. You name it."

"And when was the last time you did something productive for your business?"

Moni chewed on her lower lip. "It's been at least a week."

"Okay, what if you tell yourself you'll do one new thing for your business each day. You can do more if you like, but at least one."

She shook her head. "That would be great, but right now, I'm stuck. I'm not sure which direction to move in next."

He studied her. "Up until now, how have you chosen your projects?"

"I made a list."

"Okay, what's the next item on the list?"

She held her head between her hands. "Well, there were a few Internet-related projects that are no longer an option. I also have an idea for accessories for young girls, but that would involve setting up a focus group and recruiting attendees. I don't know."

"So, the one thing you need to do today is make a list of everything that would be involved in setting up this focus group."

Moni rubbed her temple. "I have some ideas for a bunch of products marketed toward preteen girls. When the time was right, I was hoping to just drop by a middle school and recruit on the spot, but it's summertime. School isn't even in session."

"You're telling me you need a handful of twelve-year-old girls?"

She sighed. "That's right, do you have some in your pocket?"

He nodded, laughing. "This is your lucky day. My brother just conned me into hosting a slumber party for my niece, Tara, and five of her friends from cheerleading camp. They all descend upon my house next Saturday night. Maybe you can try your products out on them? In exchange for my letting you use them as guinea pigs, you can help chaperone the party. I have no idea how to entertain six twelve-year-old girls."

Moni stared at Grant. "You're kidding, right? You just happen to be having your twelve-year-old niece over next week?"

"Yes, you can thank Keith and the shoddy plumbing system in his apartment building for that."

She thought for a moment. "I wonder if I could pull this off. You said there will be six girls total?"

He nodded.

A grin began to spread across her face. "I think I have enough samples to go around. This just might work out."

"Now, before you get too excited, remember the deal. You have to help chaperone. At least until the girls go to bed—and Lord only knows when that'll be."

"It's a deal. Maybe I can get Summer and Candy to help out, too."

"The twins? What's the deal there? Are they still staying with you?"

"Yes, they're my roommates. They don't have anywhere else to go, and I like the company."

Grant raised brows and shook his head. "Okay . . ."

Moni cocked her head to the side, studying his expression. "I can tell by your tone that you don't approve."

"It's not my place to approve or disapprove. I'm sure you know what you're doing."

Moni bristled. Suddenly Grant reminded her of Burt. Whenever he thought he knew better, he took that same tone. He never gave her enough credit when it came to important decisions. Out here, so far from Burt and her friends, she'd almost forgotten what it felt like to have the fear of disapproval influencing her actions. Even if she did make a few mistakes, she was enjoying the freedom to stand, or fall, on her own.

"I do know what I'm doing," she said firmly. She set her water bottle aside. "I guess I should get back to work now."

Grant stood, turning toward the fence. "Looks like you're almost done."

Moni started to rise, then remembered her ring. She had just assured him she knew what she was doing and didn't want to discuss how or why she'd gotten a body-piercing, so as she stood, she picked up her bottle and held it in front of her belly. "Yes, one more coat of stain should do it."

"Great job," he said, nodding at her workmanship. "You know I was skeptical from the beginning, but it looks like you've pulled it off. I'll let you finish up." He turned and headed back into the house.

Moni pulled on her work gloves and reached for her paintbrush. Her mind was already filling with plans for a line of fashion products for girls.

Grant walked back into the house, pleased that he and Moni were able to have a friendly conversation after their awkward parting last week.

He started to head upstairs, then turned back around. He'd gone outside to discuss what had happened between them, and had never actually brought it up. Now that they were back on speaking terms, it might be easier to discuss their last encounter.

He still felt a little guilty about the way they'd left things. She'd looked genuinely upset at the time, and even though she maintained the story that she'd been busy, he knew she'd been dodging him.

Grant walked back out on the lawn and called Moni's name.

She turned immediately, and a flash of something glinted in the sunlight. Her stomach was twinkling at him.

"What's up?" she asked, pulling off her gloves and walking up to him.

He couldn't tear his eyes away from her navel. Pierced? "What the—"

Her hand immediately moved to cover her belly ring. "Oh."

"You pierced your navel?" In his head, he heard his accusing tone, but he couldn't seem to help himself. For quite some time, he'd been transfixed by the tight ripples of her abdomen. As irrational as it seemed, he took her belly ring as a conscious attempt to drive him out of his mind.

She smiled sheepishly. "It was kind of a spontaneous act."

Grant's entire body went hot. "What is this obsession with your stomach?"

Moni's brows knit. "What?"

"Do you even own a full-length shirt?"

Her chin lifted. "What do you mean?"

"You know, the kind long enough to actually tuck into your waistband? I don't know what is with fashion these days. They make tops for five-year-old girls and sell them to grown women. Now, as if walking around half naked isn't enough, you make sure to draw focus to your tight abs by sticking something bright and shiny in your navel—yeesh."

Moni, who wrapped both of her arms around her middle, was now staring at Grant with a look of wide-eyed shock.

Heat suffused Grant's face as he realized how he must sound. He was ranting like a lunatic. He couldn't think of a way to logically explain his outburst, so he didn't bother.

"I'm sorry. I—I'll talk to you later."

Moni was posing in front of the mirror that evening when Summer poked her head into her bedroom.

"What on earth are you doing?"

"Do you think I walk around half naked?"

Summer giggled. "Honey, did you forget who you were talking to?"

Moni winced at her faux pas. At that moment, Summer was wearing a purple miniskirt and a matching tube top under a white shirt that was entirely see-through.

"Sorry. I don't know what I was thinking."

Summer came into the room and sat on the bed. "What's all this about anyway?" she asked, poking through the pile of tops and blouses on the bed.

"He's right. Most of my summer tops are midriffs."

"Who's right? Grant?"

"You guessed it. He caught sight of my belly ring and nearly blew a gasket. He went on and on about women's fashion today, yadda-yadda-yadda."

Summer snickered. "You may not realize it, love, but that's a good thing."

She shook her head in confusion. "It's a good thing that he all but called me a tramp?"

"No, it's a good thing that he's noticing. He may have gone a bit crazy, but that's only because you drove him there."

"That's ridiculous. It didn't sound like he was paying me a compliment."

"Put these back where they belong, and don't think twice about changing your wardrobe." Summer picked up a stack of tops and handed them to Moni.

Moni took the clothes, still feeling confused.

"Don't worry," Summer said, on her way out. "You'll figure it out eventually."

It took Moni all week to prepare for her slumber party focus group, but by Saturday she was ready. She'd assembled a selection of free samples for all of the girls to try.

She went over to Grant's early that evening to help him prepare for the arrival of the girls.

"Having you here as backup takes a load off my shoulders, Moni," Grant said, helping her set up a table for punch and cookies. "I baby-sat my sister's kids the other night, but that was a little less nerve-wracking because they're boys. I can at least remember what it was like to be one of *them.* I don't have the first clue how to amuse a bunch of twelve-year-old girls."

She laughed. "Girls aren't as complicated as you think. All you have to do is supply plenty of pizza and videos and the girls will do the rest."

Moni pulled out her box of carefully assembled samples. She was actually excited about the opportunity to show the girls her products. They were just the kinds of things she would have loved to have at their age.

Grant tried to peek into her box. "Whatcha got in there?"

She pushed his hand away. "Girl stuff. I don't want to unwrap anything until the girls arrive. I got my sample maker to put the samples in cute little pink bags. The girls will love them."

Grant shrugged, stepping back. "Okay, well they should be here any minute now."

Sure enough, less than ten minutes later, they heard the loud motor of Keith's Porsche.

Tara came to the door by herself. "Where's your dad?" Grant asked, looking over her shoulder.

The girl stepped into the foyer, carrying a black duffel bag with the letters DKNY printed on the side. "He and Mom took off. They're spending the night at a resort spa in Tijuana."

Grant rolled his eyes. "They'd better be back by Sunday night."

"Don't worry." Tara flipped back her red blazer to reveal a shiny silver pager hooked to her jeans. "I can send him a text message any time."

Before Grant could get the door closed behind Tara, another car pulled into the driveway. One by one, girls began to accumulate in the living room, which reached a crescendo of high-pitched squeals and giggles.

Grant leaned over to whisper to Moni. "I can hardly believe there are only six of them. Right now it sounds like an entire high school pep-rally."

She nodded, studying Tara's friends. Moni had always arrived at sleepovers wearing faded jeans and sweatshirts. These girls looked like they were dressed for a night on the town in spaghetti-strap tops, colorful glittering pants and full makeup.

Before she could say something to Grant, one of the girls approached him. "Mr. Forrest?"

"Yes?"

"Hi, I'm Leah," she said formally, holding out her hand for Grant to shake, which he did, rather tentatively.

"May I use your phone? My cell is dead." Leah held up a purple phone. "I've got to call my stylist. If I don't make appointments at least three weeks in advance, I get wait-listed."

Moni blinked at her and Grant pointed toward the kitchen. "It's in there."

Moni and Grant exchanged puzzled looks. "Are you sure these girls are twelve?"

He shrugged. "I'm pretty sure. Why?"

"Designer clothes, pagers, cellular phones—I didn't know twelve-year-olds were into those things."

When Leah finally joined the other girls, Moni decided it was time to get started. She moved to the front of the room and asked for their attention.

"Girls, before your slumber party gets underway, I was wondering if you would mind giving me some feedback on some new products under development for girls in your age group. You'll be able to keep free samples of everything I show you today. How does that sound?"

"Cool."

"Sure, no problem."

"I just love free samples."

The girls all nodded and smiled in agreement.

Moni removed one pink bag from the sample box then handed it to Grant, who was standing beside her. "Do you mind passing these out for me? There's enough for each girl to have one."

Grant nodded and began distributing the bags among the girls. When he was finished, he took the empy box and moved to the back of the room.

"Okay, girls, please take the first item out of the bag. It should be a small hair clip like this one," she said, holding up a translucent pink barrette.

Each of the girls did as they were instructed.

"You'll notice that it looks like any other stylish hair accessory," she said, unsnapping the clasp. "Until you put it in your hair."

Moni fastened the clip to a section of her hair and it began to light up like a Christmas bulb. "It's actually a 'glo-clip.' Try it."

The audience of girls began to flicker. Moni pointed to a redhead who had placed the glo-clip at the end of her French braid. "Tell me, what do you think?"

The girl unsnapped the barrette and stared at it. "Honestly?"

"Yes, of course. I want honest opinions from all of you."

The redhead wrinkled her nose, looking around at her peers. "Well, I'm sorry, but I think it's kinda lame."

"Lame?" Moni repeated. "Anyone else?"

The other girls chimed in with agreement.

"I agree with Becky," Leah said. "This seems like something that, I don't know, maybe a younger kid would like."

Moni frowned. "How young?"

The girls looked around at each other and seemed to reach a consensus. Tara spoke up. "Like, six or seven?"

Stunned, Moni tried not to react. "I hear what you're saying. Of course, you girls are too mature for glowing barrettes. Let's try something else. Please take the pink compact out of your bags."

At first she'd wondered if makeup was a bit too old for preteen girls. She hadn't been allowed to wear makeup until she was seventeen. But, after seeing this crowd, she breathed a sigh of relief that she hadn't removed the compact at the last minute.

"As you can see, it comes with scented eye shadow, flavored lip gloss and glitter blush. There are five funky color palettes that you can mix and match—"

She was in the middle of her spiel, when a hand shot up from the audience. "Do you have a question?"

A beautiful dark-haired girl who looked closer to sixteen than twelve gave her an appraising look. "Is this makeup noncomedogenic?"

"Noncomedo . . ." She made eye contact with Grant at the back of the room who just shrugged, trying to hide his snickering behind his hand.

"It means it won't clog your pours," the girl said with a haughty tone.

"Well, I'm not—" Before she could finish another hand shot up. "Yes?"

"Who designs these products? I only use Char Blanco Products—well, I used to use *Belle Rouge*, but it's too drying."

"You should try *Majik*," Leah said to her friend. "It has a moisturizer built in. I use the facial scrub and the body wash."

A spontaneous conversation about the benefits of exfoliation followed.

Moni stood before the girls in disbelief. No wonder they thought hair clips were too young for them. They were all twelve going on thirty-five. She wouldn't have known a thing about exfoliating and noncomedogenic makeup at twelve. In fact, she didn't know anything about those things now.

She quietly placed the compact back into the bag. "Why don't we move on to the next product," she said after loudly clearing her throat for their attention.

Moni decided to skip ahead to the cream of the crop. If the girls weren't interested in light-up hair baubles, they certainly wouldn't get a thrill over a musical belt. The last item was her favorite. If the girls liked this, none of the other products would matter.

The girls were poking around in the bag. Tara looked up first. "What are these? Stickers?"

Moni smiled, feeling her excitement building again. "Actually, they're decals. You can use them to decorate your blue jeans."

She'd worn her favorite faded button-flies for the occasion. "Let me show you how they work."

Moni picked up the decal of a beautifully painted butterfly. "You see, the glue is tinted a pale blue so it fades right into the denim. The best part is that you can soak them in water and they'll come right off, so you can decorate your jeans all over again. You never have to worry about wearing those same old jeans. With these decals everyday can—"

She paused in the middle of her excited gush and studied the blank expressions on each girl's face. "You hate them, don't you?"

None of the girls would meet her eyes. Tara must have felt sorry for her, because she stood up, holding out the pink bag. "You know, Moni, we really like these bags. They're great, aren't they girls?"

"Yeah, they're so cute." All the girls agreed.

Moni sighed. "I didn't make the bags."

"Oh," Tara said, sitting back down.

The girls fell silent for the first time that evening.

Moni tried to shake it off. "Look, I've taken up enough of your time." She walked around and collected the bags, then tossed them back into the box.

"You're going to have a lot of fun tonight. After you have punch and cookies, we'll order whatever kind of pizzas you like."

"Cookies?" The little redhead sounded appalled. "I'm on low carbs this week."

"Uncle Grant," Tara said, standing up again. "We don't want pizza. Can we have sushi instead?"

Chapter 12

Grant and Moni were sitting in the kitchen a few hours later, sipping coffee. The girls had finally settled down to watch the latest Austin Powers DVD in the next room.

"I've officially crossed the female young-adult market off my list," Moni said. "I can't believe how out of touch with them I was."

Grant smiled. "It's not your fault. Tara's my niece. I see her all the time, and I still had no idea how mature twelve-year-old girls are these days. Why don't you try creating something that matches their current interests?"

Moni folded her arms across her chest. "Nope. I learned something very important from this focus group. I was trying to capitalize on the fad aspect of the preteen market. The point of fads is that they come and go like the afternoon rain. By the time I rework my product line for twelve-year-old miniature adults, it will be en vogue to be girlish again. I'd never get ahead of the curve. I need to have more control over my business than that."

Grant regarded her with sympathetic eyes. "I see what you mean." They each sipped their coffee in comfortable silence.

Finally, he turned to her. "So, what's next on your list of perspective businesses?"

At the moment, after dumping three perfectly good ideas in the trash bin, Moni wasn't sure what her next move should be.

"Actually, I'm thinking of doing something radical."

Grant got a wicked glint in his eye. "What? Athletic wear for house pets? Or, let's see, you can teach yoga to senior citizens."

Moni fell silent. She'd always suspected that Grant didn't take her business acumen seriously.

Noting the expression on her face, he appeared immediately contrite. "Did I offend you just now? I was only teasing you."

Sighing heavily, Moni realized it wasn't worth getting worked up over. At the rate she was going, why *should* he take her seriously?

"It's okay. I'm used to being thought of as fluff."

"Moni, I don't think—"

She grinned. "Forget it. Really. At this point, I'm wondering if I shouldn't take the money and do something else with it. I could take a very long vacation and see the world. I could go back to school and get my masters degree in business administration or something. I could even set up a charitable foundation. People have been throwing these ideas at me for months. They're all reasonable uses for the money. Maybe it's time to start looking into it."

Grant slouched back in his chair, shaking his head. "No, you can't give up just because you didn't hit the jackpot on your first coin. How many people get the chance to live their dreams?"

She shrugged. "I'm not giving up my dreams so much as admitting that maybe I don't really have any. Right now, the only thing I would be giving up on is wasting time. Can you believe I actually took a job last week?"

He looked incredulous as Moni recounted her adventure in Old Town that led her to take a part-time job in a florist shop.

Finally, he shook his head. "You may as well help out since you have the experience, but working doesn't mean you have to abandon your business plan."

She pushed away her empty coffee cup. "I have a lot to think about."

He was quiet for a moment and then shouted, "I've got it."

His sudden outburst startled Moni so much that she almost jumped out of her chair. "You've got what?" she asked, placing a hand over her rapid heartbeat. "Whatever it is, keep it to yourself."

"Why don't you put your aunt's banana love bread on the market? I know it would be hugely popular."

Moni laughed. "Grant, I know you love my aunt's bread, but I have no intention of selling it."

He looked disappointed. "Why not?"

"For one thing, Aunt Reggie always used to say, you only bake banana love bread for those you love." A blush warmed her cheeks as she realized she'd baked the bread for Grant twice.

"I-I mean—in the 'love thy neighbor' kind of way," she stammered. "The gift of banana love bread wouldn't be special if you could go to the market and buy it any time."

"But—"

"Listen," Moni interrupted, swiveling around to stare at the empty doorway.

Grant leaned forward, his eyes darting around the room. "I don't hear anything."

"I know," Moni said, pointing to the kitchen clock. "The movie the girls were watching should be over by now. Why are they so quiet? I have trouble believing even *these* girls would go to bed before ten o'clock at a slumber party."

"Let's go see what they're up to."

They both went to the kitchen door and peeked out. All six girls were huddled in the middle of their island of sleeping bags, whispering.

Moni and Grant exchanged curious glances.

Grant entered the room with Moni at his back. "How was the movie, girls?"

The huddle split and all eyes turned toward them.

"It was pretty good," Tara answered.

"What are you all doing," Moni asked.

The girls giggled, exchanging whispers. "Why don't you ask *them*," one of the girls said, jabbing Tara in the ribs.

Tara rolled her eyes. "Okay, maybe you two can help us with something."

Grant looked pleased. "What is it?"

Moni, who knew there were no limits to childhood curiosity, started backing toward the front door.

"We were wondering"—a red stain crept up Tara's neck—"why do boys kiss with their tongues?"

Grant blanched, turning toward Moni, who was already scooping up her box. She pulled her purse from the coat hook.

"I've got to be getting home, Grant. Have fun girls."

Grant shot her a desperate look, but Moni pretended not to see it as she slipped out of the door.

Moni let herself into the house a few minutes later and found the twins curled up on the couch watching a movie. She dropped her box and her purse at the door with a huff.

Summer put the television on mute. "From the sound of that sigh, I'm guessing things didn't go well with the teenyboppers."

Moni plopped down on the sofa beside Candy. "You've got that right. I had no idea that twelve-year-olds girls are so sophisticated. My products were, I quote, 'so five minutes ago.'"

"I can't say I'm surprised." Summer shook her head. "That's why I refused to get within ten feet of them. Kids and me just don't mix."

"You poor thing," Candy said, wrapping an arm around Moni's shoulder. "So, what's next on the agenda? You know Summer and I can help, don't you? You've been so kind to let us move in here. I only have summer classes Tuesday and Thursdays. You can count on us for all the free labor you need."

"That's for sure," Summer chimed in. "Since I'm not crazy about going back to dancing or waiting tables, I'm at your service. I even wrote down some ideas in case you're running out. Want to hear them?"

Moni let her head fall onto Candy's shoulder. "Maybe in the morning."

She was sick of talking about her failed business ideas. The whole concept was becoming overwhelming. She had a psychology degree, but no desire to go back to school for her Ph.D. Without that, there weren't many options for her in that field.

It really was amazing how small the world

had become once it had opened up to her. She had the money and the time to really make something happen, yet nothing was clicking into place. She was exhausted—both mentally and physically.

Moni stood, raising her arms over her head in a long stretch. "I think I'll go to bed now."

"Wait," Summer said, grabbing a slip of paper from the coffee table. "One of your friends called while you were out. She sounded really excited on the phone."

Moni took the message Summer handed her. It was from Akiko. "It's late. I'll call her back in the morning. I have an afternoon shift at the flower shop tomorrow. Good night, girls."

After a restless sleep, Moni woke up early Sunday morning. Candy and Summer had established a routine of sleeping until noon, so Moni ate a bowl of cereal and read the paper aloud to her fern, Marley.

Just before she left for the flower shop, she remembered Akiko's message. She dialed her friend's number and Jim answered the phone.

"Moni, I'm so glad you called. Akiko has been dying to talk to you. Hold on, I'll put her on."

"Moni," Akiko said.

"Listen, Akiko, I'm on my way to work, but I wanted to make sure—"

"I'm pregnant!"

"What?" Moni sat down on the closest piece of furniture. Luckily, that happened to be the arm of the sofa. "Did you just tell me you're pregnant?"

"Yes, can you believe it? We just found out last night. I have a doctor's appointment tomorrow to confirm it, but four home pregnancy tests can't be wrong."

Moni's shock finally released its hold on her vocal cords and she screamed into the phone. "Eeeeh! Congratulations—this is amazing."

"I know. I couldn't wait to tell you. I know I was never the maternal type, but I'm happier than I ever thought possible."

Something that felt distinctly like a brick lodged in her throat. "You and Jim will be great parents," she said, blinking back the tears that had formed in her eyes.

"Thank you, Moni. I know you're in a rush. But, thanks for calling me back. I couldn't relax until I'd told you the news. We can talk more later."

On the drive to work, Moni was surprised by the mixed bag of emotions she was experiencing. She was thrilled that her best friend was going to have a baby, but part of her also felt jealous. This bothered her most because it didn't make any sense.

Why should she feel jealous of her friend's pregnancy? She didn't even have a husband. *But she could have had one*, a small voice whispered in the back of her mind.

If she'd stayed in Dunkin, she and Burt would

be married by now. They might have even been planning a family of their own. Was that what she really wanted? Had walking away from that life been a mistake?

No.

The answer came to Moni without hesitation. She'd walked away from Burt because she wasn't ready for that life. It *had* been the right thing to do. She knew that much. The only reason she was even questioning her decision now was because her business wasn't coming to fruition.

Sure, going back to Dunkin to marry Burt would have been so easy. They would invest her inheritance in a tire shop for Burt and a new flower shop for Moni. She wouldn't have had to think about anything. Her future would be clear cut.

But she'd left Dunkin because she *didn't* want to take the easy way out. She didn't *really* love Burt. Not the way he loved her. Her attraction to Grant had made that clear.

She'd come to California to make her own way. She was doing that. It might not be smooth sailing, but she was taking responsibility for her mistakes. Out here, there wasn't anyone to come to her rescue, and that's what she needed—to fly without a safety net.

As Moni parked her car in the Old Town employee lot, things had fallen back into perspective. She wasn't going to give up. She'd come all this way to succeed or fail by her own hand, and in that sense, she was a success already.

Vera, her new boss, was pulling up the window shades as Moni entered the store. "Great, Little Miss Perky is here. It's time for my cigarette break," she grumbled, pulling a pack of Virginia Slims out of her apron pocket.

Moni rolled her eyes and walked to the back room to store her purse. She'd given up trying to draw Vera out of her funk the first day on the job. Why waste time on the impossible?

The day passed quickly for Moni. Working in the shop brought back so many memories of working with Aunt Reggie that she almost expected to turn around and see her any minute. But instead of making her feel sad, the constant reminders of Aunt Reggie made her feel warm inside.

It felt good to have control again. She'd made several suggestions to improve the shop, and since Vera didn't seem to care either way, Moni could do whatever she wanted. She bought a new computer system to bring the accounting software up to date and reorganized all of the inventory. Now a brightly painted sign listing all their flowers by common and Latin names hung on the back wall.

When she was at the flower shop, Moni knew her efforts were making a difference. She also enjoyed interacting with the customers. She was even enjoying the light barbs she traded with Vera.

"Vera, don't forget to wrap those tulips in tissue. You don't want the petals to get crushed."

"Pardon me, Miss Sunshine."

"No problem, Madame Hurricane."

The customers giggled whenever the two of them would get into it. Eventually, Moni learned not to get embarrassed the way she had the first time she got angry with Vera's cracks and shot one back at her.

When Moni got home that evening, she decided to stop by Grant's before going inside. Tomorrow was the last day of the month, and she wanted to make sure she would get credit for finishing the fence on time, even though she wanted to repaint the fence. She wasn't happy with the way the new stain blended with the old. Unfortunately, the new stain, in her opinion, was prettier than the original one.

Moni rang Grant's doorbell and he answered right away. "Moni," he said, stepping aside for her to enter the house. "I should close the door in your face after the way you ran out on me last night. The deal was for you to stay until the girls went to sleep."

"Aw, was poor Gwant afwaid of some itty-bitty-wittle girls," she mocked, following him into the kitchen. "It was getting past my bedtime. I knew you could handle it on your own."

She paused, cocking her head to one side. "How *did* you handle it, anyway?"

"What?" Although Grant's gaze was locked on her, his attention appeared to be on something else. "Oh, you mean that kissing question. I cheated—I told them to ask their parents. Then I put in another DVD to distract them. Thirty minutes in, they were all asleep."

Moni laughed. "Ask their parents? I can't believe they let you get away with that."

He shrugged. "They were disappointed, but they knew they weren't going to get a decent answer out of me. I wasn't about to touch that one with a ten-foot pole." Grant continued to study her with open curiosity.

Moni felt herself become flush. Feeling self-conscious under his direct gaze, she looked down to make sure she didn't have a gigantic stain on her blouse. "What's the matter?"

His attention was focused on her waist. "Why are you so dressed up?"

Moni looked down at herself again. This morning she'd put on a short-sleeve white blouse, a herringbone vest and a narrow black skirt. She'd finished the outfit with a pair of chunky black sandals. "I worked at the flower shop today."

"Oh," he said, looking disappointed.

She narrowed her eyes, unable to figure out Grant's odd reaction.

"Anyway, I just came over to tell you the fence repairs are done, but I'm not happy with the way the stains match. Do you mind if I take a couple of extra days to—"

Moni stopped to study Grant. He was still looking at her quite strangely. "What's the matter with you?" she asked.

He turned away. "What do you mean?"

"You're looking at me funny."

He continued to avoid eye contact. "I don't know what you're talking about."

She felt a spark of temper. "Look, I remember what you said about my clothes. I'm fully covered right now, so I don't know why you were looking at me like that."

"Like what?"

Moni stared at him, trying to decide if he was deliberately being dense. "I don't know. Like there's something wrong with the way I'm dressed."

Finally, he brought his gaze up to meet hers. "There is."

Her fists clenched at her sides. "What could possibly be wrong with my clothes now? You fuss at me for showing too much of my stomach, and now that it's covered, you're *still* not happy?"

His eyes traveled down the line of her body. "Is your navel still pierced?"

Genuinely angry now, Moni rubbed her temples with her fingers. "What on earth does that have to do with anything?"

Grant took a step toward her. "It's driving me crazy."

She lifted her head in surprise. "What is?"

His voice was low, and he was close enough that she could almost feel his breath on her face. "Not being able to see it."

"My piercing?" She took a step backward.

"Your navel." He stepped forward. "I wasn't fussing at you because you show too much of your stomach. I was mad at myself for letting it get to me?"

She swallowed hard. "What's getting to you?"

"You. And those tight abs. When you got your belly button pierced, I thought I was going to lose my mind."

Suddenly, Moni felt like she'd been *very* naïve. Summer's words came back to her. "You mean you *like* my stomach?"

He nodded.

She giggled. "You were upset because you're attracted to me."

He nodded.

A rush of feminine power washed over her. "And you can't control it, can you?"

He shook his head.

She smiled wickedly. "You must hate that," she said, closing the space between them. Feeling their mutual attraction build between them like an electric charge, Moni gave in to the moment.

Placing her hands on either side of his head, she brought her lips up to meet his. Grant's arms locked around her as he kissed her back with full force.

Moni knew she had Grant's full attention, and that gave her a sense of power she'd never felt before. Unlike their last encounter, *she* was in control.

Letting her fingertips slide back from his face, she moved them behind his ears and down his neck. Grant released an almost catlike purr as her fingers finally locked behind his neck.

Testing her power again, she pushed her tongue into his mouth and was rewarded with another instantaneous reaction—this time in solid, physical form.

Her stomach fluttered as heat suffused her body. There was that passion again—she released a soft moan herself. It was addictive.

Unlocking the fingers behind his neck, she ran her hands over his shoulders and downward, until they were pressed firmly against his chest. She backed him up to the kitchen counter.

"What are you doing to me?" he whispered.

"Shh." She yanked his shirttails out of his jeans and began undoing the buttons. When she'd bared his chest, she let her fingers run free on his soft dark skin.

Grant threw his head back and gnashed his teeth. She was making him crazy and that knowledge almost made Moni's knees give out.

One strong hand pressed into her back, pulling her close as his other hand peeled off her vest and made short work of her blouse's buttons. Burying his lips in her neck, his hands slipped into her neckline.

Moni clung to him as waves of new sensations took over her body. His touch was so gentle, she was almost tortured with anticipation as his fingers played on her skin. His lips nipped, sipped and sucked at the sensitive spot just below her ear.

"Oh my . . . mmm." Moni gripped his back, feeling like a piece of driftwood in the ocean. He was the only thing keeping her afloat. Yet drowning in pleasure didn't seem like a bad way to go. She didn't want these feelings to end.

And then something changed. She felt his body grow tense. She swallowed the sudden rush of panic welling up inside her.

Grant pulled back from Moni, his hands still inside her blouse.

Oh no. He's finally remembering that I'm a virgin. He's going to send me home just like he did before.

He pulled his hand from inside her shirt, holding it closed with one hand. "We can't do this."

Her heart sank. There was such a rushing of thoughts in her mind, she almost didn't hear his next words.

"Not here . . . on the kitchen counter." He scooped her up, into his arms. "We'll be much more comfortable in my bed."

Moni buried her face in Grant's chest, trying to hide her urge to weep with relief. As he carried her into the bedroom, and she saw his neatly made bed, another thought came to her mind.

"Grant?"

"Yes, baby?"

"Why are your sheets pink?"

He chuckled in her ear, as he settled her on the bed. "That's a long story . . . one I can't get into right now. You understand, don't you?"

She nodded, forgetting the question. Her eyes fastened on Grant as he stripped off his shirt. His hands unzipped his jeans and he pushed them down over his hips.

Lying there, watching him undress, she finally grasped the full impact of what was about to happen. A niggling of anxiety cropped up.

Naked, Grant climbed onto the bed and pulled her into his arms. He kissed her slowly, even though she could feel an urgency just below the surface. As his lips engaged hers, she was barely aware of Grant removing her clothes.

His movements were patient, reassuring, and she felt safe. Naked beneath his nude body, Moni finally relaxed. He must have sensed her body decompressing, because he slowly became more aggressive.

Moni sighed and moaned with each new

touch, trying to explore his body as much as she could before getting caught up in the next sensation.

He tested her body for readiness with his fingers. It felt strange at first, but Moni slowly grew to like the increasing pressure.

She was well on her way toward satisfaction when Grant replaced his fingers. Her body stilled and tears sprang to her eyes as she struggled to adjust, despite his preparations.

Grant was patient, and once again, she grew accustomed to the pressure. He began to move inside her and the pressure began to build entirely new feelings.

A new sense of panic sparked up. She was afraid the pressure would be taken away before she found what she was looking for. Moni was surprised to find herself voicing her thoughts.

"Don't stop. Oh, Grant, that feels so good. Please don't stop." She clutched at his back at the same time trying to press herself into him with each thrust.

"Oh my—don't . . . oh please, don't stop."

Their bodies were slick from their frenetic motions, and Moni felt herself ever closer to her peak.

"Baby, you're killing me." His voice was ragged. "I'm trying to hold on for you, Moni."

The breathless, passion-thick sound of Grant's voice pushed her over the edge. She cried out in pleasure as her body finally found the release it had been seeking.

Grant's own voice joined hers as the strokes of his body quickened to an almost superhuman pace.

Moni threw her head back in surprise as the ultimate moment she'd thought had passed, crested and rose a second time.

As she trembled with the aftershocks of her second peak, Grant's body arched and collapsed against hers.

Chapter 13

After they'd made love, Moni had fallen right to sleep. Grant, on the other hand, couldn't rest. He lay in bed beside her, watching her chest rise and fall.

What had he been thinking? The answer to that question was simple. He *hadn't* been thinking. If he'd thought things through, then this cute little minx wouldn't be lying beside him.

And that thought was more upsetting than the utter futility of their current situation.

It was a mistake. He'd known this was coming, and he knew their relationship couldn't go anywhere. So it was indeed a mistake, but it was one he didn't regret making.

How much longer could he have gone on obsessing over her? When Moni was close by, it was impossible to ignore the riotous reaction his body had to her. Looking down at Moni, he resisted the urge to run his hand along the bare expanse of shoulder peeking out from the sheets.

This outcome had been inevitable. Maybe now he'd have a shot at concentrating on his book. Now the anticipation, which had become a ghost in the room whenever Moni was around, would stop haunting him.

Grant had finally gotten what he needed—but not without a price.

Sleeping with Moni was the cure-all for his current hang-ups, but it also made things a hell of a lot more complicated between them.

For heaven's sake, he was her first and only lover. There was a lot of responsibility that came with that. For that very reason he'd done everything in his power to keep her at arm's length. He just wasn't the man to offer her all the hearts and flowers that came with this scenario. She wasn't a woman of the world. She was a small-town girl with small-town values.

Grant knew she'd been terribly hurt when he sent her home after almost making love to her in his living room. Now she was probably under the impression that he had changed his mind about wanting a relationship.

How could he look her in the eyes and explain the truth to her? Especially after he'd taken something so precious from her.

Breathing deeply, Grant tried to swallow the sickening wad of guilt swirling in his gut. Man, he had to be the biggest jackass ever. Moni deserved so much better than what he could offer her right now. There was no way to give her the whole "it's not you, it's me" speech without sounding like a cad.

Grant rolled away from Moni and slipped out of bed. He started pacing the room. There was no easy way to handle this delicate situation.

As soon as his feet hit the floor, Moni sat up in bed with a start. Her eyes darted around in obvious disorientation, until her gaze finally settled on Grant. She jerked the bed sheet up to her chin.

"How long was I asleep?"

He glanced at the digital clock on his night table. "Not more than twenty minutes. How are you feeling?"

She averted her eyes in shy reserve. "I'm okay. Do you think I could use your shower?"

He nodded toward the door connected to the master bedroom. "Of course. Help yourself."

"Thanks," she said with a voice barely above a whisper. She started to slip out of bed, stopped, then searched the floor for her clothes.

Grant grabbed his shirt and handed it to her. She slipped it on, buttoned it up to her chin and skittered into the bathroom.

Grant frowned, staring at the closed door. Poor little thing. Her shy display of modesty just made him want to hug her. He wanted to wrap her up in his arms and let her know everything was okay. Then he'd kiss her until she lost her inhibitions all over again.

His lower body went hot remembering how eager she'd been just a short while ago. If he hadn't seen it with his own eyes, he might never have believed it. With his own ears, he'd heard her beg him not to stop making love to her.

He heard the shower turn on in the bathroom and Grant closed his eyes on the image of Moni naked, stepping under the hot spray. It was all he could do not to go in there and join her.

Grant got to his feet. "What the hell is wrong with me?"

He had to say the words out loud to jolt himself back to reality. He needed to back out of this relationship, not make it more intimate.

Grant pulled on his clothes and left the room. He hoped putting some physical distance between himself and Moni would give him the space he needed to think things through.

Moni stood in Grant's shower trying to come to grips with what had just happened between them. She let the water run over her face.

Moni Lawrence was no longer a virgin.

She smiled a private smile. Making love was everything she'd hoped it would be. Aside from a bit of tenderness between her thighs, it wasn't nearly as painful as she'd feared. Grant had been a patient and gentle lover.

"Lover." Moni repeated the word slowly and began to feel sad.

Grant had all the qualities she looked for in a man. He was incredibly intelligent, considerate and he had a sense of humor. He was also handsome, sexy and she could add excellent lover to the list. Even though she didn't have any resources for comparison, she knew he had to be better than just average.

After what they'd just shared, Moni knew Grant was the kind of guy that she could fall in love with . . . and her heart ached.

Why had he come into her life now—before she'd had the chance to get her act together? Now she'd started down a road she wasn't ready to travel.

The fact of the matter was that she was raised with old-fashioned values. Aunt Reggie had been a modern woman, but she'd still taught Moni the important role sex played in a committed relationship.

She was grateful for this new experience, because now she knew true passion wasn't just a myth. And she also knew that it was something she would have never shared with Burt Reynolds.

Making love with Grant also illuminated one other thing in Moni's mind. She just wasn't the type of girl who could sleep around. Her skin grew hot as she remembered the things she'd said and done not too long ago in Grant's arms. The thought of being that intimate with just anyone was impossible to fathom.

She'd just given Grant her virginity. There was no doubt that he realized the enormity of that act. He was definitely the type of man to take the responsibility seriously.

Moni didn't regret the experience one iota, but now she was really uncertain how to handle the consequences.

Instability was a completely new feeling. Growing up in Dunkin surrounded by an extended family of friends, she'd never had much to worry about. She'd come to San Diego, far from those friends, to try out her independence. It was a scary feeling. And her life seemed more out-of-control lately than ever before.

She was afraid that if she let herself get caught up in a relationship with Grant, she'd abandon any chance she had to follow her own path. Grant was a leader. He already seemed to have his act together. Moni knew that he would naturally try to take care of her. And, as confused as she was feeling these days, it would be so easy to let him.

She'd walked away from one relationship because it would have stood in the way of her independence. She still hadn't figured out who she was and what she wanted to do with her life. If she didn't walk away from Grant, too, the last few months would have been in vain.

But how could she walk away from such a good thing? Grant was an amazing man. She could really fall in love with him.

She could really lose herself in him, too.

Moni reached up and turned off the water. Snagging a pink towel from the shelf above the sink, she wrapped herself up and took a seat on the toilet cover.

There was clearly no such thing as sex with no strings attached.

Suddenly, her life seemed more complex than ever.

After getting dressed, Moni sat on the bed for several minutes. She felt like such an idiot. She and Grant had just made love—the most intimate act two people could share—and now she wasn't even sure if she could face him.

"There you are," Grant said, leaning against the doorframe.

Moni stood, self-consciously wringing her hands. "Hi."

"Are you going to stay up here all day?"

She released a nervous laugh. "Of course not."

For a few minutes, they both stood there, letting the uncomfortable silence hang between them. They both began to talk at once.

"Do you want to—"

"I guess I should—"

"You go ahead," he said politely.

"No, that's okay. You first."

He shrugged. "It wasn't important. I already forgot what I was going to say."

Moni's palms felt moist, so she wiped them on the back of her skirt. "I was just going to say that I should probably get home now."

Grant straightened and backed out of the doorway so she could pass. "Of course. I'm sure you've got . . . lots of . . . things to do."

She slipped passed him and looked over her shoulder as she started down the stairs. "You too. I mean, I don't want to keep you from . . . whatever you . . . were planning to do this evening."

He followed her down the steps and opened the door for her. For a few seconds they just stood there staring at each other.

Finally, clearly at a loss for words, Grant said, "I'll call you."

The words sounded so forced and cliché. Moni pushed open the screen door. "Um, yeah. I'll be around tomorrow—you know, working on the fence . . ."

"Right, right. So I'll . . . see you then?"

She nodded, waving over her shoulder as she bolted through the door.

Moni didn't know if Grant was watching her as she crossed the street, but she wasn't about to look back to check.

"You two know more about these things than I do," Moni said to Candy and Summer that night. "What should I do? Grant says he's not looking for a serious relationship, and that's good, because I'm not looking either. But regardless of what we say, it's going to be hard for one of us not to get our feelings involved."

The three women were sitting around on the living room floor sipping strawberry margaritas. It had taken two margaritas for Moni to screw up the courage to tell her friends what had happened between her and Grant.

Summer stretched out her leg to nudge her sister with one of her purple-painted toes. "I don't really see what the problem is, do you?"

Candy gave her twin an exasperated look. "Of course I do. Moni's afraid that getting involved with Grant will interfere with her goals."

"Why does it have to interfere with her goals? Grant is one hot hunk of a man. Why can't she have her cake and eat it, too?" Summer snagged the margarita pitcher and refilled Moni's and Candy's glasses.

Moni put her glass on the coffee table and pushed it out of her reach. She was already confused, and it was getting harder to think rationally by the minute.

"Do you think I'm overreacting to this whole thing? Maybe it's no big deal. I know a lot of people don't take sex as seriously as I do."

"Don't try to second-guess your feelings, Moni." Candy said, squeezing her shoulder. "I don't blame you for feeling confused. I mean you've been waiting for weeks for this guy to admit he's interested. And now, instead of taking you out on a date, spending time getting to know you, he takes you straight to bed. He's the king of sending mixed signals."

Summer shook her head at Candy. "You're

being too hard on the guy. He was trying to do right by the poor girl. He knew she was a virgin, and he was trying not to take advantage of her. It's not his fault that she's a hot little number and the heat finally got to him. The guy is only human."

Candy rolled her eyes. "I think you were a man in another life, because you sure think like one."

"Why is the belief that two healthy, attractive adults have the right to enjoy each other a male thought? It's simply a fact."

"Girl, there is nothing simple about it. Emotions are involved here. Moni's afraid of falling in love. If they fall in love, she's going to put all of her energy into him instead of her business."

Moni sat back and watched the twins go back and forth like a devil and angel warring for control of her conscience.

They were the embodiment of her present dilemma. Part of her just wanted to roll with her new feelings and worry about the consequences later—much later. But the other part of her was scared to death of making another mistake like the one she'd made with Burt.

"Moni, I think the only thing you can do here is just be honest with Grant," Candy advised. "Tell him you're not ready for a relationship right now and that you can only offer him friendship."

"Friendship?" Summer snorted. "No way, you can't let this guy slip through your fingers. You want him. He wants you. You have to go for it."

"You have your nerve giving her relationship advice after that fiasco with Nigel."

Summer's eyes went wide. "Oh, no you didn't."

"I think these margaritas gave me a headache." Moni stood up, rubbing her temples. "I'm going to head upstairs to bed. Thanks for the advice, girls. I'm just going to sleep on it for now."

As she trudged up the steps she could hear the girls continuing to bicker.

"Do you see what you did? You gave her a headache," Summer barked.

"It was your crappy margaritas that gave her the headache, dodo bird."

"If anything made her sick it was your bad advice . . ."

Moni grinned as she shut her bedroom door. In a few moments, she knew the sisters would be laughing again as if their little squabble had never happened.

It was nice to have girlfriends out here. Summer and Candy were like night and day, but she'd become so close to them in such a short period of time. Whenever she was feeling down or, in this case, completely confused, their antics always had her smiling again in no time.

* * *

Monday was a record-breaking writing day for Grant. Instead of using life as an excuse to avoid his book, he'd started using his book as an excuse to avoid his life.

Every time he gave himself a moment to think about Moni, he became racked with guilt. He knew he had to call and talk to her, but he didn't have the first clue as to what he might say. So instead of dealing with his unsettling feelings about Moni, he wrote.

Grant's fingers flew over the keyboard, barely keeping up with the rapid pace ideas were coming to mind. When the phone rang, he ignored it. He didn't take copious breaks to check e-mail, watch the news or play with the cats for a change.

At last count, Grant had written forty-two pages, and his mind was still whirring with ideas. Trent Black was trapped on a boat in the middle of the Pacific Ocean with a suspected murderer, and Naomi, his love interest and side-kick, was right by his side. As it turned out, the little scrap of a girl had a black belt in Tae Kwon Do and proved to be very useful when Trent got into a bind.

Grant hadn't known this particular tidbit when he'd sat down to write that morning, but as the adventure began to reveal itself to him, he began to hit his stride.

Finally, only the call of nature was able to tear Grant away from the computer. After relieving his bladder, he noticed that not only were his fingers and wrist sore from overuse, but he was also famished.

He headed to the kitchen for food and caught sight of Moni outside painting his fence. Instantly, like a needle skipping across a record, Grant's whole world stopped. He stood on the stairs watching her through the sliding glass doors.

Keeping thoughts of Moni at bay was only possible when he was busy writing. Now he had to admit that he couldn't continue to avoid her.

They'd made love yesterday. If he didn't make some kind of contact, she'd think it was just a one-night stand. He didn't know what to call the intimate time they'd shared, but the last thing he wanted to do was hurt her. He wanted her to know that even though he couldn't give her what she needed right now, she meant a lot more to him than a fling.

Grant took a break from lamenting to realize that Moni was in fact painting his fence. Not just the new fence posts, and not just the old ones. She appeared to be painting his entire fence a totally new color.

Any other day, he would have been out in the yard in a heartbeat questioning her actions. But, after studying her work for a few minutes, he realized that the new shade of tan matched the facade of his house much better than the original rust-colored stain. So he left her alone, partly because he still didn't know what he would say to her after they finished talking about fences and paint.

Still, he had to address their situation somehow. Walking over to the kitchen phone, Grant decided to leave Moni a message. He knew she wasn't home, and he could at least initiate contact without having to get into issues he wasn't ready to confront.

When Moni returned home from painting Grant's fence, she was worn out. She'd almost stayed in bed that morning because she'd been afraid to repeat the awkward dance she and Grant had performed the day before. But he never came out of the house.

At first she'd been relieved that he'd spared her the embarrassment. As the day grew later, though, she began to become concerned that he was avoiding her as much as she wanted to avoid him. Despite her feelings, the idea that he wouldn't want to see her was particularly upsetting.

It was something of a comfort to return home that night and find a message from him on her voice mail.

"Hi, Moni. This is Grant. I'm sorry I didn't get the chance to come outside and talk to you, to-

day. I woke up early to write and found myself on a really good roll. I got off to a slow start with the book, and it just sank in that the summer isn't going to last forever. So, even though I've been working at a feverish pace, I didn't want you to think you weren't on my mind. You are—and as soon as I come up for air, we'll get together. Okay? I guess we'll talk soon. Bye."

Moni replayed the message twice more before erasing it. It was good just to hear his voice. Taking a deep breath, she dialed his number. She had no idea what she should say to him, but she knew it was time to stop running from her fears. They had to talk.

She was surprised to get his answering machine.

"Hi, Grant. This is Moni. Thanks for your message. I've been thinking about you, too. . . . I'm really glad to hear your book is moving along. You may have noticed that I started painting your fence. I should be finished tomorrow. It's not quite the stain you had before, but I think you'll like this paint so much more . . . but um, if you don't, I can always put it back the way it was. Let me know. Well, uh, good luck with your writing. Good night."

Moni spent Tuesday morning working at the flower shop and the evening finishing up the paint job on Grant's fence. Unfortunately, one of the men at the hardware store next to the shop told her that, since she hadn't bought water-resistant paint, she was going to have to treat the fence with a coating of sealant.

She was so tired after painting the fence she decided to save the paint treatment for the next day. When she returned home that night, she had a new message from Grant.

"Hi, Moni. Grant here. I was a bit surprised when I first saw what you'd done with the fence, but you're right, I do like it much better. You're a sneaky one, but good work. This morning I went to the courthouse and filed paperwork stating that you'd completed the repairs to my satisfaction. Now we can call it even between us. You should get your copies of the forms in the mail. I hope, uh, I hope things are good for you. I don't know why it seems like ages since we've spoken in person. My book is really coming along. If I keep up this pace, I should reach the halfway mark by the end of the week. Well, I guess that's all for now. Um, take care. I'll see you soon."

Moni wanted to call him back right away, but the girls came home right then with grand ideas of eating dinner out to celebrate Summer's new job as a hostess at a high-class restaurant downtown. She wanted to treat them all to steak and lobster at her new place of employment. They didn't get home until late, so Moni didn't call Grant back until Wednesday morning.

"Grant. I can't tell you how glad I am to hear that you like the paint. I'm even happier to hear that things are settled regarding our little matter of the fence. My Aunt Reggie always used to say, 'If you can't get along with your neighbors, who are you going to turn to when your basement floods?' Well, I guess we're more than just neighbors . . . but you know what I mean. I mean, I'm not trying to imply that we're—you know, anything more than what we are . . . this isn't coming out right. Do me a favor and erase this message, will you?"

Moni was so embarrassed at the rambling message she left on Grant's answering machine, she didn't check her own messages again until Thursday morning. By then Grant had left her two new messages.

"Moni, I didn't erase your message. You're right, we are more than just neighbors. We're more than friends. I think one of the reasons I've been playing telephone tag with you all week is because I haven't quite figured out where that fits into my life right now. But, I do want you to know that I don't regret anything that's hap-

pened between us. You—you're very special to me. Um, good night."

Grant's second message was left that morning and it got straight to the point.

"I've had enough of this, Moni. I think we need to talk in person. If you're free tomorrow night, I'd like you to come over for dinner. We have a lot to talk about."

Moni picked up the phone and dialed Grant's number.

"Hello?" The sound of a live voice startled her.

"Wow, there's a real man behind the voice. I'd gotten used to speaking with your machine."

"Would you like me to put it on the line? Maybe you'd prefer to have dinner with my machine."

"No, that's okay. I was calling to accept your invitation for dinner. I agree. It's time we sat down and talked."

"I'm looking forward to it. Friday night . . . around six-thirty?"

"I'll be there."

"Ouch!" Grant shoved his burnt finger between his lips as he balanced the hot pan of chicken lasagna in one mitt. The clock over the oven read

6:24. Moni would be there any minute, and he was still rushing around the kitchen.

Why he was going to all of this trouble he still wasn't sure. When he'd first decided to invite her over for dinner, the plan was to prepare something simple and casual so that they could talk.

Something "simple" had become more elaborate as the day wore on. He'd gotten a little carried away at the grocery store. It had been quite a while since he'd had an occasion to prepare food for more than one person.

Once he'd realized his dinner was turning into an elaborate affair, he felt obligated to set the mood. Next thing he knew, there was a white table cloth on the dining room table with matching place mats and napkins. He had votive candles surrounding a crystal vase of fresh white flowers.

He couldn't help feeling a hint of chagrin as he surveyed his presentation. How was he supposed to explain his reservations about their relationship in front of a romantic candle-lit dinner? His subconscious was clearly working against him. But it was too late now.

The doorbell was ringing.

Grant dashed back through the kitchen touching up any remaining spills. He checked his clothes for food stains, then pulled open the door.

Dressed all in white, Moni was a refreshing sight in her summer dress and sandals.

Suddenly, Grant wasn't sure whether to kiss her, hug her or shake her hand. He leaned forward as she opened her arms, and they did an awkward dance that ended with him kissing her cheek during a quick embrace.

She held a bottle of wine out to him. "Aunt Reggie always told me that you never go into someone's home for dinner without a gift. I don't know what you're serving, but I know nothing about red wine. So I took a chance and brought white."

"That's perfect." He took the bottle and ushered into the house. "Thanks for coming."

"Thanks for having—oh, my goodness. You set a beautiful table."

He felt his face flush. "It's too much, isn't it? I got a little carried away."

She pressed her fingers to her lips. "It's lovely. I can't remember anyone going to this kind of trouble for me before."

When Grant saw the brightness of unshed tears in her eyes, his heart melted. Seeing that look on her face just made him want to please her all the more.

Once Grant placed the food on the table, they sat down to eat, and he served the wine Moni brought over. After an awkward toast, they fell into an even more awkward pattern of small-talk.

Every time Grant wanted to bring up their ill-fated romance, he backed down. He was usually quite good with words, and had fed many a client just the right lines to "let her down gently."

For some reason, now that he was wearing those shoes, the right words just wouldn't come. He'd look across the table at her and get lost in her golden eyes. She really looked stunning that evening. Her white dress flattered her dark skin, revealing just enough to keep his imagination active.

"How are the plans for your parents' anniversary party coming along?" she asked after draining her wineglass.

Grant reached for the bottle to give her a refill. "We've gotten most of the big details taken care of. I think the only vendor we're still searching for is a florist. I didn't realize how much a few flowers cost around here. Keith went way over budget hiring a semi-famous band that he just had to have. Now the floral budget we agreed on is cut in half."

She seemed to visibly perk up. "Now you're speaking my language. You know the shop I work for can do the flowers for your party. The owner's a little difficult to deal with, but because the shop is located in an historic area, she gets a good discount from the wholesalers. I know I could get you a really good deal."

"Really? I don't want to impose—"

"Oh, don't think twice about it. Just leave it to me to handle the details."

Grant smiled. "Thanks, in that case, I'd really appreciate your help."

He looked down and noticed that Moni had barely touched her dinner.

"Are you okay? If you're not hungry right now, I can wrap it up for you to have later. Or if you don't like it, I can—"

"Oh, no-no, please. It's delicious. I think the reason I'm having trouble eating is nerves."

"Nerves? Moni, what do you have to be nervous about?"

She stared at her plate not meeting his eyes for several long seconds. "There's something that I need to say to you, and I'm not quite sure how to go about it."

Grant's heart started beating faster. Dear Lord please don't let her say she's in love. He had no idea how he'd handle such a confession.

"If you have something to say, the best thing to do is to just put it out there."

Grant tried to brace himself for whatever she was planning to tell him.

Moni put down the fork she'd been using to play with her food. "I'm really overwhelmed by this nice dinner you prepared. The table setting is beautiful. So romantic—it's, it's more than I could have ever imagined. And I really appreciate your going to all this trouble."

Grant felt a huge lump in his throat. He couldn't sit there and let her go on. "Moni, please stop. You don't have to keep thanking me. I—"

She held up her hand for him to pause. "Really, what I'm trying to say is . . . I don't think it's fair for me to sit here and keep leading you on like this."

"What?" Grant felt his jaw slacken as his fork hit the plate with a loud clatter. "Leading me on? I don't under—"

"Grant, you're a wonderful man. The kind of guy any woman would want to be with. Unfortunately, I just don't think I'm in the right place in my life to get seriously involved. That probably sounds really awful after what's happened between us. . . ."

Grant sat back in his chair and gaped openly at Moni. "This is unbelievable."

Moni frowned, wringing her hands. "I know and I'm so sorry. After all you've done—"

He threw his head back and laughed wholeheartedly. He laughed until he felt the moisture of tears in his eyes.

This time it was Moni's turn to sit back and stare at him, completely dumbfounded.

"I'm sorry," he finally said, wiping the tears from his eyes. "The reason this is so unbelievable is that I've been sitting here racking my brain over how to tell you that we can't continue a romance, and all this time you've felt exactly the same way."

Moni crossed her arms over her chest. "Are you serious? You brought me over here to dump me?"

Grant sobered. "Relatively speaking. . . ."

She glared at him. "So why did you bother with the nice dinner and the candles and the whole romantic setup? Just so you could get my hopes up and then tell me to get lost? What kind of jerk are you?"

"Wait a minute . . . are you actually mad? Didn't you just tell me that you don't want to get seriously involved right now?"

"Well, yes, but—"

He raised his voice. "So what? Your little speech is only valid if you get to be the one to break *my* heart?"

"Well, no," she said, starting to laugh. "I know I'm being silly. But, you could have at least had the decency to *act* heartbroken, you cad," she joked, throwing her napkin across the table at him.

"Hold on, if you give me a minute maybe I can muster up some tears. Will that help?"

"Nope. Too little, too late." They laughed until their mutual laughter began to die down.

Moni thrust her hand out for Grant to shake. "So are we agreed? Just friends?"

He took her hand. "Just friends."

"Whew, that's a load off my mind." Moni picked up her fork and gave him a big grin.

"And it's a good thing, too, because now my appetite is back. I'm starving," she said, finally digging in to her food.

* * *

Moni was surprised at how drastically the mood had changed once she and Grant had cleared the air. The awkward silences and the shyness that had been so prevalent in their relationship since they'd slept together had finally dissipated.

After dinner, which was filled with constant chatter and good humor, they started watching a movie on cable. Without thinking twice, Moni snuggled up to Grant's side on the couch. He slipped an arm around her shoulder and they relaxed to watch the movie in comfortable silence.

Until the onscreen romance began to heat up. At that point, Moni felt Grant beginning to squirm.

She was feeling a bit uncomfortable herself. Finally, without either of them saying a word, Moni lifted her head. She found Grant staring down at her.

With only their eyes speaking, their heads drew together like magnets. Within seconds they were making out full-on.

Pulling away to catch her breath. Moni framed Grant's face with her hands. "Wait a minute," she whispered.

Grant's face delved into the crook of her neck, tasting the sensitive skin there with the tip of his tongue. "What's wrong?"

She swallowed hard, trying to remember what her train of thought had been. "Um, I thought we were going to be just friends?"

He lifted his head slightly. "This seems pretty friendly to me," he joked. Then he sat back against the couch, untangling their embrace. "I guess you're right. We shouldn't be doing this, should we?"

Moni shook her head no as she sat up, trying to arrange her clothes back into place. They sat for a moment, contemplating the situation in silence. She turned to face Grant, feeling sheepish.

"The thing of it is . . . I'm not really sure that I mind."

He was watching her closely. "Not sure you mind what?"

"Bending the rules." She shrugged. "What's a little kissing between friends?"

"Yes, but it's bound to lead to more than that . . ."

She stared down at her hands, feeling her cheeks heating up. "True. On the other hand, since we both feel the same way about a serious relationship—"

Grant nodded eagerly. "That's right. I understand your position. You understand mine."

"So . . ." She smiled at him.

He started lowering his head. "So . . ." Then his lips found hers and their bodies settled back on the sofa.

After just a few moments of kissing, it became clear that neither of them was interested in holding back or taking things slowly.

Moni nipped at his earlobe playfully. "Maybe we should go upstairs?" She kissed his neck. "Unless you'd rather just do it here?"

Grant pulled away. "Actually, I have a better idea."

Moni pulled her legs underneath her on the sofa, leaning toward him. "What is it?"

He winked at her. "Wait here."

"Where are you going?"

His grin was wicked. "I'll be right back."

Moni sat on the couch for what seemed like an eternity. She stared at the movie playing on the television set without really seeing it. Her mind was racing.

She felt excited about being with Grant again. They had come to an agreement, and it hadn't been nearly as difficult as she'd feared.

In the back of her mind, she knew that maintaining the title of "just friends" while they were having sex wasn't as black-and-white as they were making it out to be. There were bound to be emotional issues to deal with later.

But, at present, Moni didn't care about any of that. She'd come out to San Diego to be bold. Why couldn't she have a carefree contemporary relationship?

Finally, she heard Grant's footsteps on the stairs. He came halfway down and paused.

Moni stood. "Where have you been? What were you doing?"

He motioned toward her. "You'll see. Come on."

She followed him upstairs to the master bedroom. She stopped in front of the bed, but he gestured for her to keep going.

He led her to the bathroom and pushed open the door. Leaning forward to peek in, Moni couldn't believe her eyes. Grant had placed candles all around the perimeter of the Jacuzzi bath tub. Floating in the water were white rose petals from the flowers on the dinner table.

Pressing her hands to her cheeks, she turned to face him. "I can't believe you did all this for me."

He drew her into the bathroom and shut the door. "We had to get it right this time. We rushed through everything so fast the first time."

Moni just stared up at him, unable to find the words to express how she was feeling.

Grant pulled her close, pushing the straps of her dress off her shoulders. First he kissed her lips. Then he kissed her neck and finally he rained soft slow kisses on her shoulders.

Moni felt her heart pounding rapidly. She forced air into her lungs so that she wouldn't faint. Her knees were growing weaker by the second.

"I thought you deserved a little romance this time." Grant loosened his grip and with a little encouragement, her dress floated to the floor. "We've got all night, and I'm going to take it very slow."

Chapter 14

At six A.M. Saturday morning, Grant's phone started ringing. Moni, who he'd discovered was a light sleeper, bolted upright in bed and sat forward with her hands over her ears.

Groggily, Grant snatched the cordless telephone receiver off the base and promptly dropped it on the floor. Getting up to pull it out from under the bed, finally brought him out of his sleepy stupor.

"Hello?"

"Good morning, buddy."

Still disoriented, Grant couldn't place the voice. "Who is this?"

"It's Mitch. Sorry to wake you up so early, but I have some important news."

Grant climbed back into bed beside Moni and she curled up against his side. "What's going on?"

"Last night I proposed to Shelly. We're getting married."

Grant exhaled. "That's fantastic. Congratula-

tions, man—wait a minute," he said, noticing
that the clock radio read 6:05 A.M. You waited
eight years to ask your girlfriend to marry you,
and you couldn't wait until a decent hour to call
and tell me about it?"

"There's a good reason why I called this
early."

He played with the curls on Moni's head as
she traced circles around his navel with her fingers. "I'm listening."

"We're getting married in Las Vegas. Today."

Grant swallowed hard. "Did you say today?"

"That's right, Grant. I need a best man, and
you're it. I can have a first-class ticket waiting, if
you can get to the airport by noon."

"You got it. I'm there." His hand stilled in the
Moni's hair. "There's one thing, though."

"What is it?"

"Well, you see I'm—"

"You're not alone, are you?"

"What are you—psychic?"

Mitch laughed. "You dirty dog. Who is it? The
attractive nuisance?"

"Shut up."

"Perfect. Two first-class tickets coming up. We
can make it a double wedding."

"Very funny. Listen, I can take care of—"

"Don't you dare. This is going to work out
great. All of Shelly's girlfriends are flight atten-
dants, too, and they're working today. Moni can
help Shelly get ready and be our second witness."

Grant grabbed a pen and pad from the night table and wrote down all of the flight information. When he hung up the phone, Moni raised her head.

"What's going on? Are you going somewhere?"

"How do you feel about Las Vegas?"

Moni ran home to pack, barely able to contain her excitement. She'd never been to Las Vegas before.

As soon as she came through the front door, Summer and Candy came out of the kitchen.

Summer winked at her. "I guess your little date last night went well."

She grinned at the girls, feeling her cheeks flush. "No time to talk. I've got to pack for Las Vegas," she said, dashing up the stairs.

Candy squealed and followed Moni into her room. "Omigod, you two aren't running off to get married, are you?"

Moni paused in the middle of tugging her suitcase out of the closet. "Are you kidding me? Of course not. What gave you that idea?"

"Well, you didn't come home last night," Summer said from the doorway.

"And you ran in talking about Las Vegas. What else are we supposed to think?" Candy finished.

"Not that." Moni hoisted her bag up onto the

bed. "You're definitely not supposed to think that. I don't know where Grant and I stand. I think we both just decided to go with the flow."

"And the flow is taking you to Vegas?" Candy asked.

"Actually Grant's best friend is getting married. Apparently he's been dating his girlfriend for eight years, and they finally decided to tie the knot." Moni started throwing piles of underwear into her suitcase.

"Whoa, whoa," Summer said. "How long are the two of you going to be away? You've got enough underwear in there to last you a month."

Moni took a handful and put them back in the drawer. "I like to have extra."

Candy sat down on the edge of the bed. "Why is it that a man will wait years to propose then suddenly want to get married right away?"

Moni shrugged. "I've never met the guy, so I can't speak on the situation. All I know is that he's buying Grant and me tickets to Las Vegas so we can be witnesses at his wedding."

Summer pulled a few dresses out of the closet. "Kid, you're going to have a blast in Las Vegas. It's my favorite city in the world. I'm going to give you twenty-five bucks to put on the roulette wheel for me."

"No problem. I don't know how much free time we'll have for gambling, though."

"Oh, you've got to at least play the slots.

They're perfect for a first-timer like you. You'll probably win something."

Moni finished packing her suitcase and surveyed her roommates. "Are you two going to be all right here by yourselves?"

"Sure, don't you worry about a thing. We'll watch the place for you. We'll even talk to Marley, if you want."

Though Summer was quick with the reassurances, she thought she saw a worried look pass over Candy's face.

"Um, okay." She glanced down at her watch. She still had time to shower and change before she had to leave for the airport. "Why are you two up so early on a Saturday morning?"

"Because the phone—" Candy was abruptly cut off by Summer. "We couldn't sleep," she said loudly.

Something tingled Moni's spine. "Both of you couldn't sleep?"

Candy's laugh was a tad forced. "You know how selfish my sister is. If she can't sleep, she wakes me up so I can keep her company."

"Okay, well, I'm going to jump in the shower. I'll say goodbye before I leave. I'll also leave the hotel information so you can reach me if you need me."

Summer ushered Moni into the bathroom. "You have a nice mini-vacation, girlfriend. Don't worry about a thing."

As Moni stepped under the shower spray, she

realized that there was something in Summer's tone that did make her worry.

Flying first class was another new experience for Moni. The two couples sipped champagne while Grant harassed Mitch with jokes about shotgun weddings, Elvis officiants, and drive-thru wedding ceremonies.

Moni took a liking to the bride and groom right away. Mitch was laid-back and friendly while Shelly had an irreverent sense of humor that had Moni hanging on her every word. By the time their plane landed in Las Vegas, her stomach hurt from laughing so much.

This was the closest thing to a whirlwind adventure that Moni had experienced since her big move. A limousine met them at the airport and drove them straight to the Bellagio hotel on the Las Vegas strip.

That's where the two couples parted ways until the ceremony scheduled for six o'clock. While Mitch and Shelly rushed off to enjoy pre-wedding pampering at the spa, Moni drank in the sights and sounds of her first trip to Las Vegas.

"This place is everything it's cracked up to be, and more," she said, dropping her overnight bag on their hotel room floor. "Those fountains are incredible. I can't wait to see the strip lit up at night. I want to experience the entire spectacle of Vegas."

She walked through the room, checking out the balcony view of the strip, the minibar and bathroom.

Grant made himself comfortable on the enormous king-size bed. "Does everything meet with your approval?"

Moni came out of the bathroom, wearing the terry-cloth robe she'd found there. "There's a telephone in the bathroom and these robes are heavenly. I've always wanted to stay in a hotel classy enough to supply robes."

He chuckled. "Unless I'm mistaken, you are now a woman of means, you should learn to get used to this kind of luxury."

Moni joined Grant on the bed. "I'll never get used to it. At least I hope I don't."

She snuggled up to his side. "So, what's the deal with your friends? Why did they wait eight years to get married?"

Grant played with her hair, letting the springy curls slide through his fingers one by one. "Apparently Mitch has the opposite problem that I had. I got married too easily, he had issues with commitment."

"Wow, you two are a pair, aren't you," she joked. "I hope you don't go into all your personal details with your clients."

"Fortunately for us, it's rarely appropriate to talk about our own personal experiences in therapy sessions. Sometimes I'll do it to put someone at ease, but even then I usually keep it very general."

Moni turned to face him, leaning on her elbow. "I was just teasing. I'd imagine you're an excellent therapist. You're so easy to talk to and so compassionate."

He shifted position so that he was lying on top of her. "Why thank you, my dear." He leaned down and kissed her long and slow.

When he lifted his head, she touched his lips with her fingertips. "Do you miss your regular job?"

He leaned back against the pillows, staring up at the ceiling. "At the moment I do."

She frowned. "Why at the moment?"

"Because right now, I think it would be a hell of a lot easier to be a therapist than a writer."

"I thought you said the book was going well."

He rubbed his forehead. "Um . . . I get a few moments of clarity, strung between page after page of monotony. Things picked up a little when I introduced a new character recently."

She sat up, interested. "Will you tell me about your book? Maybe talking about it will help."

He seemed to think the prospect over for a few minutes. "No . . . I don't think I'm ready to talk about it just yet." He pulled her into his arms. "Besides, we're on a vacation. Neither of us should be doing anything that even remotely resembles work."

His face took on a wicked grin. "That is, of course, unless you'd like to discuss your current business prospects."

Moni straddled Grant. "No, you're right. No work talk. There's so much of Las Vegas, and so little time to explore."

"Well, since I've been here several times before, and this is your first visit, the itinerary is up to you." He glanced at his watch. "We've got three hours. What would you like to explore first?"

Moni slid her hands inside his shirt. "You."

At six o'clock sharp, Moni stood at the front of the Bellagio's east chapel with Grant and Mitch as Shelly appeared in the doorway.

When Moni had heard that Grant's friends were eloping in Las Vegas, she'd half expected for the four of them to end up in an Elvis chapel in the middle of the night. But, earlier in the chapel dressing room, Shelly had explained that just because she'd waited years for the proposal didn't mean she'd accept any old cheap and cheesy ceremony. It was truly amazing the exquisite splendor they were able to arrange on short notice.

As the first strains of the "Wedding March" played throughout the chapel, Shelly began her descent down the petal-strewn brocade aisle in her elegant white sheath dress.

She looked toward Mitch and saw raw emotion in his eyes as he struggled not to shed the tears that had welled in them. Moni pressed her hand to her chest as her own eyes began to fill.

As Shelly joined Mitch at the altar, she and Grant took their seats on the front pews on either side of the aisle.

"Good evening," the white-robed minister announced. "And welcome to this happy occasion, the marriage of Michelle Andrea Gilbert and Mitchell Nelson Taylor. We are gathered here today for one of the happiest occasions in all of human life, to celebrate before God the loving and joyful union of a man and woman who have chosen to spend their lives together in the bonds of sacred matrimony."

Moni had pictured her wedding day a thousand times, and it was difficult now not to picture herself standing at that alter. Not long ago, she was engaged to marry Burt Reynolds, but she'd always had trouble visualizing the two of them standing together in the Dunkin Baptist Church.

But, today, probably because the images were so real for her now, she couldn't help seeing herself in her white gown, bouquet in hand, standing before the minister. Only, instead of her typical faceless groom, a tuxedo clad Grant filled those shoes.

Moni blinked, forcing herself to concentrate on the ceremony taking place right in front of her.

Moni watched the couple, dabbing at her

eyes. She was beyond childish fantasies now. The only reason she was picturing Grant was because she'd spent so much intimate time with him lately. That didn't mean she wanted to marry him.

Why, she wasn't even in love with him.

Moni sniffed. She was in a mature relationship that she and Grant had both agreed wasn't leading to anything serious. She was going to show Grant that she could handle it.

Grant watched his best friend getting married as though he were watching it in a dream. The love between the couple was so strong it was almost palpable.

He glanced across the aisle and saw Moni dabbing tears from her eyes. She was watching Shelly and Mitch recite their vows with rapt attention. Grant found himself smiling at the open joy he saw on her face.

Moni had a very tender heart, he thought to himself. She'd shown herself to be a sentimental and emotional person. It wasn't at all surprising that she'd cry at the wedding of two people she'd only met that morning.

Even though she'd expressed her desire not to get serious, Grant couldn't help wondering if someone with such an open heart could handle a purely physical relationship.

He swallowed hard, beginning to worry that

such a sentimental occasion would have an impact on Moni's perception of their relationship. The last thing on earth he wanted was to break her heart if she made the mistake of falling in love with him.

Grant felt a sinking in the pit of his stomach. He'd seen this scenario time and again in therapy. Often when no-strings-attached relationships were proposed between couples, it was the woman that eventually fell in love. He'd seen that women had a tougher time separating sex and love.

Inevitably, this would be something they'd have to deal with. He knew it last night when they decided to cross the friendship line. Still, he'd set out on a course he didn't know how to change. Moni was an adult. He just prayed she could hold the reins on her own heart.

Grant was so caught up in the melee of his own thoughts he almost missed his cue.

The minister cleared his throat. "May we please have the rings."

Grant stood and offered the rings to the officiant.

The minister blessed the rings, handing one to Mitch to place on his bride's finger.

Mitch repeated after the minister, "Michelle, I give you this ring as a sign of my love and faithfulness."

Shelly, her voice shaking with emotion, repeated the ritual giving her ring to the groom.

And when the minister finally pronounced them husband and wife, before they shared their tender kiss, even Grant felt the sting of emotion in his eyes.

Moni thrust three quarters into the Wheel of Fortune slot machine. "This has been a fantastic trip. I can't believe we've only been here one day. It feels like three."

Granted nodded. "That's part of the charm of Vegas."

After the ceremony, the four of them ate wedding cake and sipped champagne in the chapel before going to the Prime Steakhouse in the hotel. They ate the meal of a lifetime, over several romantic champagne toasts, before Shelly and Mitch retired to the Presidential Suite to celebrate their honeymoon.

Moni and Grant would be flying back to San Diego the next afternoon, but Mitch, optimistic that Shelly would accept his proposal, had arranged in advance for them to spend the coming week in St. Lucia.

Since they only had a few hours left to experience all that Las Vegas had to offer, Moni wanted to fit in as much as possible.

After dinner, Moni and Grant spent a few hours dancing the night away at the Rum Jungle nightclub in the Mandalay Bay hotel.

On the way back to the Bellagio, she'd insisted they walk the strip, stopping at each hotel in between so she could sample each theme.

Now, back in the casino of their own hotel, Moni was dead set on losing every last dime she'd brought to gamble—that is, except the twenty-five dollars she'd doubled on Summer's behalf playing 36 black on the roulette wheel.

She jerked down the handle of the slot machine and watched the little wheels spin. "Nothing," she said, cheerfully. "Aren't you going to play anything? I can understand not wanting to play roulette or blackjack, but the slots should be tame enough for you."

Grant shook his head. "No thanks, watching you is just fine."

Moni laughed. Admittedly, she'd started out the night a little tipsy from all the champagne and dancing, but she'd sobered up hours ago. It was nearly three A.M. and the casino had quieted considerably.

"Come on, Grant. You're missing all the fun. If quarters are too rich for you, I saw some nickel machines over there."

He shook his head firmly. "I don't gamble. I already told you that."

Moni continued to feed the machine, which finally rewarded her with three more quarters. "Is it because of your brother? Is that why you won't gamble?"

He frowned. "Of course not. I just think it's a waste of time."

She cocked her eyebrow at him as she pumped her winnings back into the hungry mouth of the machine. "A waste of time or a waste of your brother's genius? Didn't you tell me he's good at it?"

Grant rolled his eyes. "My brother's penchant for getting lucky has nothing to do with my distaste for gambling. It's just something that never turned me on. But I do think if my brother lost a little more often, he might eventually come to his senses. Everyone knows how this racket works, eventually, the house always wins."

Moni grinned, pulling the handle one last time. "Well, that's certainly true in my case. I'm pretty much out of quarters. I think I lost all the money I came to lose. After this last spin, I'm out."

Grant sighed with relief. "Great, then maybe we stand a chance of catching a few Zs before we have to get on the plane this afternoon."

She handed Grant her last quarter. "You play it."

He waved her off. "Lose your money so we can go back to the room. If you don't want to sleep, I can think of some other things we could do."

Moni grabbed his hand and pried it open, placing the quarter in his palm. "I insist. Maybe you're luckier than I am."

Again, he rolled his eyes. "Okay, let's get this

over with." He stuffed the quarter in the machine and cranked the handle.

"Wheel of Fortune" sounded out from the machine.

Grant jumped, visibly startled as the Wheel began to turn. "What happened?"

She jumped up and down, clapping her hands. "You hit it. You hit the Wheel of Fortune. Whatever amount it lands on, you win."

Grant gaped open-mouthed at the machine.

At quarter to six in the morning, Grant stood on the balcony alone. Moni had come back to the hotel room exhausted and had fallen asleep almost immediately.

He, on the other hand, knew from experience that trying to get to sleep at this point would be fruitless. The past two days had been incredible.

He turned and stared back through the open double doors at Moni asleep on the bed. It was hard to deny the reason for his recent contentment. Moni was like a breath of fresh air. Experiences he'd gone through many times were suddenly brand-new when he shared them with Moni.

In the past, since he'd never been much of a gambler, he had always seen Las Vegas as an excessive desert haven for debauchery. This time it had felt like an enchanted playground. Their time together here had also been very romantic.

He shook his head as he stared out at the expansive lake in front of the hotel grounds. He couldn't believe he'd actually won money with just one turn at the slots. It had only been a hundred and twenty-five dollars, but from one quarter, that wasn't bad.

He felt his cheeks heat with chagrin as he thought back on the way he'd spent the remainder of the night. It must have been beginners luck that set him off, because after winning the first time, he'd been struck by the fever.

Grant, who'd initially wanted to rush back to their hotel room, had insisted that they stay in the casino and try out a few more games.

He'd been like a kid in a candy store. First, he'd tried a few hands of blackjack, followed by a turn at the roulette wheel. Without seeing much luck there, he returned to the slot machine that had paid him so well.

After diligently feeding the machine, he'd actually managed to double his money. But his fever still held and eventually he watched all the money slip away. His streak had gone cold.

Ultimately, he had no regrets. For the first time in his life, he'd actually had fun in a casino. He'd won some games, lost most of the others, but the thrill of the play had been worth it.

His brother's lifestyle didn't seem quite so foreign to him now. Grant also had to admit that Keith had changed a lot lately. Ever since starting a family, he gambled significantly less than he used to. His life didn't involve as many dramatic highs and lows. Clearly he realized that he had to provide more of a stable household for Tara's sake.

Grant found himself laughing out loud. He also had to admit that his brother won significantly more than Grant had that night. After the reckless way he'd gambled away his profits, he had no right to judge his older brother.

His tired but wired mind was still rolling with thoughts. He kept replaying Mitch's wedding ceremony in his mind. It was hard not to imagine what Moni would look like up there.

He knew she would be beautiful. His daydream went from a simple muse to some kind of surreal fantasy. Blinking rapidly, he tried to push the unexpected thoughts away.

Instead, another thought came to mind. He'd learned tonight that sometimes pleasure was worth the gamble and the consequences. Relationships were very much the same way.

Even purely sexual relationships were a gamble. He'd come to terms with that fact as he watched Shelly and Mitch say their vows to each other.

He was crazy to think that he and Moni could be friends and lovers without getting their feelings involved. In the back of his mind, he'd always known that fact.

In the past, he'd gambled on the game of love and lost. Twice. He'd been fairly certain that he wasn't interested in going down that road again.

But now he realized it was all about timing. The key to winning was knowing when to bet it all and knowing how to quit while ahead.

Without making the conscious decision, Grant knew his money was already on the table. The choice now was to let it all ride or walk away while his pride was still intact.

Swallowing the lump in his throat, Grant turned once again to watch Moni. Unfortunately, this time the choice had already been taken out of his hands.

He walked into the bedroom and closed the balcony doors. Careful not to disturb Moni, Grant climbed into bed beside her. He had to bet it all.

He was already in love with Moni.

❧ Chapter 15 ❧

"Hello, I'm home," Moni called as she entered the house a little after four o'clock Sunday.

The twins appeared at the top of the stairs. "Hey Moni," Summer said.

Candy asked, "How was your trip?"

"Las Vegas was amazing. I can't wait to go back sometime." Moni happened to glance at the answering machine. "Wow. There are twenty-seven messages on the machine."

Candy shot Summer a glaring look. "You were supposed to erase those."

Summer pressed her hands to her head. "Oh no, I forgot."

Puzzled, Moni hit the play button. Nigel's voice filled the room. "Summer. . . . You can't hide from me forever. I see you—" Moni stopped the player.

"Omigod, are all these messages from Nigel?"

Rolling her eyes, Summer nodded. "He's been driving by the house and calling randomly."

"Don't worry," Candy said. "We called the police. He'd left by the time they arrived, but they patrolled the neighborhood in case he came back. Tomorrow we're going to file for an Order of Protection against him."

"I can't believe this." Moni walked across the room and curled up on the couch. "All this went on last night? Why didn't you call me?"

"We didn't want to worry you," Summer said.

Candy nodded. "It's actually better that you were away. We wanted to get this all taken care of before you got back. You were so kind to let us stay here, we didn't want to bring all of this chaos to your house."

"Don't worry about me," Moni said. "Are the two of you all right? I thought this was over. I can't believe Nigel has been stalking you right under my nose."

Summer sat down beside her and patted her knee. "Sweetie, don't worry. This comes with the territory with men like Nigel. After I get the Order of Protection tomorrow, it will be like none of this ever happened."

"I think you're taking this too lightly," Moni said, feeling worried for her friends. "I broke off an engagement with a fellow I was dating back in Dunkin. Burt wasn't happy about it, but he sure enough wasn't going to follow me across the country to tell me so."

Candy took a seat on the other side of Moni.

"I didn't know you were engaged. Why did you break it off?"

Moni shrugged. "I just don't think he was 'the one,' you know? We were great friends but he never gave me shivers."

Summer winked at her. "But Grant gives you shivers, doesn't he?"

She felt herself flushing. "No comment. We're getting off track, here. Are you sure this Order of Protection will take care of Nigel? I would have expected him to give up long before now."

Summer rolled her eyes. "You don't know guys like Nigel. He's not still harassing me because he loves me or anything like that. He's just mad because I left before he was done with me. Nigel likes to be in control. Once he's certain he's gotten me so frightened that I won't leave my house, he'll forget about me."

Candy crossed her arms, shooting her sister a bitter look. "Let's hope that happens before your *next* job."

"Oh hush, Candy," Summer said.

Moni frowned. "What does that mean?"

"Summer lost her new job Friday night because of Nigel's antics at the restaurant."

"*Friday* night? That was before I left town. Why didn't you tell me?"

"Don't worry," Summer said, "I'm going to find a new job. And even though you haven't asked for any, Candy and I would like to pay some rent."

"Rent is not the issue. I can't believe he got you fired." Moni shook her head. "What a pig."

"You've got that right," Candy agreed.

"Well, we've wasted enough time talking about that fool, Nigel. We've got much more interesting things to talk about. Like how was your trip to Las Vegas?"

Moni got up to get her purse. "Next time I go to Vegas, I'm bringing you—because your money was a lot luckier than mine," she said, handing her friend fifty-dollars.

Monday morning Grant slept later than usual and, therefore, was still in bed when the phone started ringing around 9:30.

"Hello?" he said, groggily.

"Grant, I need a favor. Be a love and send me an invitation to your parents' anniversary party."

Still sleepy, Grant's full attention hadn't kicked in yet. "Excuse me, who is this?"

"Charlotte. Come now, Grant, it hasn't been *that* long, has it."

"Charlotte," he repeated slowly. "What is it you want again?"

"An invitation to your parents' anniversary party."

Suddenly Grant was awake and fully alert.

"What? Why on earth should I send you an invitation to the anniversary party? I could barely get you interested in family events when we were married."

"Now, Grant, that's just not true. I've always loved your family. I just had a lot of work commitments that conflicted with your little gatherings."

Grant rolled his eyes. "Then I'd have to assume your sudden interest in my family now has to do with work."

"It's my understanding that Simon Brockwell, the famous criminal attorney, is a good friend of your father's. Ever since he appeared on "Nightline" my boss has been after me to get a story with him. I'm certain he'll be at that party."

Grant had to hand it to her. She didn't even try to hide the fact that she was willing to use his father's connections to further her career. It was so typical of Charlotte.

"Yes, Brockwell is on the guest list, Charlotte. But you most certainly are not."

"Well, add me."

"I can't do that."

"Why not? If you're inviting that new-age airhead Katrina, you certainly have room for me."

"Where did you hear that Katrina was invited?"

"From your sister. I called her first. She started

having one of her stuttering fits, and I told her my cell-phone battery was dying. I figured I'd better deal directly with you."

"You really are a piece of work, do you know that? The extent of your nerve is really appalling."

"Come on, Grant. Let's not play word games. You can either make things easy on the both of us, and issue me an invitation. Or I can find my way there some other way, but you know I always get what I want."

He felt his anger rising and refused to waste any more energy on this conversation. "Okay, Charlotte. You're right, no more games. Let's negotiate. I'll speak with my father and see if he can arrange an introduction between you and Brockwell . . . let's say, over lunch. That way, *you* meet Brockwell, and *I* don't have to see you at the party."

"Now you're talking, Grant. That would be perfect. You can call my secretary with the final arrangements," she said, and hung up the phone without further pleasantries.

Grant stared at the telephone realizing that he'd been tricked. Charlotte had never wanted to attend the party in the first place. All she wanted was to meet Brockwell, and he'd played right into her hands.

He replaced the receiver in the cradle. Oh well, he thought, it was worth it to keep her out of his hair.

* * *

Moni sat at her computer, sipping coffee as she stared at her business spreadsheet. Her list of business prospects was getting ever shorter.

Now that she was nearing the bottom of the list, she knew exactly why those projects had ended up there. At one time, they'd all seemed like viable opportunities, but now they just seemed silly.

She couldn't work up even a tepid interest in any of the remaining business ideas on the list. What could she possibly do now?

Before she could work herself deeper into her funk, the telephone started ringing. She put down her coffee. "Hello?"

"Hi, Moni. How are you?"

"Akiko. It's good to hear from you. Nothing much has changed on my end. How's the mommy-to-be?"

"No significant changes yet. But that doesn't keep Jim from watching my every move. He seems to think I'm a china doll that might fall off a shelf and break."

"I'm sure that will pass once he gets used to the idea of your being pregnant. Right now it's still new."

"I hope you're right," Akiko said, sounding tired. "I'm not getting out much these days. I'm going to have to live through you. Tell me about your carefree single life."

Moni brought Akiko up to speed on the understanding she and Grant had come to and their weekend trip to Las Vegas.

"Wow, I thought you said nothing had changed. Sounds like everything's changed. Grant sounds like a great guy . . . but, how are you going to keep yourself from falling for him? I have to admit, I don't think I'd be up for that challenge."

She chewed on her lower lip, wondering how to explain something to her friend that she hadn't completely worked out for herself. "I don't want to make the same mistake I made with Burt."

"Grant doesn't sound like he's anything like Burt. Burt was a small-town guy with a simple view of life. If you'd married him, you'd always wonder what else was out there for you."

"Exactly."

"But what does *that* have to do with having a serious relationship with Grant? How long can the two of you maintain a pretense of emotional freedom?"

Moni felt the need to defend herself. "It's not a pretense. I've got my hands full trying to figure out what I'm going to do with the rest of my life. And Grant has a lot of baggage, too. Did I tell you he's been divorced twice?"

"Twice? Really?"

"Yes. I know he doesn't want to risk going through all of that again. But, we have fun together. I don't see why it can't be as simple as that."

"Okay, Moni. I just want to make sure you're

happy. If this is what you want, then I'm glad for you."

"This is what I want," she said more confidently than she felt.

Grant drove home from the driving range that afternoon feeling exhausted. With Mitch still away on his honeymoon, he'd been forced to hit a few balls at the course on his own, and the solitude had given him nothing but time to think.

How could he have let himself fall in love with Moni? That was exactly what he'd been trying to avoid. Here he'd been so worried about whether or not she could handle the kind of relationship they'd agreed upon, and as it turns out, *he* was the one who'd gone and broken the one and only rule.

It was too much of a risk. He couldn't let himself continue to spend time with her when he'd only be falling harder. If that hadn't been clear before, it was certainly clear now that he'd spoken with Charlotte.

Women were always different before they knew you were in love. Charlotte had been the one to pursue him. She'd been subtle about it, of course, but she'd been very attentive. But, once they'd made love for the first time, she'd known she'd had him. That was the end of her equal participation in the relationship. From then on, his mission, or rather her mission *for* him, was to please her.

Moni already had that darned DDS thing working in her favor. He was setting himself up for trouble. There was no two ways about it. It would probably confuse her at first, but he had no choice but to cut things off before they got too crazy.

Grant pulled into his driveway, noticing a monstrous black pickup truck parked in front of Moni's house. Beside the truck a blond man in jeans and a T-shirt sat on the curb.

Puzzling over the identity of this man, Grant entered his house. Had Moni called a handyman or something?

Before he had time to dwell on it further, his doorbell rang.

He pulled it open to find the blond man standing on his doorstep. "Yes? Can I help you with something?"

"Do you know the young lady who lives across the street?" he said with an all too familiar southern accent.

"Moni? Uh, yes I do."

"By any chance can you tell me when she might be getting home? I've been waiting on her for going on two hours now."

"Um . . . I think she's due back from work around four o'clock. Why? Are you a friend of hers?"

"I guess you could say that." The man cocked his head, giving Grant a wide grin. "I'm her fiancé, Burt Reynolds."

❧ Chapter 16 ❧

Grant felt his body grow cold as he stared dumbstruck at the man before him.

"Her *fiancé*? Moni didn't tell me she was engaged."

Burt shrugged, continuing to grin. "Well now, technically we're on a break, but I've come to take her home." He said the words as casually as if he'd said he'd come to wash the windows.

Grant stepped out of the doorway to make room for Burt to enter. "Why don't you come on in and wait for Moni. She shouldn't be too much longer."

"Well, thank you. I sure do appreciate it. It's mighty hot out there."

"No problem. Can I offer you a drink?"

Burt followed Grant into the kitchen. "If you don't mind."

"Would you like ice?" he asked more politely than he felt. Burt nodded and Grant handed him a tall glass of lemonade.

"Thank you very much," Burt said.

He watched the other man drain the glass, thinking he'd never have pegged this blond, blue-eyed Adonis as Moni's type.

How in hell would you know what her type was? his subconscious chided him. Clearly this guy had been enough her type for Moni to get engaged to him.

But, despite Burt's opening words, Grant had every confidence that Moni didn't still consider Burt her fiancé. She'd mentioned a high-school sweetheart that she'd left behind, and although she'd neglected to mention their engagement, she'd spoken with clear finality.

In fact, she'd emphasized the fact that Grant had been able to give her something this Burt character could not.

For a moment, Grant selfishly felt his chest swell with pride, but he immediately began to pity the poor guy. Here he'd driven all this way, and he was going to have to return home empty-handed.

Grant got Burt another glass of lemonade and even made him a sandwich after he realized the guy had been on the road for four days, living just on fast food.

He sat down across from Burt as he bit hungrily into the sandwich. "So? You said you've come to take Moni home."

Burt swallowed. "That's right. I think the sudden death of her Aunt Reggie really shook her up. It's understandable that people can act out of character after something like that. Now that Moni's had some time to work things out in her head, I'm willing to bet she's ready to come home."

Grant felt his heart climb into his throat. "What makes you say that? Have you talked to her?"

Burt took another large bite from the sandwich. "Nah, I thought it was best to surprise her. Let her emotions govern her first reaction to seeing me." He got a wistful look on his face. "I sure have missed her."

Grant sighed heavily, trying to mask his relief that Moni hadn't sent for him. "I'm sure you have. She's . . . she's something special."

Even though Grant had been all set to break it off with Moni before things got any more complicated than they already were, he now knew that was impossible.

The insane jealousy that coursed through him when Burt had identified himself as her fiancé told him all he needed to know. He wasn't ready to let her go.

Burt polished off the rest of his sandwich, leaning back in the chair. "Yeah, things sure aren't the same in Dunkin without Moni. We used to watch Redskin games, go cat fishing and play Grand Theft Auto on Playstation II. Cutter Brown just got the latest version, so I play with him sometimes, but he's not nearly as good as Moni."

Grant nodded, surprised by the direction of the conversation. Confirming Moni's classification of their relationship, it definitely seemed that Burt missed Moni more as a friend than a lover.

Grant found himself falling into his role as counselor. "Have you considered how you'll handle it if Moni's not ready to return home with you?"

Burt shrugged without giving it a second thought. "Why wouldn't she want to come home? That's where all her friends are."

Grant nodded solemnly. "I think she's started making some new friends here in San Diego."

"Her new friends can visit her in Dunkin. The people back home have known Moni since she was knee-high to a grasshopper. They're all asking after her. I'm sure once she hears how much they all miss her, she'll start feeling homesick."

Grant nodded again, realizing that Burt was very confident in his position. He honestly didn't understand why Moni wouldn't want to go back home where he felt she belonged. But, knowing what Grant knew of Moni . . . Burt was in for a big disappointment.

As Moni drove down her street, the sight of the black pickup parked in front the house almost caused her to stop the car.

"Burt. Omigod, it just can't be Burt's pickup."

Pulling into the driveway, she rested her forehead on the steering wheel. "Please don't let it be Burt's pickup."

Moni looked around and didn't see the owner of the truck anywhere in sight. Warily, she got out of her Jeep and entered the house. Candy and Summer had gone to the courthouse, so neither of the girls could have been home to let Burt into the house.

Maybe her imagination was getting the best of her, she thought, trying to calm down. Maybe one of her neighbors just happened to have a visitor with a truck like Burt's.

She'd just managed to convince herself of that lie when her doorbell rang. Her stomach dropped. Before she opened the door, she knew who would be on the other side.

"Hi, Moni. Surprise," Burt said, pushing back the door to give her a big hug. As she peeked around Burt's arm, she saw Grant standing in the doorway with a cryptic look on his face.

"Hi, Moni," he said. "I thought you'd be anxious to see your *fiancé*."

Moni eyes went wide as she pulled out of Burt's embrace. "Oh, Burt, is that what you told him?"

He grinned widely. "Of course."

"Why? You know that isn't true."

Burt shook his head at her in that way that infuriated her. "Moni, Mama said you were going through a phase with your aunt dying an' all, and I should give you some time. So I did. But now that you've had time to think things through, it's time to come home. Everyone in Dunkin misses you."

"First of all, Burt. We're not engaged any-more. Second of all, Mother Reynolds has got this whole thing wrong. I'm not going through a phase. And I can't *come* home because I already *am* home."

Burt sighed heavily rubbing his temples with two hands, clearly taking in Moni's words.

She was almost afraid to see Grant's face as she shifted her gaze in his direction. He was watch-ing the whole scene with open amusement.

A fact she found more irritating than com-forting.

Burt finally looked up. "Okay, Moni . . . are you saying you need more time? Because I guess I could stay here for a few more days, but I need to get back to the tire shop next week."

Moni frowned. "Why would you stay, Burt?"

"Well, I'm not going to let you pack up and move by yourself."

She smacked her forehead giving Grant a pleading look. He just shrugged, shaking his head. "Burt, I'm not moving. I thought I made that clear. Why would I come all the way across the country to live if I was going to go back to Dunkin after a couple of months?"

Burt shook his head sadly. "I'll just have to

stay till I convince you, then. Daddy can run the shop until we get back."

"Hey, why weren't we invited to the party?" Summer said, standing in the open doorway with Candy right on her heels.

"This is hardly a party," Moni snapped.

"Okay, sugar, I'm sorry." She came inside and stopped in front of Burt. "Now, who do we have here?"

Burt gave her his sparkling grin. "Hiya ma'am, name's Burt Reynolds. I'm Moni's fiancé."

Moni shot him a glaring look. "Stop telling people that."

"Why? It's the truth."

Summer ignored the exchange. "It's a pleasure to meet you, honey. I'm Summer," she said, boldly checking him out.

"Down girl," Candy said, grabbing her arm and pulling her back from Burt.

He blinked. "Wow, twins."

"Double your pleasure," Summer said with a wink.

Candy jerked Summer's arm harder. "Hi, I'm Candy. Clearly, you all are in the middle of something. We'll just get out of your way," she said, dragging her sister into the kitchen.

Burt gaped after the two women.

Moni looked at Burt and then looked at the kitchen. She'd never seen *that* look on his face before. *Interesting.*

"Burt? Hey, Burt?" Finally she had to snap her fingers in front of his face to get his attention.

"Huh?"

"I think you should go home."

"Why, I just got here."

Moni crossed her arms. "Well, where are you going to stay? Because I hope you don't think you're staying here." She knew how tight Burt could be with money and was hoping the idea of an indeterminate amount of time in a hotel room would discourage him from staying on.

"We've got plenty of room," Summer called from the kitchen.

"Shut up," Candy scolded.

Burt shrugged, never losing his good-natured smile. "I can sleep in my truck if need be."

Moni opened and closed her mouth. She knew he'd do it in a heartbeat.

Finally, Grant spoke up and not a moment too soon. "I don't think the neighbors would appreciate that. Sandra down the street is an overzealous busybody and would probably call the police."

"See, this doesn't sound like a good idea, so—" Moni started.

"But, I don't have a problem with you staying with me."

Burt's face lit up as he turned to pump Grant's hand gratefully. "Are you sure? 'Cause that would be awfully kind of you."

"Sure, it's no problem at all. There's plenty of room at my place."

Burt threw up his hands. "Well, I guess that settles it. Thanks, Grant."

Moni pressed her lips together in a tight line. "Yes, *thanks*, Grant."

He just winked at her.

"No, he doesn't look like that guy from 'The Fast and the Furious,'" Summer stated emphatically to Candy. "He looks so much more like Bo Duke from 'The Dukes of Hazzard.'"

Moni rolled her eyes. She'd been listening to the twins go on and on about what a hunk Burt was throughout dinner. There was no argument that Burt was a handsome man, but that didn't mean Moni wanted to marry him.

Summer winked at Moni. "I have to admit, I'm surprised at you, girl."

She shrugged. "Why?"

"I didn't think you country girls new anything about jungle fever."

Moni sighed heavily. "You know, I went through this same thing in college. Everyone thinks just because I'm from a small southern town that we're all backwards and segregated. I'm starting to think you big-city types have got it twisted."

"What do you mean?" Candy asked.

"In Dunkin, we all know each other. We're all family. We don't worry about race or gender or any of that other petty stuff. It's when I go out into the so-called 'real world' that folks start hassling me about how I'm supposed to talk, or who I'm supposed to date or how I'm supposed to act because I'm Black or a woman or southern—"

Summer nodded. "Touché, girlfriend. You're absolutely right."

"Now, can we move on to more important things?" Moni asked.

"What's the matter?" Summer asked, clearing away their dinner dishes.

"Isn't it obvious? I need to figure out how to get rid of Burt."

Candy nodded. "I guess the fact that he's here proves that he's not taking no for an answer."

"Exactly," Moni answered. "I still can't believe he just showed up out of the blue like this."

"Well, you can handle this situation the way my sister handles bad break-ups. You can get a restraining order."

"Hey, that's not funny," Summer called over her shoulder as she loaded the dishwasher.

Moni rested her chin on her hands. "She's right. The difference between Burt and Nigel is like apples and oranges. But he still doesn't seem to get it. I'm never going back home with him."

Summer closed the dishwasher and came back to the table.

"It sounds like he knows that here," she said tapping her chest. "But he hasn't accepted it here." She pointed to her temple.

"I don't know what more I can do to get through to him."

Candy shook her head. "This really is pretty funny when you think about it. Your ex-fiancé is across the street, bunking with you current love interest. How crazy is that?"

Moni pressed her hands to her cheeks. "I don't know what Grant was thinking when he offered to let Burt stay with him."

"Have you talked to Grant about Burt?" Candy asked.

Moni shook her head. "Not recently. I'd mentioned leaving my high school sweetheart behind in Dunkin, but I don't think I told him we'd been engaged. Fortunately, he didn't seem angry about it."

Summer shrugged. "How could he be angry? The two of you are going out of your way not to establish a commitment."

"That's true," Moni said. "But it's still a very awkward situation. I mean, can you imagine what the two of them must be talking about over there?"

Summer giggled. "Hopefully they're not comparing notes."

"They wouldn't dare." Moni's cheeks grew hot. "Would they?"

"No, I'm sure they're doing no such thing," Candy said.

Moni chewed her lip. "It's possible, though. I

mean, what if Grant tells Burt that we're . . . you know . . . involved?"

Candy waved her off. "Why would he do that?"

Summer shook her head. "I don't know, men do a lot of peculiar things when they're jealous."

Moni straightened. "I don't think Grant's jealous. Why should he be?"

Summer examined her manicure. "I could give you a lot of reasons, but there's no sense in you getting all worked up over it. Tomorrow you just go over there and tell that boy what's what and send him home."

Moni sighed. "I wish it were that easy."

The next morning, Moni rang Grant's doorbell. A few moments later, he opened the door. "Well, look who's here." He leaned forward and planted a solid kiss on her lips."

Moni just gaped at him. "Where's Burt?"

He led her into the house. "Don't worry, he's in the shower." Then he pulled her into his arms and gave her a long, slow kiss.

Moni let herself relax into the embrace for a minute before squirming free. "You sure are taking this whole thing well."

Grant shrugged. "Do you want some coffee?"

"No, thanks. How did things go with you two last night?"

"Just fine. We watched some television. Talked about sports. We got along fine."

Moni frowned. "Don't you find this situation even the slightest bit awkward?"

"Awkward?" He poured coffee into his mug. "No, not really."

Moni crossed her arms across her chest. "Well, why not?" It was starting to bother her that the idea of her with another man didn't faze Grant in the least. If one of his ex-wives showed up claiming to still be married to him, she certainly wouldn't like it.

Just because they weren't officially a couple, didn't mean he had to be so darned understanding. It wouldn't have hurt him to demand an explanation, at least.

Grant leaned against the counter, sipping his coffee. "I'll admit this isn't the most ideal situation. Sure, I was caught off guard at first. I mean this burly, blond lumberjack-type shows up claiming to be your fiancé—it was a little odd. Especially since you never even mentioned that you'd been engaged. But, I'm a grown man, what do you want me to do? Sit here and cry about it?" He took down a mouthful of coffee and slammed the mug on the counter.

His even tone had slowly intensified with each syllable, and suddenly Moni realized that Grant's calm, cool, and collected routine had just been an act. He was jealous.

She smiled.

Then she walked over and slipped her arms

around his waist. "Okay, as long as you're not upset."

He hugged her, then pulled back to look down at her. "So what are you going to do about this situation?"

"Well, I can only think of one solution."

He was already nodding.

"I'll have to go back home with him," she teased.

"That's right—what?"

"I'm just kidding."

They heard the shower turn off upstairs, and after a moment, the bathroom door opened.

Moni looked up at Grant. "He'll probably be down in a minute. Do you mind if I talk to him alone?"

"No problem. I have to get started writing for the day anyway." Grant headed for the door and then paused. "Are you going to tell him about us?"

"Do you want me to?"

"Don't you think it will make things easier? If he knows you're involved with someone else, he'll have to accept that you're not going home with him."

"That's true." She nodded. "But, Grant, he's not going to understand if I explain where things *really* stand between us. I may have to tell him we're serious about each other."

"That's fine. I'll even play along. It'll be torture, but I'll suffer through it somehow." He leaned down and kissed her on the lips.

Moni reached up and wrapped her arms around his neck as the kiss deepened. Grant pulled her closer by applying gentle pressure at the small of her back. She released a tiny sigh.

Finally Grant pulled away, looking down at her with blatant passion in his eyes. And for a moment, Moni forgot all about Burt and what she had to do next.

The sound of footsteps on the stairs brought her back to reality. Grant turned around, moving past Burt. "Good morning, buddy. I've gotta get to work." He nodded to Moni. "I'll see you later."

"Hi, Burt," Moni said, feeling a bit like a guilty child. Could he tell that she and Grant had just been kissing?

She didn't want to break the news to him that way. What she had to say was difficult enough for Burt to accept. He'd driven three thousand miles just to get his heart broken all over again.

She pulled out a chair and sat down at the kitchen table. "Burt, we need to talk."

Burt made a beeline for the coffeepot. "Look, Moni, I already know what you're going to say. But I don't think you've given me a fair shot. Maybe if I stay out here a while, and we start dating again, you'll realize that I'm right. We're meant to be."

"Come over here and sit down. There are some things I have to tell you that you haven't heard before."

Burt, wearing a wary expression, took his cup of coffee and sat down across from her. "You're not going to change my mind no matter what you say."

"Burt, I've found somebody else."

"Whoa . . . except that." He stared down at his cup. Finally, he looked up at her. "Well, who is he?"

Moni didn't know just how to phrase the words.

"It's not—Is it him?" Burt pointed toward the stairs.

She nodded.

Burt slapped his hand to his forehead. "Good Lord, why didn't you say something sooner? Here I am staying in the man's house." He shook his head.

"I didn't know you were coming and everything happened so fast. I tried to explain my feelings, but you didn't want to listen. You always think you know what's best for me. The whole reason I moved so far away was so that I could figure out what's best for myself."

Burt shook his head, still staring down into his coffee. "He seems like a nice enough guy, but geez, I feel like such an idiot. Does he treat you right?"

"He's been wonderful. But, Burt, I need you to

realize that this isn't about me and Grant. . . . It's about us. I love you to death. You were my closest friend in Dunkin. But what we had wasn't the kind of love that people base marriages on."

Burt sighed, giving her a pleading look. "How do you know unless we give it a try?"

"Burt, I just know. And if you really think about it, I think you know, too. The fact is, Dunkin is a small town, there aren't a lot of people to date. We tried seeing other people in college, but I don't think either one of us really gave it much effort. Don't you want to see if there's someone out there more right for you?"

Burt gave her a sweet smile. "Moni, how could there be anyone more right for me than you? You're my best friend. We like all the same movies. Play the same games. Read the same books. I don't know any other girls I can share those things with."

She reached across the table and took his hand. "What you've just described is a beautiful friendship. There's a lot more to love than just sharing common interests and having fun together. There's another important element that we've never shared. It's something that I think I've found with Grant."

Burt's cheeks flamed bright red. "You mean in the bedroom?"

She nodded. "You and I never could seem to make that work."

He ducked his head. "But you and he—"

She swallowed hard, nodding her head. "But that's only because you and I were always meant to be friends. We weren't meant to be lovers."

Burt let out his breath in a huge whoosh. "I see what you're saying." After a moment of silence, a wistful look crossed his face. "I have to admit, I am a little curious about dating other women. Being out here does make you aware of the possibilities."

She squeezed his hand. "See. I'm glad you understand."

Burt scooted away from the table. "I guess I ought to get my stuff and clear out of here."

"Wait. Don't rush off. You haven't caught me up on all the gossip in Dunkin. Despite everything that's happened, I'm hoping we can still be friends."

Burt gave her a shy smile. "I wouldn't have it any other way."

A few days later, Grant rang Moni's doorbell. When she opened the door, he said, "Is the coast clear over here?"

Moni laughed, letting him in the house. "I'm the only one here, is that what you mean?"

He grabbed her around the waist and pulled her against him. "That's exactly what I mean. Burt disappeared about an hour ago. I thought I'd take a chance and see if you're alone over here."

"Yes. The girls took Burt sight-seeing today.

I'm so sorry for all of this. When I suggested Burt stay on in California for a few days, I didn't mean for him to impose on you."

"It's no trouble. But, I am starting to miss the privacy. You and I haven't had any *alone* time, if you know what I mean?"

She laughed. "Oh, I know what you mean. I think Burt will be heading out this weekend and then you'll have the place all to yourself."

"These past few days have actually been so hectic, I barely noticed Burt. My parents' anniversary party is Saturday night. I've been running around trying to take care of all the last-minute details."

"I'm sure the party will turn out great. And don't worry about the flowers, I plan to deliver them myself."

"That's fine as long as you know you're attending the party as my date."

Moni smiled and Grant started nibbling on her neck. "Why didn't you end up going sightseeing with the others?"

"I told them to go without me so I could catch up on some work."

Grant lifted his head. "Oh, am I interrupting your work?"

She laughed, pulling his head back down to hers. "Only if you consider eating fudge ripple ice cream and watching 'All My Children' working."

Grant started backing her away from the door.

"Good, then I say we take advantage of this rare time alone."

The sound of screeching tires floated through the open window. "What's that?"

Grant didn't turn around. "It's just a car."

Moni looked passed him out the window. "The car is pulling into your driveway. Someone's getting out."

Grant's heart rate picked up as he turned around. His mother's car was parked in his driveway and she was carrying a suitcase up to his front door.

❧ Chapter 17 ❧

Grant ran out of the door and jogged across the street. "Mom, what are you doing here?"

Moni followed behind him.

The older woman turned around. She had a stylish short haircut with streaks of silver running through it like highlights. She wore a purple jogging suit and carried a Louis Vuitton suitcase in her hand.

"Oh, there you are, Grant. Sweetheart, could you please do me a favor? I need to stay in your guestroom for a few days."

Grant blinked, clearly dumbstruck. "Well, actually there's someone already in the guestroom. But, wait a minute, why aren't you staying at home with Dad?"

She sniffed, lifting her chin. "I'm leaving your father."

"*What?* You can't be serious." Grant threw his hands up.

Moni could only imagine what must have been going through Grant's mind. Here he was planning a fiftieth anniversary party for his parents, and his mother was standing on his doorstep claiming she was leaving his father.

She touched his elbow. "Grant, why don't you take your mother inside and get her settled. I'm sure Burt won't mind sleeping on the sofa."

His mother looked past Grant to Moni. A friendly smile spread across her face. "Hello, dear. I'm Sylvia Forrest, Grant's mother."

Moni shook her hand. "It's a pleasure to meet you. I'm Grant's neighbor, Moni Lawrence."

"Oh, how nice. How long have you been here?"

"Just a few—"

"I can't believe this," Grant muttered. He held the front door open. "Mom, why don't you come inside and explain to me what's going on here."

His mother went into the house, and Moni decided she'd better head back home so Grant could sort things out. "I'm just going—"

Grant grabbed her wrist and pulled her into the house. "Oh no you don't. You've got to stay and help me keep my sanity."

Moni sighed, following Grant and his mother into the living room. The last thing she wanted was to get in the way. She leaned against the arm of the sofa nearest the door so she could slip out if things got too personal.

Grant paced the room. "Can I get you a drink?"

Sylvia leaned back against the cushions and crossed her legs. "Oh no, dear. I'm fine."

"Good. Then please tell me why you're here."

"Well, both Samantha and Keith have children so I figured you would be the best choice."

"No, Mom, that's not what I mean. Why did you leave Dad?"

Her upper lip stiffened, and she crossed her arms across her chest. "Oh, your father. I just don't think I can live with that man anymore."

"Where is this coming from? Neither of you mentioned that you were having trouble."

His mother sat there in stony silence. She was clearly still very angry.

"Don't you want to talk about this?"

She huffed. "Not particularly. You'll probably just take his side anyway. I need to go to the powder room," she said, getting up and leaving the room.

Grant turned his gaze to Moni's. "I can't believe this. I must be trapped in some nightmare that I can't wake up from."

Moni shrugged, uncertain how to help him. "If your mother doesn't want to talk, maybe you should speak with your father. Maybe he can tell you how this all got started."

Grant snapped his fingers. "You're right. I'm going to call him right now."

While Grant was on the phone in the kitchen, his mother came back to the living room and sat down on the sofa. She picked up a magazine from the table and began flipping through it.

Moni, deciding she had nothing to lose, went over and sat down next to her. "I understand how you must be feeling," she said. "Men can be very difficult to deal with."

Mrs. Forrest let the magazine rest in her lap. "I'm glad someone understands."

Moni nodded. "Yes, it's just a fact of life that sometimes couples fall out of love."

Mrs. Forrest gave a start. "Well, I wouldn't say that we don't love each other anymore . . . I just can't live with him."

"Oh, I see. Is it his temper? Some men aren't very good at controlling their anger."

The older woman slapped her thigh. "Oh goodness, no. Charles? He's as gentle as a lamb."

"Ahh, I see," Moni said, even though she didn't. "But, you can't live with him. That's a shame after so many years together—how many has it been?"

Her lips tightened. "We're coming up on our fiftieth wedding anniversary."

Moni made a tsking sound. "Fifty years. Well, I suppose some things just can't be fixed. No matter how many years you invest." She gave her a sidelong glance. "I assume you're keeping the house? You could probably take in boarders so that it doesn't feel so empty."

"Well—"

"It's really so much better that you're doing this after your kids have grown up. It'll still be an adjustment, but I'm sure Samantha and Keith will work out some kind of agreement with you. You know, so you and your husband can visit the grandchildren on opposite weekends."

Moni hoped if she laid it on really thick, Grant's mother might realize she hadn't thought things through. Judging by the shocked look on the other woman's face, she guessed it was working.

"Oh my, I—" Mrs. Forest sputtered.

Grant burst out of the kitchen. "Dad's on his way over. He should be here in about fifteen minutes."

"You called your father?" his mother asked.

"Yes. I'm sorry, Mom, but I think you and Dad need to talk things through. He says he has no idea why you stormed out of the house."

"It figures. We've been married all these years, and he still doesn't get it."

Grant sat down beside his mother. "Now, I know you're angry, Mom. But will you please talk to Dad when he gets here?"

"Well . . ." She glanced at Moni. "Since you've already called him, I guess I can listen to what he has to say."

Moni patted her hand to comfort her. "That's a really good idea, Mrs. Forrest."

Despite Grant's clock-watching, pacing and looking out the window every few minutes, it didn't take his father long to show up. As soon as the car pulled up in front of the house, Grant dashed out to drag him inside.

If Moni wanted to know what Grant would look like in thirty years or so, all she had to do was look at his father. The family resemblance was striking.

Grant led his father into the living room and stood between his parents. "Now that I have you both here, will one of you please explain what happened?"

Charles Forrest shrugged, looking completely perplexed. "The whole thing is just plain ridiculous. If you ask me, I'd say your mother's gone and flipped her lid."

Sylvia Forrest came to her feet. "Are you saying I'm crazy?"

"If the shoe fits."

Mrs. Forrest turned to Moni. "Now do you see why I left him?"

"Uh . . . I-I—" Moni stuttered.

"And just who might you be, young lady?"

"Dad, this is Moni. She lives across the street."

"Across the street? The girl who drove through your fence?" Mr. Forrest asked, chuckling.

Mrs. Forrest turned to her. "Oh, was that you? Well, you did an excellent job on the repairs. I never even would have noticed—"

"Excuse me," Grant shouted. "But can we please get back to the issue at hand? That would be the two of you—my parents—splitting up after nearly fifty years of marriage."

"I just got tired of living with a tyrant. I won't do it anymore," Mrs. Forrest said, sitting back down on the couch and folding her hands into her lap.

"A tyrant?" Mr. Forrest was indignant.

"That's right. He makes all the decisions. Takes care of everything and never once asks for my opinion. He never wants to know how *I* might like things done or where *I'd* like to spend our second honeymoon."

Grant's father threw up his hands. "Oh, is that what this is about? I was trying to do something nice for you. All you had to say is that you don't want to go on a cruise."

"How can I? You already bought the tickets. Nonrefundable."

Grant turned to his mother. "Is that all, Mom? If you don't want to go on a cruise I'm sure Dad will cancel the tickets and take you somewhere else. Isn't that right, Dad?"

"That's what I told her, but she still wasn't happy," Mr. Forrest groused. "Instead she packed a bag and tore out of the house. If you hadn't called, I would have had the police out looking for her."

"Is that true, Mom?"

She cocked her head, crossing her arms again.

"It's not about the cruise. It's the principle of the matter."

Grant looked confused. "What principle?"

His father shook his head. "Hell if I know."

Moni, feeling a bit conspicuous, raised her hand. "Forgive me for butting in, but I think I see what's going on here."

All eyes in the room turned toward her.

"I think what Mrs. Forrest is saying is that she would have liked for you to discuss things with her before you bought the tickets." She turned to Grant's mother. "Am I right?"

"That's right."

"But I did discuss it with her. I asked her if she wanted to take a second honeymoon for our fiftieth anniversary. She said yes, so I made the arrangements."

Moni raised her hand again. "But, did you ask her *where* she wanted to go?"

Grant's father looked confused. "I don't have to ask. I know what she likes. Sunshine. Tropical weather. So I booked a cruise to Hawaii."

Grant frowned. "I thought you loved Hawaii, Mom."

The woman sighed. "Of course I do. That's not the point. It's not that I don't like the cruise. It sounds wonderful. But, after all these years, a woman of my age should be able to make some decisions for herself."

Both Forrest men looked at each with identical puzzled expressions.

"Mrs. Forrest, what I hear you saying is that the cruise itself isn't the problem. It was just the last one of a long line of decisions you feel you didn't get to participate in?"

"Exactly. Charles picked our home and surprised me with it. This is the place where I would spend my life raising our kids, and I didn't lay eyes on it until it was bought and paid for. He told me when it was time to quit my nursing career to raise a family. He told me how many kids we should have."

Mr. Forrest shook his head. "Are you telling me you never liked our home? You didn't want to quit nursing? You didn't want three children?"

"No, I'm not saying that at all," Mrs. Forrest said. "I'm not saying they weren't good decisions. They were, but I would still like to have been a part of making them."

Grant looked at his mother. "Mom, have you been unhappy all these years?"

"No, Grant. Of course not, but when you get this far in a marriage you start to notice things. I see these young girls running around with careers and their independence, and suddenly I feel like a child. I have someone to plan my day and make my decisions. I don't want to go on like that. I have ideas."

She looked over at her husband. "I know you every bit as well as you know me. Why can't you trust me to decide what's best for you sometimes?"

He stood there quietly for a moment. "Sylvia, I didn't know you felt this way. Why didn't you ever tell me?"

She looked down, shyly. "I did. Just not in so many words."

The older man threw up his hands again. "Hell, I'm seventy-two years old. I'm *tired.* You say you want to take over making all the decisions for a while, you're welcome to it."

Mrs. Forrest looked surprised. "Charles? Do you really mean it?"

He snorted. "Of course I do. Do you think I like bearing all the responsibility? Do you think it's easy making all the decisions, trying to anticipate your needs—because if you're not happy I'm not happy. It's a lot of work. If I'd known you wanted the job, you could have taken over years ago."

Grant's mother crossed the room into her husband's waiting embrace. "You really don't mind if I make some of the decisions from now on?"

He smiled lovingly at her. "Just as long as your next decision is to come back home with me, and the one after that is to spend the *next* fifty years as my wife."

"Done," she said, and he leaned down to kiss her.

Grant sighed in relief. "Oh, thank God that's over."

Moni gave him a thumbs-up.

"Sorry about that." Grant's father picked up

his wife's suitcase. "We're going to get out of your hair now. Sylvia? What should we do for dinner?" He looked over his shoulder and winked at Grant.

She smiled. "I think you should take me out tonight, Charles."

"Great, there's a nice little sea—I mean, where would you like to go?"

"How about that nice little seafood restaurant by the bay?" Mrs. Forrest said, closing the door behind her.

Shortly after Grant's parents left, Burt, Summer and Candy returned from their sight-seeing trip. Moni and Grant never got to enjoy their time alone together.

Still, Grant had learned an important lesson that day. When you had something as special as what he had with Moni, you didn't just walk away from it.

He'd been dwelling too long on the mistakes of his past, that he almost made an even bigger one. When the *right* woman for him had finally come along, he'd almost pushed her away.

The sensitive way she'd stepped in to help his parents work things out made him love her all the more. He'd never even told her how he felt about her. It was time to change that.

Despite the fact that she claimed she wasn't ready for a serious relationship, he knew in his heart she loved him, too. She was such an open person, it showed on her face every time she looked at him.

After the way she got him through his parents' near breakup, he wanted to find some really special way to tell Moni that he loved her.

Even more important than telling her, he had to show her. He just didn't have any idea where to start. As Grant thought about the time he'd spent with Moni and the things that were important to her, an idea began to form in his mind.

Grant reached for the phone. It was time to call in an old favor. He knew just the thing that would make all of Moni's dreams come true.

Moni was reading the paper at the kitchen table the next morning when the telephone rang. "Hello?"

"Hi, Moni. It's Grant. Do you think you could come over for a few minutes? There's someone here I'd like you to meet."

"Oh sure, no problem."

"Did you make the banana love bread I asked for?"

She looked at the cooling rack above the stove. "Three loaves, just like you wanted. But, I have to warn you, Grant. If you keep gobbling down banana love bread the way you do, you're going to need Weight Watchers."

"I'm willing to take the risk. Will you bring the bread over when you come?"

"Of course. I'll be there in a minute."

Moni piled the three bread loaves on a tray and gingerly carried them across the street. Grant's door flew open before she'd stepped onto the porch.

"Here let me help you with those," he said, taking the tray out of her hands.

"I can manage—oh, well, okay." She studied him. "What's gotten into you? You're wearing the widest grin I've ever seen."

He paused just outside the kitchen. "I have a really big surprise for you."

Moni clapped her hands together. "I love surprises."

She followed him into the kitchen and saw a tall man in a suit standing there.

"Here she is," Grant announced. "Moni, I'd like you to meet Robert Keene. He's the president of the Universal Foods Corporation."

Moni sent a puzzled glance in Grant's direction, but stepped forward to shake the man's hand. "I'm Moni Lawrence, Grant's neighbor. It's a pleasure to meet you."

He pumped her hand eagerly. "Oh, I've heard quite a lot about you, Ms. Lawrence."

"Oh, please call me Moni." She took a seat at the table. "But, you've got me at a disadvantage. What is all of this about?"

"In due time, Moni," Grant called. "First things first."

He carried a slice of Moni's banana love bread over to Robert and placed it on the table before him. "Wait until you taste this. You'll see it's everything I told you about and more."

Moni began to get a sinking feeling in the pit of her stomach. "Grant? Please tell me you didn't—"

"Shh," Grant said, pointing toward Robert who was savoring the slice of bread.

"This is brilliant. A hint of lemon, but a strong banana flavor and what else? Cinnamon?" He looked at Grant with a wide grin on his face. "Oh yes, this is definitely a product we can work with."

"Yes," Grant said, punching the air.

Moni swallowed hard, staring from Grant to Robert. "Will someone please tell me what's going on here."

"Oh, sure—" Grant started but Robert held up his hand, smiling broadly.

"Grant, may I?"

"Absolutely."

Meanwhile, Moni was feeling sicker by the minute.

Robert picked up an art board and passed it across the table. "Moni Lawrence, this is your future."

"My future?" She took the board. "Omigod."

Sketched in full color on the art board was a packaging mockup of Aunt Reggie's Banana Love Bread.

"What do you think?" Grant asked, clearly thrilled.

"This has to be some kind of mistake. I never gave my permission for this."

"Don't worry about this." Robert rushed to appease her, taking the board out of her hands. "It's just something I had my art department draw up to give you an *idea* of what the product could look like. You, of course, would have full control over the final packaging."

Moni looked back and forth between the two men. "Why are you talking about this as if it's a done deal? My aunt's banana love bread isn't for sale."

Robert reached into his vest. "Grant said you might need some convincing. Shall I give you a quote?"

Moni stood. "You can put your checkbook away, Mr. Keene. This isn't about money."

Grant rushed over to her. "Moni, Universal Foods is behind the Mrs. Wilder's Cookie franchise. He could have Aunt Reggie's Banana Love Bread at food stands in every mall."

Moni glared at Grant. "I already told you I didn't want this." She turned to Robert Keene. "I'm so sorry Grant wasted your time, Mr. Keene. But we won't be doing business together."

She turned and headed for the front door. Grant followed her outside. "Wait, Moni, what's wrong?"

She spun around. "What do you mean what's wrong? How can you even ask me that?"

He shook his head. "I don't understand.

You've been having so much trouble with your business lately, I just wanted to do something to help you. I thought if I got Robert here to help you see the possibilities—"

"What? That I'd realize you were right all along about my going into the food business? I *told* you I didn't want this. I don't want to sell Aunt Reggie's banana love bread recipe."

"Why? For sentimental reasons?"

Moni snapped. "No, simply because I don't want to be in the food business. I've told you this time and again. You refuse to listen, don't you?"

Grant went still. "But—"

"Now you've gone and wasted that important man's time. Did you really think I'd change my mind just because you showed me some fancy poster?"

"I'm sorry . . ."

She nodded, not sure when she'd ever felt this mad. "Good, because you should be. Didn't you learn anything from your parents yesterday?"

"I—"

"That's too bad, because I don't have fifty years for you to figure this out." She started stalking across the lawn. "I knew falling in love with you was a mistake."

"Moni, wait." He ran to catch up to her. "Honey, I've fallen in love with you, too."

Moni felt her chest burning. She should have been overjoyed to hear those words. Instead, all she felt was overwhelming pain. "I'm sorry. I can't see you anymore."

"What are you talking about? Just because I made a mistake? I'm sorry. I get it. This was your thing I shouldn't have interfered."

She swallowed hard. "I knew this would happen. It wasn't meant to last anyway, remember? That was the deal. I'm just holding up my end."

She turned away.

Chapter 18 🔔

Grant stood staring out at the panoramic ocean view from one of the many windows of the Hotel Del Coronado ballroom. It was an hour before guests were due to arrive for his parents' fiftieth wedding anniversary party, and all he could do was shake his head. He'd been planning this evening for months, and now, he'd rather be anywhere but here.

He watched with disinterest as the staff moved tables and set up chairs around him. The only thing he wanted was for the bar to open early. He'd never been much of a drinker, but, at that moment, he couldn't think of one good reason for not getting stinking drunk that night. Samantha and Keith were perfectly capable of handling things on their own. In fact, it was time he started letting go of the reins and allowing them to figure their problems out for themselves.

Moni had shown him that much. He may not learn fast, but when he finally learned his lesson, it stuck. Too bad he hadn't gotten the hint from

Moni a bit sooner—before he'd blown it with her entirely.

Two men held the ballroom doors open as a giant Ficus tree decorated with white lights was carried in. Grant, who, up until now, had been paying little attention to the setup, was immediately drawn to the person carrying the tree. It was clearly a woman, evidenced by the small hands with pink-polished fingers and the sparkling red heels showing below the oversized flower pot.

Several of the hotel staff gathered around, trying to help her carry the tree, but the woman stubbornly gripped the unwieldy tree, teetering and tottering until she finally plopped it down in front of the podium.

Then Moni stood upright, brushing leaves from her red dress.

"Now, that's what I call a dress," Grant muttered, feeling a familiar tightening in his groin.

By design, it was a simple dress with spaghetti straps and a modest V-neck. The dress whisked over Moni's curves, barely hinting at the temptations hidden beneath. The dress's sexy hemline waved and curled a few inches above Moni's ankles. But the best feature by far was the daring split that shot up to the middle of her thigh.

The dress was a killer, but there was also something else that caused Grant to hold his breath. Her hair. For the first time, she wasn't desperately trying to tame it with barrettes, bands, scarves or clips. She let it curl freely around her face.

Her trademark look of youthful innocence was nowhere to be seen. Gone was the fragile, helpless little thing who'd driven her car into his pool earlier that summer. He saw her as a woman—strong, sassy and just a little bit out of control. But that wasn't a bad thing. It was the kind of out of control that made a man want to throw her over his shoulder and carry her up to the bedroom.

Had she changed that much? Grant shook his head, sensing that she hadn't. He knew he was finally seeing her clearly—the way she'd always been. He was the one who'd changed.

Grant noticed that he wasn't the only one who felt the intensity of Moni's presence. Several of the hotel staff stopped moving furniture to ogle her as her hands smoothed over the fabric of her dress.

"If she's trying to torture me, she's doing an excellent job so far," Grant said through his teeth. Then he was moving across the ballroom, hoping she wouldn't turn, see him coming, and bolt.

She did turn, but instead of fleeing, she met his gaze directly and waited for him to reach her.

"I wasn't sure you'd be here tonight," he said, stopping in front of her.

"I honor my commitments," she stated simply.

"Look, can we please talk?"

Moni nodded and Grant felt a rush of relief overtake him.

"Absolutely," she continued. "I've got two dozen more of the ficus trees. Where would you like them?"

"I don't care about the trees. I want to talk about us."

"I'm here to do the flower arrangements for the party. And I'm here to celebrate with your parents—because I like them, and because I feel partly responsible for getting them here tonight. But I'm not here for you. And I'm not here to talk about us."

Grant's heart wrenched hearing Moni speak to him so coldly. This was the woman who always had a smile on her face, no matter how bad things got. This was the woman who bent over backward to make other people happy. This was the very same woman who had confessed to him that she'd never told anyone one off in her lifetime.

He knew he was dangerously close to becoming her first. Instead of letting that happen, he let go. Hadn't he vowed to stay away from serious relationships after the last divorce? He should have taken a piece of his own advice.

Shoving his hands in the pockets of his tuxedo pants, he took a step back. "Well, thanks for coming tonight. My parents like you, too. They'll—" He swallowed, remembering the kind words his father had said about Moni a few days ago. "They'll be happy to see you."

Grant turned and walked back across the room. He looked down at his watch. At least the bar would be open in a half hour.

Moni released the breath she'd been holding as Grant walked away.

"You did the right thing. You did the right thing. You did the right thing," she muttered, hoping she'd soon begin to believe it.

She couldn't bear that she was the one who'd caused Grant to have that crushed look on his face. Chewing her lip, she turned away. This time, she had to stand her ground. She'd worked too hard for too long to abandon the whole thing now. Moni knew she'd thank herself later.

That fact didn't keep her from feeling miserable right now.

Guests began to arrive at seven o'clock sharp and Grant took his place at the bar. He'd ordered a double martini, hoping to obtain the maximum effect as soon as possible.

"You're drinking already?" Samantha said, coming up behind him. She pulled the drink out of his hand and set it on the bar. "Shouldn't you wait for the champagne toast after Mom and Dad arrive?"

Grant reached for his drink. "I'm thirsty now." Samantha took the drink from him and handed it back to the bartender. "Get rid of this, and please don't serve him anything before the champagne toast."

The bartender nodded and Grant threw his hands up. "What are you doing?"

"The question is what are you doing? This is not the time or the place to start drowning your sorrows."

Grant took a few steps away from the bar, out of the bartender's earshot, and Samantha followed him. "What makes you think I have sorrows?"

"I saw your neighbor in the lobby. Keith told me the two of you had been dating. Judging by the shape you're in, and the look on her face, it's not hard to figure out the two of you aren't together anymore."

He blew his breath out in a rush. "I'm not sure we ever were together. Anyway, this is for the best."

"That's not true and you know it. You need to fix this. Go out there and talk to her."

Grant stopped in his tracks and faced his sister. "Since when are you so bossy?"

"Since I decided you needed a little bossing."

He shook his head, noticing that his sister seemed to be doing better than ever. Carl finally got tired of hearing her complain and suggested she start working from home. She hadn't called with an erroneous complaint in nearly two weeks.

"Don't you want to tell me about your latest affliction? Some new anxiety or phobia you think you're coming down with?"

"Don't change the subject—besides, I'm feeling just fine. We were talking about you. Don't try to squirm out of it. Let me help *you* for a change."

That struck a chord with Grant. Moni had walked away from him because he'd tried to help her and it backfired. Why did he think he was supposed to be the savior to the world? Clearly, he *was* the only one who seemed to need help at the moment.

Grant took another deep breath, but this time he released it slowly. "Okay, you win." He put his arm around her and led her toward the doors. "Let's go outside and talk."

"Hey, this dress wasn't expensive." Samantha said, clearly moved that he wanted to confide in her. "Go ahead and cry on my shoulder."

"Whoa, this place is amazing. Am I too late for the surprise?" Summer asked, skittering up to Moni's side.

"Summer, what on earth are you doing here?" Moni said, quickly looking around to see if Grant had seen her yet.

"Why, crashing of course. You didn't think I was gonna miss a fancy-schmancy shindig like this, did you? The Hotel Del Coronado is *da bomb*. Everyone knows that."

"But, Summer, Grant may get upset if he sees you here. This is a surprise for his parents."

"First of all, what do you care what *he* thinks? Second, I plan to behave myself, don't worry. I may even find me a rich man to marry. Look out, girl, it's *on* tonight."

Moni shook her and then shrugged. Aunt Reggie always used to say, "If you find yourself knee-deep in mud, you may as well lay back and take a bath." Moni intended to do just that.

She hooked her arm through Summer's and headed toward the bar. "We're both single ladies. Point me toward the cute bachelors."

A few minutes later, Moni and Summer were standing by the grand piano chatting with two of the players from the Los Angeles Clippers. Apparently Grant's father was an attorney for a lot of important people. Over Summer's shoulder she saw two things that were sure to upset Grant more than Summer. Entering the ballroom was Grant's first wife, Charlotte. Farther into the room, at the buffet table was his second wife, Katrina.

Moni quickly surveyed the room but Grant was nowhere in sight. "That's not my problem anymore," she said to herself.

"What did you say?" the basketball player closest to her asked, leaning down to hear her.

"Uh, how tall are you, six-four?"

He grinned at her. "Well, actually, I'm . . ."

Moni knew he was talking, but she couldn't

focus on his words because Grant had just entered the ballroom with his sister.

"Thanks for the talk, Sam. I feel a lot better," Grant said as they entered the ballroom.

Samantha leaned over and gave him a quick hug. "I'm glad I could help."

Getting over his feelings for Moni would be difficult, but, after talking to his sister, he was beginning to feel like he could face anything. He knew he had the support of his family.

Grant saw that his brother seemed to have been watching for them. He pulled away from his wife and strode over to them. "There you are," Keith said when he'd reached them.

Grant looked down at his watch. "We've got plenty of time before Mom and Dad get here. By the look on your face, you'd think we were late."

"It's not that—"

Samantha kissed Keith on the cheek. "I'm going to find Carl and the kids. See you two later."

"Hey, I see you brought Janet. I guess everything is working out?" Grant asked.

"Yes, we're getting back together . . . for good this time."

"Congratulations, bro. How did you finally convince her to stick it out?"

"We're going into business together. We're going to open Forrest Auto Repairs."

Grant clapped his brother on the back, "All right."

"Yeah, I finally realized that if I wanted to keep my family together, I had to make some changes. I can work on the cars while Janet runs the business."

Grant nodded without speaking.

"So how are you? Samantha seems to be under the impression that there's trouble between you and Moni."

"Yeah, she and I are over."

"What ha—"

The look on his face must have clearly stated that he didn't want to talk about it.

"Never mind, that's not why I came over here. I have bad news, Tater."

"What is it? If you tell me Dad's car broke down on the freeway . . ."

"No, it's worse than that. Your ex-wives are here."

Grant's body went cold. "What? Both of them?"

"Yup."

He closed his eyes, took a breath, then opened them again. "Okay, where are they?" he asked, wishing Samantha had let him start drinking when he'd wanted to.

Keith just shook his head and pointed. Both Charlotte and Katrina were standing in the center of the room, beside the grand piano. They were both talking to Moni.

Grant spun around and started off in a different direction.

"Where are you going?"

"To the bar. This is going to be a long night."

"I never realized the two of you felt that way. How come you never told him?" Moni asked.

Katrina shook her head. "He doesn't want to hear it. Not now."

"Well, I still think—" Moni was cut off by a series of melodic electronic tones.

"Honey, I think your purse is playing 'I Believe I Can Fly,'" Charlotte said, pointing to her evening bag.

"That's my phone. I'm not expecting any calls." She looked down and saw Burt's cell-phone number flashing in the screen of her phone. "Please excuse me," she said, walking out of the ballroom.

When she was out of earshot from the party guests, Moni pushed the talk button. "What's the matter with you, Burt? You know you shouldn't be calling me here."

"Moni, we've got a problem," Candy shouted into the phone.

"Candy? What's going on?"

"You'll never believe what this idiot—"

"I am not an idiot. I didn't know," Burt called from the background.

"Shut up and drive," Candy shouted, then returned to Moni. "Burt answered the phone and Nigel was on the line. He said he was Summer's cousin and this fool told him exactly where to find her."

"You all knew she was going to crash the party?"

"Of course. Didn't you? Anyway, Nigel's on his way there right now. You've got to get her out of there."

"Where are you two?"

"We're about ten minutes away. Warn Summer about Nigel. We'll be there soon."

"You're coming here? Wait—" Moni said, but Candy had already hung up.

Moni looked at her watch. It was almost eight o'clock. Grant's parents were supposed to be there any minute. She could just imagine the spectacle that could break out if she didn't get Summer out of there before Nigel showed up.

Rushing back into the ballroom, she scanned the room for her friend. Finally she spotted Summer flirting with an older gentleman that Moni vaguely recognized as a prominent political figure.

Moni took a deep breath and started across the ballroom. She hadn't gotten too far when someone tapped her on the shoulder. She turned. "Oh. Hi, Keith. I was just on my way to—"

"Moni, I wanted you to meet my wife, Janet."

Moni couldn't hold back the wide smile that spread across her face. She held out her hand.

"Janet, it's a pleasure to meet you. I've heard so many good things about you."

Moni exchanged enough polite words with the couple so as not to be rude when she excused herself. Thank goodness Summer had not moved. Once again, Moni began crossing the ballroom, and, once again, she was stopped—this time by Keith's daughter, Tara.

"Hey, Moni, I'm wearing the scented eyeshadow from the free sample you gave me. How do you like it?" She fluttered her eyelids.

"Tara, I thought you and your friends said you hated the scented eye shadow."

The girl looked a bit embarrassed. "Well, maybe some of them thought so. I don't think I agreed with them." She shrugged her shoulders and clearly abandoned her attempts to cover her chagrin. "Come on, Moni, you know how kids are. We go along with whatever our friends like. I actually think the eye shadow is cool."

"Great. I've got a whole case of it at home, and it's all yours."

The girl's face lit up and she rushed off to tell her father she was getting free makeup.

Moni shook her head. That was exactly why she decided not to market any more products exclusively to teenagers. They were way too fickle.

Turning around, Moni looked across the room and saw that Summer was no longer there.

"This is just great," Moni muttered as she did another scan of the room.

Before she could track down her friend again, the lights dimmed, indicating that Grant's parents were about to enter the room.

Throwing her hands up in defeat, Moni gathered with the rest of the guests to shout surprise as the doors opened. The lights went up and flashbulbs started going off to capture Mr. and Mrs. Forrest's expressions.

There was a lot of crying, hugging, speeches and singing, and in the melee Moni had no idea how she was going to find Summer.

Then a flurry of movement caught Moni's eye. Burt and Candy had arrived and were clearly arguing with Summer. Moni rushed over to them.

"What's going on? Summer, you've got to get out of here. Nigel will be here any minute."

"I refuse to be a victim any longer," Summer said, her voice full of bravado. No doubt fortified by the wine she'd been drinking.

"This has nothing to do with being a victim," Candy said, taking her sister by the arm. "This has to do with staying safe."

Summer pulled out of her sister's grasp. "No. I won't run. If Nigel comes here, I'm not going to back down from him. If I do, he'll never leave me alone."

"Summer, this isn't the time and certainly

isn't the place to take a stand." Moni glanced around nervously, still seeing no sign of Nigel.

"I've had enough of this crap," Burt said suddenly. "Woman, if you don't know what's good for you, that's your problem. But I'm not gonna sit here and watch you suffer."

Moni should have expected Burt to stalk off, and in fact, that is exactly what he did. But not before he scooped up Summer and tossed her over his shoulder.

Summer was so stunned she didn't even fight Burt as he carried her out of the room. The crowd noticed what was happening and several people began to applaud.

Candy looked at Moni. "That's just great. How the heck am I supposed to get home?"

"Cheer up, your party is a success," a female voice said from behind him.

"Yes, I told you that your parents wouldn't mind having me here," said another female voice.

Grant didn't even turn around. He continued to sit at the table, watching his parents dance, hoping his two worst nightmares would just fade away.

Instead, they both pulled up chairs. "We need to talk to you," Charlotte said. "You need to listen to us before you make another mistake."

Reaching up, he began to massage his temples. "Why should I take advice from the two of you—especially since neither one of you is supposed to be here?"

Katrina grinned broadly. "I sold the concert tickets on eBay so I could buy this Versace dress. Isn't it hot?" she asked, spinning around.

Grant rolled his eyes and turned his gaze to Charlotte. "What about you?"

"Brockwell canceled our lunch meeting. I had no choice but to try and catch him here," she said, shrugging.

"Never mind all that," Katrina said. "Moni is perfect for you. Are you going to let her get away?"

Grant turned in his chair, facing them both for the first time. "What did you just say?"

"Look," Charlotte said. "Katrina and I have been talking—"

"And you've obviously been talking to Moni, as if I wasn't in enough trouble without the two of you jumping into the mix."

"Yes, as a matter of fact, we have been talking to Moni. She's a nice girl. Just your type, and she loves you."

He went still. "Did she tell you that?"

Charlotte smiled. "She didn't have to. It was written all over her face."

Grant turned away again. "You'll have to forgive me if I don't take your word on this. I've seen no evidence that either of you would recognize true love if it bit you on your collective behinds."

"Ooh, so bitter," Katrina said, shaking her head. "Yes, I know. Having both of your ex-wives counseling the love counselor seems a bit crazy. But, answer one question for me, Grant. Do you want to end up alone?"

"If it means not having to deal with any more crazy females, then maybe I do," he lied.

"Brace yourself, Katrina. We're going to have to tell him."

Grant looked from one woman to the other, wishing for the second time that he'd made good on his promise to get completely plastered.

Moni looked at her watch and sighed with relief. It was almost 9:30, and she'd seen no sign of Nigel. Summer and Burt were long gone, so maybe it was time for her to relax and enjoy herself.

Moni ate dainty hors d'oeuvres, sipped champagne and made small-talk with some of the most fascinating people she'd ever met. She'd just begun a fox trot with Grant's father when she spotted trouble.

Nigel strolled into the ballroom as though he owned the place. Moni immediately recognized the two men flanking him from the raid on Grant's place. They were all dressed in tuxedos, blending with the other party guests, so that only Moni knew they didn't belong there.

She missed a beat and almost tripped on Mr. Forrest's foot.

"I'm sorry, dear. My fault," he said graciously.

When she tripped again, he slowed down. "Are you all right?"

Moni pulled away gently. "Thank you for the dance, Mr. Forrest. But there's something I need to do. Right now. Happy anniversary," she said, hoping she'd be able to keep it that way.

Picking up the hem of her dress, Moni tried to weave through the crowd on the dance floor as quickly as possible. Because she was so short, it was hard to see through the throng of swaying bodies. She just hoped she could reach Nigel quickly enough to tell him Summer had left a long time ago. Hopefully then he'd leave quietly.

She reached the end of the dance floor and caught sight of Nigel and his buddies. They were making a beeline for Grant, who was dancing with his mother. He looked the happiest Moni had seen him all night, and her heart ached.

Turning around, she headed back through the dancers. She reached Grant and his mother just as Nigel and his friends did.

Nigel tapped Grant on the shoulder as though he meant to cut in.

"Grant, watch out," Moni called.

Grant turned around and found himself nose to nose with Nigel Montgomery. "What are you doing here?"

Moni rushed to Mrs. Forrest's side and guided

her off the dance floor. If Grant and Nigel got into a fight, Moni would just die if Grant's mother were caught in the middle of the fray.

"What's going on? Who is that man?" Mrs. Forrest sputtered as she allowed Moni to take her arm.

Moni didn't have any good answers for the older woman, so she chose to ignore the questions. "You should be safe here, Mrs. Forrest. I'll be right back."

Then she dashed back to Grant and Nigel.

"I just told you, I don't know where Summer is."

"I know where she is," Moni called from behind them.

Nigel turned to face her. "You again. Where is she?"

"She left hours ago. She's not here."

Nigel seemed to mull that over for a minute. "Oh, she left?"

"Yes."

"She's not here?" he asked again.

"That's right. I saw her leave."

"Really? Then who is that over there," Nigel pointed behind her and Moni turned, praying it wasn't who she thought it was.

"That's Candy."

Nigel grinned. "How did I know you were going to say that." He brushed past Moni to go after Candy.

"Wait," Grant said, grabbing Nigel's shoulder. "You weren't invited to this party. You and your goons have to leave."

Moni had no warning when Nigel reared up, catching Grant square in the jaw with an upper-cut. Grant's head snapped back and he staggered backward but didn't fall.

She saw red. Moving instinctively, she grabbed a serving tray from a passing waiter and brought it down on Nigel's head, complete with shrimp dip and crustless toast.

One of Nigel's goons grabbed Moni by the waist and Grant moved with lightning speed to pull her away.

Moni was vaguely aware of an all-out brawl erupting around them as she became the rope in a human tug-of-war.

The clamor of shattering glass, startled gasps and screams, and pained grunts roared in her ears. The confusion overloaded her senses, and Moni wasn't sure just what was going on around her.

The next thing she knew she was falling forward into Grant's arms as they collapsed in a heap on the floor. Police officers and hotel security were everywhere.

Grant's arms tightened around her as she lay on top of him. "I knew I'd get you back into my arms sooner or later," he said.

Then the fog began to clear from her brain.

Grant was holding her, and she felt safe and comfortable. Too comfortable.

Pulling away, Moni scrambled to her feet and ran from the Hotel Del Coronado ballroom.

❧ Chapter 19 ❧

Grant sat on his bed watching the eleven o'clock news. His parents' fiftieth anniversary party was the top story.

"And in a related story," the blond reporter said, standing outside the Hotel Del Coronado. "Nigel Montgomery, son of billionaire Forbes Montgomery, was arrested in the ballroom brawl that took place here this evening."

"In addition to the assault charges he acquired for instigating the fracas this evening, it seems the younger Montgomery, owner of an adult nightclub in downtown San Diego, is wanted for multiple charges of assault and harassment along with bail jumping and attempting to violate an order of protection."

Then they cut to a clip of Moni's roommate Candy, who'd been interviewed earlier that evening.

"I think that punk got just what he deserved. He's in deep—" Her expletive was beeped. "His daddy's money ain't gonna get him out of trouble this time."

"Ms. Rayne, did you witness the events this evening?"

Candy tossed her braids over her shoulder and gave the camera a brilliant smile. "I saw the whole thing. It happened just like this . . ."

Grant's phone started ringing, and he turned the television sound down with his remote. "Hello?"

"Hey, Grant, it's Dad. Mom's here, too. Did you see the news?"

He sighed. "I was just looking at it. Look, I'm so sorry about the way things—"

"Hush, Grant. Stop apologizing already," his mother said. "I told you, this is the most excitement I've seen yet. I'm starting to really look forward to what the next fifty years hold for your father and me."

"Yes, but they ruined—"

"Boy, didn't your mother tell you to hush? We didn't call to hear you whining. We wanted to say thank you for the wonderful party. So, there was a little fight. No harm done. The police cleared out the thugs and your mother and I danced the night away."

"It *was* a lovely party. And it was so nice to see you, Keith and Samantha work together for a change. You've all made us very proud."

Grant smiled. "Thanks, Mom. Thanks, Dad."

"It was also nice to see your young lady again.

But, we hardly saw the two of you together. Is anything wrong?"

He hadn't told his parents that he and Moni weren't a couple because he hadn't wanted to spoil the evening. If three thugs and a fistfight hadn't spoiled their anniversary, he had no intention of telling them the truth now.

He'd tell them eventually. Just not now. "No, there isn't anything wrong. I'm glad you two enjoyed the party despite everything. It's been a long day, so if you don't mind—" Grant feigned a yawn, knowing he'd probably be awake half the night.

"Of course, you get some rest," his father said.

"Don't be shy now," his mother said. "We may be old, but we're not stupid. Moni's there, isn't she? Tell her good night for us."

"Sylvia, don't put the boy on the spot."

"Now, Charles, I just want him to know that we were young once, too. We know what goes on when two young people are in love."

Grant closed his eyes, trying not to scream out loud. "Good night, Mom. Good night, Dad."

He hung up the phone harder than he should have. Glancing toward his bed, Grant turned away. He was way too wired to sleep.

Reaching up to unknot his bow tie, Grant entered his office. The scrolling marquee of his computer's screensaver taunted him. YOU SHOULD BE WRITING!!!

He walked right past it to the window that

overlooked his front lawn, and more importantly, Moni's house. All the lights were on inside. Burt's black monster truck was parked on the street, Summer's neon blue Kia Sephia was in the driveway and Candy's red Toyota was behind Burt's truck. But Moni's silver Jeep was nowhere to be found.

He looked down at his watch. It was 11:23. Where was she? He hadn't seen her since she'd fled the ballroom. At first he'd thought she'd gone to the ladies' room to freshen up, so he'd waited a few minutes before searching for her.

By the time he'd made the rounds, it was clear she was long gone. Grant turned away from the window, running his fingers over his scalp. Tonight had been a night of important revelations.

His mind drifted back to getting ambushed by his ex-wives. The stuff nightmares were made of. Yet, the reality had been a complete surprise.

Grant had thought both of those chapters of his life had been closed. He'd had no desire to reread or rewrite them. As a therapist, he'd naturally done more than his share of soul-searching and rationalizing, and had been certain beyond a shadow of a doubt that he'd come to terms with the failures of both marriages.

There was nothing more either of them could do to impact his life. Until they'd come to him with four simple words, "It wasn't your fault."

He'd known that, right? In fact, he'd declared it on several occasions to all who would hear him. Why should hearing the actual words make any difference.

But they had. When each woman stated that simple truth in her own way, something inside Grant had broken. Now he realized it was that last barrier surrounding his heart. The shield he'd left in place to keep himself from letting another woman get too close.

His ex-wives had given him an important gift—the hope that he could still get it right. They had seen Moni and they had seen him, and they'd known before he'd fully recognized that things with Moni could be different.

Grant turned back to the window when he heard Moni's car; she was pulling into her driveway behind Summer's car. She got out and quickly wrapped her hands around her bare arms to shield herself from the cold night air. Skittering to the door, she turned for just a second and looked toward his house.

He knew she could see him standing in the window. Then she turned and let herself into the house. Grant remained where he was.

Things just couldn't end this way. It wasn't meant to. He felt that fact in his gut. This was the same intuition he often experienced in therapy sessions. It was the instinct he let guide him to the truth when one part of a couple was holding back from the other. Or when two people were letting their fears interfere with their true potential to love.

He had to let that instinct guide him now. He needed to tell Moni how he felt, and he'd never get to sleep if he didn't do it tonight.

Moni walked into the house, and was surprised to find it so quiet, considering the fact that all the lights were on.

"Hello," she called, walking through the house and turning off lights. Apparently, everyone had gone to bed.

She paused as she walked back through the living room. Burt's car was still outside, but she was certain he wasn't back at Grant's. Why wasn't he crashed on the living room sofa?

Pulling off her shoes, Moni made her way up the stairs. Something made her pause as she passed Summer's bedroom. The door opened and she jumped.

"Sorry. Didn't mean to scare you," Burt said, coming out of Summer's room. His chest and feet were bare, and his fingers were in the process of buckling the snaps on his jeans.

Flustered, Moni averted her eyes. "Oh no, I'm sorry. Excuse me." She rushed into her bedroom, shaking her head.

Then she laughed and said to herself, "Summer . . . you must have *rocked* his world."

"You *know* I did."

Moni yelped and spun around to see Summer standing at her door, wearing nothing but her bathrobe.

"Sorry. Didn't mean to scare you," she said as she stepped into the room and shut the door behind her.

Moni collapsed on her bed. "It's okay."

Summer sat down at the foot of the bed. "Is this awkward? You don't mind, do you?"

"Mind what?"

"You know . . . Burt and me."

"Oh gosh, no. Are you kidding? I think it's . . . well, it's great. You're probably just what he needs." Then Moni paused. "You're not just playing with him, though, are you? Because I really don't think Burt's the type—"

"Girl, I think I'm in love."

Moni blinked. "What?"

"You heard me. I know it sounds crazy. He was so strong and forceful when he carried me out of the hotel. I've never felt so . . . *protected* before."

Moni smiled. Her friend's face was actually glowing.

"I heard what you said about me rocking his world and . . . well, I really think it was the other way around."

"Shut up. Burt?"

"Girlfriend, have you seen this guy lately? He's a blond god. I think you're crazy for letting him go, but hey, it works for me. And in bed, he—"

Moni shoved her fingers in her ears. "La-la-la-la-la."

"Sorry, but one girl's milquetoast is another girl's hot-fudge sundae. Hey, that sounds like something Aunt Reggie could have said."

Moni smiled. "I'm really happy for you, Summer. I think you're just the kind of spice Burt needs in his life, and, no doubt he'll be a stabilizing force for you, too. Hope this works out."

Summer rushed forward and pulled Moni into a hug. She squeezed her tight, and when Summer pulled back, she was blinking away tears.

"I'm not trying to rush into anything. But this thing with Burt—it feels so different." She sniffed and dashed the back of her hand against her eye. "It's scary actually."

Moni took Summer's hand and gave it a squeeze. "It's going to be okay. Just give it a chance."

They were just sitting there smiling at each other when the doorbell rang. Moni jumped up, sliding her feet into her slippers. "Was that the doorbell?"

Summer dashed out of the bedroom door ahead of her. "Maybe it's more reporters. I can't believe I missed all the excitement the first time."

By the time Moni reached the top of the stairs, Candy was already at the door. "Grant . . . uh, come in."

Burt came out of the kitchen eating a sandwich. "What's he doing here?"

Summer rushed up to him and dragged him

back into the kitchen. Candy looked from Grant to Moni, who had now reached the bottom of the stairs, then back to Grant. Without another word she followed Summer and Burt into the kitchen.

Moni took a few steps forward. "Hey, Grant."

He was still wearing his tuxedo, with the top two buttons of his shirt open and the bow tie hanging loose on either side. She raised a hand to her chest as if to cover that rapid beating of her heart. He still made her mouth water.

"Hi. I know it's late. But I really think we should talk."

Moni swallowed. "Okay. What did you want to talk about?"

"I want to talk about us. I know I screwed up, but—"

There was a heavy thunk and crash followed by a cry of pain from the kitchen. Moni ran around the corner to see Summer and Candy helping Burt up from the floor.

"What happened?"

"He tipped his chair back too far—trying to listen to your conversation," Summer said, looking sheepish. She waved Moni and Grant into the living room. "You two go back and have your little talk. We'll be quiet."

Moni turned to look at Grant. "Maybe we should go outside."

He nodded. "Good idea."

They stepped onto her porch and Moni shivered, immediately realizing it hadn't been a good idea to come outside. She started to turn around and suggest they go back inside, but Grant was already pulling off his jacket and wrapping it around her shoulders.

She pulled it close around her. It was still warm from his body, and it smelled of his favorite cologne. She closed her eyes trying to numb out the persistent ache in her heart.

Grant sat down on the edge of the porch and patted the space beside him. "I know 'I'm sorry' isn't enough to cover how I made you feel," he said when she'd taken her place next to him.

"I want you to know that I understand why you're upset with me, and I want to make it up to you."

Moni shook her head. "I don't think there's anything you can do."

"I know I can't help you with your business. You need to handle that on your own. I get that."

She looked up at him. "This is about so much more than just my business."

"I hear that. This is about your need to feel independent and the fact that I undermined that."

Moni sighed with exasperation. "No. This isn't about you at all." Her words were harsher than she intended them to be, and she tried to start again. "Grant, you're wonderful. You're one of the most incredible men I've ever met. Maybe at another time, in another place—"

"Whew, that sounds familiar—"

Moni realized she was repeating almost word for word the speech Grant had first given her. "I'm just trying to say that I'm still trying to figure out what I need. *That's* what I need to focus on right now. If you and I were together right now, I'd be completely focused on you."

"And I'd be completely focused on you. Love is giving *and taking*. You're the one who taught me that."

Moni stared down at her fingers. He wasn't making this easy for her. Her heart was screaming for her to give in. She wanted to let go and indulge her feelings, but she was afraid of being swallowed up by them.

"Grant. I don't think I should be with anyone right now."

"No, you don't think you should be with me. Why?"

Moni felt a hot fat tear slide down her cheek. "Because you don't believe in me."

She heard Grant's sharp intake of breath and she forced herself to keep talking even though she knew she was hurting him. "You think I'm silly, crazy, funny. You think my ideas are harebrained." She sniffed.

"I know in your heart you think you can steer me in the right direction. Give me stability, focus, sensibility."

"Moni, I—"

"Don't bother denying it, Grant. I've seen the way you look at me. Sometimes you humor me.

Other times I amuse you, but you've never taken me seriously. Not when it comes to my feelings or my dreams."

"I didn't realize I made you feel that way. Is that how you really believe I see you?"

His voice seemed so weighed down with hurt, Moni's tears started flowing rapidly. She wiped at her eyes with her hands, trying to get enough air into her lungs to continue speaking.

"Grant, I really love you, and that's the main reason I can't be with you."

"What? That makes no sense."

"If you think about it, it does make sense. If we were together, I'd start to see myself through your eyes. Eventually, your perception of me would begin to overwrite my perception of myself. I'd let you take care of me, the way I've let people take care of me my entire life. I'd work the business you thought I should work. I'd dress in the clothes that you liked best. And I'd never know what it is that *I* really want."

"Moni, I'd never let that happen."

"No. *I'd* never let that happen, Grant. Don't you remember what you told me about your clients?"

Grant shook his head.

"You said marital therapy isn't always about keeping couples together. Sometimes it's about helping two people realize that they shouldn't be together."

"Moni, I love you."

"I love you, too, Grant. I really do."

He reached out and pulled her into his arms. "Then we can make this work."

Moni let herself melt into his arms because she didn't have the strength to resist him. She needed this too. Closing her eyes, she buried her face in the warm space of his neck.

Grant's arms locked around her as though he would never let her go. For that moment in time, Moni let herself pretend this was all she needed from the world.

Grant's arms. The warmth of his body seeping into hers. His hands lightly massaging her back. The pleasant mingling scents of soap and cologne. The rise and fall of his chest, steady and comforting. The feel of the soft hairs at the nape of his neck.

His lips on her temple. His breath on her cheek. Grant's kiss. She tasted the salt of her tears on his lips. Then his tongue entered her mouth and her entire body went hot.

She let her nails rake down his back, enjoying the feel of each muscle jumping beneath her touch. They clung to each other, their kisses both desperate and urgent. It was both the most exquisite pleasure and the worst torture.

Moni pulled away from the embrace while she still could. Turning away, she covered her face with her hands.

"Moni?" Grant whispered in her ear. It was a question. Did they still have a chance? A world of emotion was expressed in that single word.

She raised her head. "Grant, it's not that I don't want to be with you. And it's not that I don't love you with all my heart. It's just that I have to put myself first this time. I have to do this for me."

She stood before she could change her mind. "You told me yourself, sometimes love just isn't enough."

Moni took off Grant's jacket and dropped it in his lap. She turned to go back into the house and saw the living room drapes swing back into place. Her roommates had been watching them.

"Moni?" Grant's voice was raw. She turned and saw him standing on the lawn, hands in his pockets.

"When I told you that, I wasn't talking about us," he called to her, then turned and walked back across the street.

Chapter 20

For the next several weeks, one day blended into the next for Grant. He didn't *feel* like he was letting himself slide downhill, he just wasn't motivated to do many of his normal activities.

Activities such as shaving, dressing well, and working on the book that was due in three days didn't seem pressing to Grant. What did seem pressing to Grant were reruns on the Game Show Network, playing spades with faceless strangers online and reading newspapers word for word.

He had these and numerous other engaging pursuits to invest his time into. He most certainly didn't have time to think about Moni.

Grant had just entered the online game room on his computer when he heard the doorbell ringing. For a split second his heartbeat picked up, but he immediately slumped back into his chair. It wouldn't be Moni. She didn't ring his doorbell anymore.

If it were anyone it was either Keith or Samantha. Grant considered ignoring the door, but instead he headed for the stairs. If he didn't make an appearance one would call the other as well as his parents and they'd all be standing on his doorstep.

"Let's get this over with," he said, yanking open the door and retreating into the house without looking at his visitor.

"Good Lord, this place is a mess."

Grant turned, surprised to hear Mitch's voice. "What are you doing here?"

"And you look like hell. What on earth have you been up to."

"Nothing," Grant said, sinking into the sofa and propping his feet on the coffee table.

Mitch stood over him shaking his head. "That's exactly what it looks like. I guess you've been burning the midnight oil trying to finish your book before your deadline."

"Well—"

"It's a good thing because I'm definitely ready for you to come back to work." His friend dropped some paperwork on the table. "In fact, I need your help with this client. Can you review her background this weekend, because I'd really like you to take over with her on Monday. She's driving me nuts."

Something in Grant's expression must have gotten through to Mitch because he paused. "Wait a minute. What's going on with you?"

Grant shrugged. "I don't know what you're talking about. I'm fine."

"No, you're clearly not fine. You're neat to the point of being certifiable, but you've got, what, like a month's worth of newspapers under that coffee table. You're unshaven. You're wearing sweats. You're telling me Moni hasn't said anything about the sloppy mess you've become?"

Grant couldn't prevent himself from wincing at the sound of her name. But he forced his voice to sound casual. "Why would *she* say anything?"

Mitch swore violently. "I get it now. How did I miss this? I know I've been caught up in my own wedded bliss lately, but how come you didn't tell me?"

Grant didn't particularly want to talk about it, but he knew it was unavoidable. Still, Mitch was going to have to drag it out of him. "Tell you what?"

"That you and Moni aren't together anymore. What happened?"

Grant snorted. "Together? And what do you mean what happened. You know we had a no-strings-attached thing going."

Mitch sat down on the love seat that faced Grant, making it hard for Grant to avoid his gaze. Instead he stared at his feet.

"I know that's what you two were telling everyone, but any fool could see the two of you had more going on than just sex. Which one of you panicked and called it off?"

Grant felt like his heart was bleeding. He hadn't discussed Moni or the way things had ended with anyone. Samantha had tried to pin him down, but he'd managed to distract her every time.

Now, even though it felt like he was prodding his wound, he couldn't resist the urge to talk. "She did."

Mitch released a pained hiss.

Grant glared at the other man. "But that's not a surprise, right? You said yourself that I should leave her alone before I dragged her down with me."

Dropping his head into his hands, Mitch cursed again. "You didn't believe that crap, did you? I was wrong. I thought you figured that out by now. You two had something special. Something you never had with either Charlotte or Katrina."

"Oh yeah, well maybe you weren't wrong then. Maybe you're just wrong now."

"No. I know I'm not wrong."

"How do you know?" Grant had meant to sound surly, but the question came out wistful.

"Because you're wrecked. Look at yourself."

Grant rolled his eyes.

"Seriously, look at yourself. I've been your friend for fourteen years. In college I saw girls come and go and afterward I saw you through *two* divorces. In fourteen years, I've *never* seen you get wrecked over a woman. What does that say to you?"

Grant stared at the rubber treads on his sneaker. "That I really screwed up this time."

"Or maybe it was finally the real thing this time."

He felt his stomach lurch. The thought that he'd lost something real for the first time only made him want to retch. "So? What am I supposed to do. She doesn't want to be with me."

"Is that what she said?"

"Yeah. She claims I don't really believe in her." Grant quickly recounted the mistake he made trying to set her up in business.

At the end of the story, Mitch flicked him on the forehead. "What the hell were you thinking?"

"I wasn't, obviously."

Mitch began pacing the room. "Let me think for a second. I think this is fixable. You just have to find a way to show her how you really feel. You know how this works. She wants to forgive you, man. She just needs you to give her reassurance that she won't get hurt. Somehow she must have been giving you a sign."

Grant dropped his feet to the floor, thinking back over the last month and a half. "I can't think of anything."

Mitch had been staring out of the front window as they talked. "Wait a minute. You haven't been running your dishwasher, but you've had time to tend to your garden?"

He shook his head. "No, of course not."

Mitch turned to look at him. "Then how come your flowers aren't dead."

"Flowers?"

The two men went outside to survey Grant's front lawn. He'd seen the flowers planted along the line of the fence. Moni had told him she was putting those down to hide the bald spots in the grass.

What he hadn't seen before were the clusters of bird-of-paradise plants in between his shrubs. For that matter, suddenly there were four more smaller shrubs that were new. He hadn't been leaving the house as much lately, and usually when he did it was late at night to raid the convenience stores for junk food.

"I guess Moni got carried away with the landscaping." He found himself grinning. "Knowing her, she probably thought the flowers by the fence made the rest of the yard look plain and she wanted to balance it out."

Mitch gave Grant a hard look. "There's your sign, man. What are you going to do about it?"

"I'm sure your wife will love these," Moni said, handing her customer yellow gladiolas wrapped in tissue.

"Thanks again for your help. Please, keep the change," he said after she tried to hand him a five-dollar bill.

As the customer left the store, Moni noticed a sharply dressed woman with three young boys enter the shop. She immediately recognized her to be Grant's sister.

Almost unconsciously, she glanced over the woman's shoulder half expecting to find Grant standing there.

"Oh, there you are, Moni." As Samantha approached the counter, her kids started to scatter around the shop. "Oh no you don't, get back here, kids. This is a grown-up store. There's nothing in here for you."

With further cajoling the children finally regrouped with their mother. "I'm sorry about that. How are you?"

Moni began to feel nervous. There could only be one reason for Samantha's presence. Well, two reasons. "Are you here to buy some flowers?"

"No, I was hoping we could talk."

She smiled politely. "Now's not a very good time for me. I'm working, but we have some really beautiful red daisies, if you're interested."

"Thanks anyway. I don't want to take up your—Johnny, stop that. Come here." Once the kids had settled down, Samantha tried again. "I just wanted to find out what's going on with you and my brother."

Moni paused, caught off guard by her blunt approach. "What's going on?"

She leaned in close, lowering her voice. "I know I must seem like a busybody to you, but I just know something's wrong and he's not talking."

Moni continued to concentrate on wiping down the counters. "Well, if he hasn't said anything, why do you think something is wrong?"

"Because every time I ask about you, he changes the subject."

"That should answer your questions, then. Grant and I aren't seeing each other anymore."

"Why not? He needs you."

Moni finally turned to face Samantha. "Grant understands why we're not together. He's accepted it and so should you." She was a bit surprised at how firm her voice sounded.

"Are you sure? Because I really think it's a mistake for the two of you to be apart. He's miserable without you."

Moni sighed heavily. She had trouble believing that. No one was more rock solid than Grant. It would take a lot more than the end of a relationship he'd claimed not to want in the first place to get him down.

"Look, I understand that you're concerned, but I have to do what's best for me. Being with Grant just isn't right for me right now. I'm sorry if that's not what you were hoping to hear, but I really can't tell you anything else. So, unless you'd like to buy some tulips, I can't help you."

Samantha nodded solemnly. "I'm sorry if I've bothered you," she said, rounding up her kids and leaving the store.

Moni held her head firm and proud until she saw Samantha head down the dirt road toward the parking lot. When she was out of sight, she pulled off her apron.

She turned to Vera, who'd been pretending to arrange some violets throughout her conversation with Samantha. "*I'm* taking a break for a change."

Moni skittered out to the back porch of the shop and not a moment too soon. She felt the prick of tears just before they slid down her cheeks.

She'd made her point, Moni thought. She was a strong, independent woman who was standing up for herself. People were going to have to take her seriously now. Why else would she allow herself to be so utterly miserable if it weren't for a very good reason?

Besides, obviously Samantha had it all wrong. If Grant really wanted to be with her, he wouldn't have taken her breaking up with him so easily. She'd kissed him off and he'd disappeared from her life.

He'd never even sent so much as a thank-you note for the extra work she'd done on his flower beds. She'd told herself she was doing it just because she couldn't bear to see the contrast of his plain yard against the vibrant fence with the new flower beds. But part of her had to admit she'd been hoping to keep the connection between them alive.

She couldn't be his lover, but she'd thought they could at least be neighborly. But obviously Grant didn't agree.

SLAM!

She heard a door swing closed behind her and turned to find Vera coming out of the store. "I didn't think I'd ever live to see the day Little Miss Sunshine clouded over."

Moni dashed away her tears. "What are you doing out here? I was actually hoping to be alone."

"What on earth are you crying about?"

"Who's watching the store?"

Vera shrugged. "Nobody, that's why I put the closed sign in the window."

"Now, why would you do that? You're losing customers."

Vera shrugged again. "So, was that lady right? You're out here 'cause you're pining for a man."

Moni couldn't believe that Vera had suddenly become so interested in her life. Aunt Reggie raised her to respect her elders, so she knew it would be going too far if she told the woman to get lost. Instead she resigned herself to the awkward company.

"I'm not pining for him. I'm reveling in my ability to make tough decisions."

Vera studied her carefully. "You love him."

"That's not the point."

"Then what is the point?"

"Um—"

Vera nudged her. "He cheat on you?"

"No."

"He a liar?"

"No, nothing like that . . . he's a good man."

"So he didn't do you wrong?"

Moni started wringing her hands. "Not in the way that you think. It's more complex than that. I don't think I can explain it."

Moni expected Vera to keep pressing her, but she fell silent for a moment. Finally, she said, "Did you know this was my husband's store?"

Moni perked up. "Oh, I didn't know you were married."

"Jacob passed away two years ago." The pain in the older woman's voice was still fresh.

"I'm so sorry to hear that."

"This store was his pride and joy. Not me so much. I was more into books. Woulda loved to have me a bookstore, but Jacob loved messing with those dern flowers."

"I see," Moni said, realizing that explained a lot.

"After he died, I kept the shop, thinking it was my way of keepin' a piece of him. But it's not the same, really. Not the same at all. Still, I come here every day, hoping I'll find a piece of him here."

Moni swallowed hard, feeling herself becoming emotional again. "I could sense your heart wasn't really in the floral business."

Vera nodded. "Yours is, though. You've got a big heart, young lady."

Moni blinked. She was fairly certain that was the closest thing to a compliment she'd received from Vera. "Why, thank you."

"So why are you being so hardheaded?"

"I beg your pardon?"

"If you keep toeing such a hard line, like you did this afternoon," Vera said sternly, "you're going to end up a bitter, lonely old woman just like me."

Moni was so taken aback by Vera's words, she just stood silently.

"I gave my heart away. I don't mind the bitterness, because I know wherever my Jacob is, he's taking good care of my heart. And when it's my time, I'll have it back again. But you . . . I don't understand you."

"Well," Moni said, looking down at her hands. "I don't expect you to. My situation is more complicated than you think."

Vera shook her head. "Pride. It all comes down to pride." She straightened. "But you say you know what you're doing so I'm not gonna meddle no more."

Moni nodded and Vera turned toward the door. "But, Missy, you'd just better be sure your pride is worth losing a good man. 'Cause I'd give my right arm to have my man back."

When Moni re-entered the store she couldn't stop reflecting on Vera's words. Not the words about Grant, those were too painful to dwell on. She was feeling a bit ganged up on when it came to Grant, and she needed some time before she could allow herself to question her decision in that regard.

What kept plaguing Moni was the flower shop. She'd known all along it wasn't Vera's dream. And she'd spent the entire summer trying to convince herself that being a florist *wasn't* her dream. But suddenly it all seemed so clear.

It was time to stop running from the truth. She would always be a florist at heart.

"Vera, I've been thinking."

The older woman didn't look up. "Don't hurt yourself, now," she said, back to her old self.

"Don't you think Jacob would be happy to know his flower shop was in the hands of someone who could love it the way he did?"

Vera shrugged. "What you asking? To buy it? It don't sell cheap. I don't know—"

Moni grabbed a piece of paper from the counter. "Why don't you let me make you an offer?" She wrote a number down and slid it across the counter.

She expected Vera to haggle a bit, so her reaction was unexpected.

Vera grabbed Moni's head in her two hands and kissed her squarely on the cheek. "I'm gonna buy me a bookstore!"

Moni went home that evening feeling emotionally drained. It had been a very big day for her. She was going to buy the flower shop. For some reason, she thought she'd be more excited about it.

She knew she'd made the right choice. It was the first business decision she'd made since moving to San Diego that truly felt right. No more floating in limbo. No more business plans. No more feeling like an imposter.

Still, as Moni let herself into the house, she knew something was still missing.

"—lots of potential customers—" Candy broke off as Moni entered the living room.

"Hey ya'll, what's going on?"

"Hi, Moni. Nothing much. Burt was just telling me what an untapped market Dunkin, Virginia, is for Web design. Out here they're a dime a dozen," Candy said.

"Oh hey, Moni," Burt called from the kitchen. He was wearing his standard attire for around the house. Blue jeans—nothing else. "I'm making hamburgers. How do you like yours?

Moni smiled. Once upon a time Burt knew exactly how she liked her hamburgers. But ever since meeting Summer, it was as though he'd forgotten all about the unrequited love he was supposed to be holding for her. And that made Moni really happy for them both. But it also made her feel just the slightest bit lonely.

"I think I'll pass on the burger for now, Burt. I'm not that hungry."

Summer came out of the kitchen looking like Burt had done a lot more than just cooking with her. "Are you sure, we've got plenty? Why don't you sit down and eat with us."

"Not this time. It's nothing personal. I just think I need to lie down first," she said, starting to climb the stairs.

As she reached the top she could hear them begin to whisper—"Do you think she's okay? She's been keeping to herself a lot. I think she's feeling down. . . ."

Moni closed her door and flopped onto the bed.

She loved her friends, but the living situation was starting to wear a little thin. Moni was unprepared for how difficult it was to live with a new couple that was happy and in love when she was trying to convince herself that her heart wasn't breaking.

She knew Burt was getting antsy to get back to Dunkin, and she had a strong suspicion Summer would be going along when he left. But she also knew they were feeling protective of her. They'd never leave her if they thought she wasn't doing well.

Maybe once she told them about buying the flower shop, it would ease their minds.

Getting up from the bed, Moni looked out her window to Grant's house. Maybe she had been too hard on Grant. If she went over there now and pounded on his door, she knew the deep aching in her chest would finally ease.

But she hadn't come to San Diego to take the easy way out. She'd always second guess herself. She couldn't make up with Grant just to make herself feel better. He'd always see her as a cute little playmate. How could she spend her life with a man that didn't take her seriously.

Moving away from the window, Moni stretched out on the bed again. She had to hold her own, no matter how much her heart wanted to surrender.

The next day, Moni got up early. After her morning jog, she planned to search for a good lawyer to walk her through purchasing a business.

Turning up the volume on her Walkman, Moni stepped through the front door and nearly tripped over a rectangular package.

Picking it up, she carried it into the house. She started to leave it on the kitchen counter and open it later, but curiosity got the best of her. That package hadn't been outside last night, and seven A.M. was entirely too early for any kind of delivery service.

As she unwrapped the brown paper, Moni discovered that it was a manuscript. Her heart started beating wildly. "Grant?"

There was a card on top. She opened it up and read:

Dear Moni,

Thank you for not only brightening up my lawn but my life as well. I can't find the right words to tell you what kind of impact you've had on me. I'm hoping my words will speak for themselves.

Love,
Grant

Moni didn't quite understand what the note meant. Why was he giving her his manuscript? What could reading his book possibly change between them?

Still overwhelmed with curiosity, Moni flipped past the title page. She was startled once again to find that the book was dedicated to her.

"This book is dedicated to my muse, Moni Lawrence. Without her, this book would have never gotten written."

Moni pressed her palm to her chest. After such sweet words she had to read on.

And read on she did. Moni sat at the kitchen table reading Grant's book until the rest of the house began to wake. Not wanting to share her precious gift just yet, she grabbed the manuscript and huddled in her room to continue reading in private.

Several times during the course of the day, she found herself crying or laughing out loud. Grant's book was truly an impressive work.

When she finally turned the last manuscript page over, Moni pressed her hands to her face and wept. He was definitely sending her a message. She hadn't realized it right away, but he'd clearly fashioned the character Naomi after her.

And this woman was no damsel in distress. She was strong, sassy, funny and endearing. Moni swallowed her tears, realizing she could finally see herself through Grant's eyes.

This wasn't an image he'd developed over night. The character introduced herself early and had grown until she was an integral part of the book. Grant really loved her. She felt so stupid for doubting that.

Moni looked at the clock and realized that she'd been reading Grant's book nonstop the entire day. It was almost seven o'clock at night.

Hoping that Grant would be home, she grabbed the manuscript and ran across the street. With her heart drumming loudly in her ears, she rang the doorbell.

Grant must have been waiting for her because

he opened the door right away and let her inside. "Moni, I see you got it."

She nodded. He looked so beautiful to her eyes. Being this close to him she realized how terribly she'd missed him. "It was wonderful," she gushed. "Truly the best thing I've ever read."

Grant's relief was obvious on his features. "Did you understand? I wanted to run across the street and beg you to take me back, but I was hoping the book would pave the way."

Moni nodded. "I understand, and thank you for not giving up on us."

He sighed, running his hand lovingly across her cheek. "Thank God the book got through to you, because plan B was not looking good. Do you smell that?"

She sniffed the air. "Oh my, did you burn something?"

He nodded and lead her into the kitchen. What she saw made her want to laugh and cry at the same time. Three burnt misshapen attempts at banana love bread cooling on the counter.

"I didn't know the exact recipe, so I was trying to improvise."

Tears of joy won out over laughter and Moni buried her face in Grant's chest. "You may need some help with the banana bread, but you got the *love* part exactly right."

Grant pulled her back so she could see his face. "I think you're the most amazing woman

I've ever known. And now that I have known you, I can't imagine my life without you."

Moni wrapped her arms around Grant's neck. "Grant, I love you so much. I was so stupid to push you away."

"Moni, I love you, too." He leaned down and kissed her hard before lifting her into his arms and carrying her upstairs.

Epilogue

Moni listened to all the wedding reception chatter and felt her heart warm. She slipped out onto the balcony to get some fresh air and reflect. Never in a million years would she have guessed that she'd be back in her hometown celebrating a wedding after leaving just a few months ago.

She missed Aunt Reggie more than ever, but being home again allowed her to feel closer to her as well.

The ceremony had been filled with love, tradition and the good old-fashioned southern charm that only Dunkin, Virginia, could provide. It had been a wedding that dreams were made of.

Grant approached her with two champagne glasses in hand. He looked incredible in his simple black tuxedo. Handing her a glass of champagne, he leaned down and kissed her cheek.

"What's that wistful look for?" he asked, smiling down at her. "You're not disappointed that our own wedding won't take place in your hometown, are you?"

Moni shook her head, staring down at the diamond engagement ring on her left hand. "No. Celebrating here with Summer and Burt was enough. Dunkin will always have a special place in my heart. And we'll be back to visit the newlyweds often, but coming back here has helped me realize how much I've changed. I'm looking forward to the wedding we're planning at the Hotel Del Coronado. It will be fun to show my friends from Dunkin my new home."

He clinked glasses with her. "To *our* home."

"And our future together," Moni said before she sipped her champagne.

"Speaking of our home," Grant said, slipping an arm around her waist. "Are you sure you don't want to sell your house and just move in with me? We spend so much time at my place anyway."

Moni grinned. "Nope. We've been over this. I'm not moving in until *after* we're married. Now that Summer and Candy have moved to Dunkin, I can experience living alone for the rest of the year. But, whenever I get lonely, you're just across the street."

Grant shook his head. "It's going to be tough sleeping in separate beds for the next eight months, but you've got the rest of our lives to make it up to me."

Before Moni could answer, Candy rushed

over to them, dressed in the same purple chiffon
bridesmaid dress Moni wore. As maid of honor,
she wore a tiny crystal tiara that matched Summer's larger crown.

Summer had insisted on the grandest wedding Dunkin had ever seen. She'd chosen
Candy, Moni and three girls she used to work
with at the Silver Spur for her bridal party, and
Moni had referred her to the best local resources
for the cake, dresses and catering. Of course,
Moni's Elegant Flowers provided all of the
flower arrangements.

"There you two are," Candy said, grabbing
Moni and Grant's hands. "Sorry to interrupt, but
Summer and Burt are about to cut the cake."

The wedding had been lovely with all the tra-
ditional elements, but it wouldn't have been
Summer's style not to add a little extra pizzazz
to the event.

Candy, Moni, Grant and the rest of the wedding guests gathered around as Summer and
Burt prepared to slice a five-tier chocolate cake
covered entirely in lilac icing. Moni had accented
the purple confection with delicate white roses
and Stephanotis. It was truly a majestic site.

Summer and Burt sliced the cake and lovingly fed each other pieces. She ended up with
icing on her lips and Burt carefully removed it
with a long kiss.

"Save it for the honeymoon," someone
shouted as the kiss lingered on.

Finally, the couple parted and Summer gave her audience a sparkling smile. "Okay, we're going to do the bouquet and garter toss a little early. Burt and I have places to be and . . . *things* to do," she said with obvious innuendo.

Moni caught the bouquet and Grant caught the garter. As the rest of the guests rushed outside to send Summer and Burt off on their journey to wedded bliss, Grant and Moni hung back.

He grinned down at her as she sniffed the lovely bouquet of lavender and roses. "Think the whole thing was fixed?"

"Probably. Everyone in this room knows that you and I are next." She winked at him, unable to resist the urge to tease him. "Third time's a charm, right?"

He ignored her joke and pulled her close with a serious look in his eyes. "There was no one until there was you. You're my first and only *true* love."

Then he lowered his mouth to hers and gave her a kiss that was filled with infinite promise.

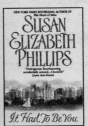